to Pete,
all the best!

Deb Norton
9-19-19

DINGLEY ISLAND

THE

STORY

SO

FAR

DEBORA NORTON

Designed and produced by:
Indie Author Books
12 High Street, Thomaston, Maine
www.indieauthorbooks.com

Printed in the United States of America

This book is dedicated to Jessica,
who told me to write it down!

Also to my children, Jessie and Caleb,
who were the inspiration for the story.

TABLE OF CONTENTS

Chapter 1 | When It All Began | 1

Chapter 2 | From Another Point of View | 7

Chapter 3 | Dreams | 10

Chapter 4 | Another Wizard? | 13

Chapter 5 | Things Are Discovered | 20

Chapter 6 | Believable or Not | 23

Chapter 7 | Private Reflections | 26

Chapter 8 | Messengers and Lookouts | 31

Chapter 9 | In the Library and the Cavern | 32

Chapter 10 | Meanwhile | 35

Chapter 11 | Some Answers but More Questions | 37

Chapter 12 | The Storm and the Battle | 47

Chapter 13 | But No One Is Suspicious | 51

Chapter 14 | The Memory of a Mouse | 53

Chapter 15 | Meeting Someone Special | 57

Chapter 16 | The Scarecrow and the Oriental Rug | 64

Chapter 17 | After the Storm | 70

Chapter 18 | One Good Omission Deserves Another | 74

Chapter 19 | Plan A and Plan B | 80

Chapter 20 | Approval | 83

Chapter 21 | Lessons and Love | 85

Chapter 22 | A Disappearance | 93

Chapter 23 | Lights in the Dark | 99

Chapter 24 | Finding the Puppies | 107

Chapter 25 | Meanwhile | 112

Chapter 26 | A Lot to Say | 116

Chapter 27 | Friends and Family | 121

Chapter 28 | Still Lost | 123

Chapter 29 | The Others on Drake's Island, United Kingdom | 126

Chapter 30 | Meanwhile, the Cat Returns with News | 131

Chapter 31 | Finding a Way Back | 135

Chapter 32 | Aaron Audran's Journal Entries | 138

Chapter 33 | Another Battle to Save a Brother | 140

Chapter 34 | Other Plans | 148

Chapter 35 | A Tragedy in Egyptian Stone | 155

Chapter 36 | A Celebration Back at the Island | 160

Chapter 37 | Audran's Journal | 161

Chapter 38 | Back at the Island, Some Villagers
Suspect Something Is Amiss | 177

Chapter 39 | What Happened in the Barn | 180

Chapter 40 | A Tour of the Cavern | 185

Chapter 41 | A Rose Garden Wedding | 191

Chapter 42 | The Beginning of the End | 193

Chapter 43 | A Saying Goodbye | 198

Chapter 44 | A Harsh Decision | 206

Chapter 45 | The Court of the Faerie | 209

List of Characters | 213

Characters That Are Not Human | 217

Places | 224

Magik Things | 226

The First Regiment of Ravens | 228

Languages Used | 229

Acknowledgments | 231

WHEN IT ALL BEGAN

It was the second night in their new home. Now that it was quiet, Ellora was sitting by the fire, reading, listening to the stillness. In the dark, the firelight was soothing, and the warmth was nice on this cool summer night. Everyone else was in bed. The day had been a whirlwind of unpacking and arranging their things. Her mother, Marjorie, knew that Ellora was sometimes sensitive to hustle and bustle, so after telling her to not stay up too late, she let her do just that. Their blended family was hard to describe to most people, so she had given up trying. For now, third cousins Daisy and Keevan and their dad lived with Ellora and her younger brother, Luke, and their mother. Keevan, who was thirteen, wanted his own room. The girls each wanted their own beds. Her brother said he would simply love living in the library. But for now, the boys shared a room.

Ellora had to wait all day for a chance to read her book, *A Wrinkle in Time*. She was just getting to a good part, and she kept reading although she was getting tired. As she turned the page, she came across a note scribbled in the margin: "Put the blue bottle in the flames" with a date. It was dated this very day! Ellora glanced at the kitchen clock, whose old clock hands were pointing just past midnight.

"Yes" the note now said, "this day, just past midnight, put the blue bottle into the fire." Ellora was alarmed. The message on the scribbled note had changed!

"Do it NOW!" The note had changed again!

Was she dreaming? Not really believing what she was doing, Ellora slowly took the blue bottle that she had always admired from the collection of old bottles on the mantelpiece. She especially liked the faint outline of a faerie engraved on the bottle, an antique that Gramma Charlotte had given to her mom. I can always take it out again she told herself as she set it carefully into the flames. As the fire spread across the surface of the design, a pleasant sound reached her ears—a faint tinkling of glass. Then the sound was of glass cracking. Ellora watched as the bottle began to spin and writhe, at first slowly and then faster.

"Too hot! Too hot!" something screeched.

Immediately Ellora took the fireplace poker and prodded the bottle out of the flames to a cooler, but still fairly hot place on the hearth. Her mouth dropped in amazement as a small creature unfolded itself from the bottle, which had stopped spinning. Enormous blue eyes in a tiny face looked up at Ellora. Its skin was like glass, shiny and new. Spiked hair began to sprout from its head and curl itself around the tiny body. Arms, legs, pointed ears appeared and then, with a poof, beautifully colored wings like a hummingbird's unfolded and beat slowly. A whiff of flowers filled the air. Ellora cautiously reached out to touch the wondrous creature when slap! A thin, barbed tail swept around and slapped her outstretched hand.

"Ouch!" Ellora cried.

What was wrong with this human? Did she not know anything? "Must not, I am still hot!" Blouette exclaimed as she slapped with her tail, her tinkling voice sounding cross. Still, this human had just released her from the spell that bound her to that awful glass prison, so Blouette decided to be polite. With her delicate wings outstretched, hand on her heart, and her tail pointed upright in the standard greeting, she introduced herself.

"Blouette. I was named by the queen, my mother. I am immensely grateful and pleased that you released me. Who art thou?"

"Ellora Donovan—"

"What place is this? Are we in Palandine, perhaps, or Herstamonix?"

"No, we are in a place called Maine—"

Again, the little creature interrupted. "Maine? what is this 'mane?' The sweeping hair of a lion? Are we in the servants' quarters? I see no guards about. What is the meaning of this?" she demanded as she stomped her foot.

Ellora giggled at Blouette's little tantrum. Was she dreaming? She looked at the kitchen clock. It was past midnight, and she had promised Mom she'd go to bed. She didn't want Daisy to creep downstairs and find her still awake, then tell her mom in the morning. Suddenly, all the emotional tension and activity of the day overwhelmed her. As much as she wished to stay awake, she could barely keep her eyes open.

"I have to go to bed now. It was nice to meet you! I love your wings—"

"I am quite tired and wish to sleep as well. You may show me the sleeping den."

As if in a dream, Ellora held out her cupped hands so the creature could step onto her palms. Her feet were very warm, and she had grown as they had briefly spoken. Her shiny skin had had lost some of its glassy sheen, but it still rippled with many hues of blue. Ellora was extremely careful as she crept up the stairs to her bedroom, which overlooked the living room. Looking down as she climbed the stairs made her dizzy, so she directed her gaze upward toward the ceiling fan. She must be dreaming. When they entered her bedroom, Blouette leaped off her palms and onto her pillow. As Ellora herself climbed into bed, the creature put up her hand.

"I am a sprite from the lands of Faerie, a daughter to Queen Merritt and Guard Sister to Marigold, the future queen. You may call me Blou. Ellora, you are human? Whose wizard's child art thou? One of magik? Or are you the seed of the Others?"

Ellora whispered, "I am a human child." She yawned, suddenly very, very tired, and settled under the covers of her bed.

"Let's talk in the morning." She fell asleep immediately.

Early in the morning, Ellora woke to the sound of growling ruckus. She turned over to see her cat and the sprite having a stern conversation. What Ellora heard were growls and hisses flying through the air, but what Blou and the cat said to each other was this:

You put me in a bottle! What a betrayal and an offense!

It was an emergency! There was no time, for the sake of the Goddess! You weren't hurt, just shaken up a bit. I don't remember the details.

Shaken up! I have been a thing of glass for nigh on so many passings of the moon that I have lost count! I have been so bored my hair is falling out. The queen will not be amused!

Sssilence! hissed Myster as he arched his back and then stood on his hind legs.

Ellora gathered the Maine coon cat into her arms.

"Myster, what's gotten into you? This is Blouette, and you can't chase her. She's not a toy and you'll hurt her!"

Myster relaxed in his beloved human's arms, moving nothing but his tail, which lashed back and forth. He stared intently at the sprite, who did not seem friendly, but looked rather menacing with her tiny clawed hands in front of her and wings beating furiously, lifting her off the bed. Ellora knew to stay away from the tail. The end had a barb with a glistening clear drop balanced on its very tip. That could not be good, Ellora thought.

Soothingly she spoke to the sprite. "This is my cat. His name is Myster, and he won't hurt you, okay?"

"What does it mean, 'okay'? He cast a spell that burned and hurt. It was horrible!"

If Myster had human eyebrows, he would have raised them at this point. Sprites were so dramatic! He began a sort of hissing-growl that sounded like words to tell the sprite a thing or two or three...

Do you remember the prophecy? You are a guard sssister are you not? You are required to give aid. This human girl is ssspecial. There are not many of her kind in this world. I have been waiting for Ellora to come of age. She is nearly sixteen. I sssee the ssigns! I sspeak with the birds, they know!

Blouette still looked angry, so Ellora turned her attention to the sprite.

"Look—"

"Look at what?"

"You aren't yourself yet. Here, lay down on this while I get us cook-ies to eat." She offered Blou a soft woolen mitten that her mother had made and that Myster had appropriated as a cat toy. The sprite eyed it cautiously, then sat cross-legged atop the pillow.

"What is a 'cookie'? I require flesh."

Ellora made a worried face, and then hurried downstairs to the kitchen to gather some items from the fridge. While she was gone, the cat and the sprite continued their conversation. This time it was quieter and some of it was telepathic, which was hard for both of them because it required more effort.

The cat began. *It has been some many moons since I cast a spell to keep you safe in the glass bottle. Many changes have come about in the queendom. The crows have been sending me messages. This world is in danger.*

Oh, everyone knows black crows lie or see things crooked, in the crow's way. I would trust the white Rahven though, Blou thought back at him.

I have neither seen nor heard from Rahven for many moons. But again, the prophecy says that when a white raven rides and the wizards, a brother and sister with purple eyes, come of age, the mountains will shake, the magik will grow, and the queen's gem will turn blood red. Myster said out loud. *There is more, but I have forgotten much.*

Blou sighed as Ellora came up the stairs, trying to be quiet, but Ellora's cousin, Daisy, stirred in her bed. Myster went to the younger girl to snuggle and to keep her dreaming, knowing she must not wake up just yet.

Ellora came in with a plate full of food for Blou, who proceeded to taste and then devour with gusto.

"Is this flesh? I enjoy its flavor. From whence does it come?"

"It's called ham," Ellora told her. "I like it too. My mother used to call it 'pink chicken'—

"Ham ... ham. It has a nice name for human food, and it tastes delicious. I require more!" the sprite demanded, her wings fluttering— which made her rise from the bed— "and some drink, of course."

"I brought tea, with honey." Ellora used the soothing voice that she used with her brother and cousins. She often was the peacemaker in the family. She could hear the others in the household getting up and moving about. She was so dreadfully tired still and would love to snuggle with the cat for nap. She drank the remaining tea and climbed back into bed, falling asleep immediately.

Blou, meanwhile, decided to fly to the rafters for a look around.

FROM ANOTHER POINT OF VIEW

Ellora's mother, Marji, was in her bedroom, which also served as an office space. She ran a small business, Island Catering, and also baked specialty cakes. The kitchen in this house would have to be renovated, she thought, or maybe she could set up a bakery in the barn—but that would take a lot of time and effort, which were in short supply right now. She was going over the costs when she became unsettled and anxious. She sipped her coffee and sighed. She decided to go out on the balcony of her bedroom, which was like a small porch. The house was lovely, but a bit strange, as if it were not finished. This balcony faced the rising sun. The kids' bedrooms looked out over the living area upon the setting sun; they were in a loft with a bathroom between the rooms. The kitchen had a porch that faced south. The library had its own bathroom and windows facing north. You could see in every direction. The long driveway could be viewed from the kitchen. The road continued past the house to the barn and off into the woods to the shore.

Marji knew there had once been a path down to the dock. Had it become overgrown from disuse? Her mother and father, Charlotte Drake and Charles Dorr, had lived in this house until the very end of their lives. Her dad had been a boat builder, her mother a librarian. Her own husband, Jeremiah Donovan, had also built boats, until his reckless behavior had cost him his life. She worried about Ellora and Luke, who both seemed to be taking his death rather well. That was odd. Luke had told her when he was very little that Daddy was going to die young. Ellora had been very quiet at the ceremony. Both children told her they had already cried, and now they were just waiting for other people to do it too. A strange twist of fate had taken her cousin's life, also. Cynthia Bradley, Daisy and Keevan's mother, a country music superstar, had died in the same accident that claimed Jeremiah. Marji was glad the elaborate funerals were over. Now they just had to pick up the pieces and get on with their lives.

"Easier said than done," she said out loud. "But we've got all summer and being here can help all of us." She had no idea why she felt that way, as if the house, the woods, and the ocean would all help their healing process. Grief is strange and affects everyone differently. She was concerned about her own kiddos, but their dad had separated himself from them long ago. Jeremiah had never clicked with his own children. He was a racing boat designer. Both children liked sailing and sailboats, especially the ones their grandfather made. It was as if Jere was mad at them for choosing Grampa Charles over him. He used to joke to her that Marcus, his best friend, was a better dad than he was to Luke and Ellora. It was true that Marcus, also a boat builder in the traditional sense, had an affection for Ellora and Luke. They spent a lot of time together in the barn with Grampa Charles, sifting through wood shavings and sawdust. The kids wanted a slow-paced kind of life. Jere was all about speed—the need for it and the lifestyle that went with it. Marcus's wife, Cynthia enjoyed that life too. Luke had known his dad would not be around when he was older though.

"I wish I could turn back time," Marji said softly to herself.

Giving in to her feeling of restlessness, she left the balcony and went to check on the girls. She smiled as she gazed at them, sleeping in their respective beds. The cat was a surprise; he wasn't sleeping with Ellora as usual. As if he'd heard her thoughts, Myster hopped down to come over and rub Marji's leg and get in bed with the older girl. This prompted the younger one to wake.

"How are you doing Daisy-day?" Marji whispered to her, using her own dad's nickname for her. Daisy rubbed her eyes and smiled. She was still uncertain of the new blended family. Finally, after longing for a sister, she now had one. But it came with another brother too, and he was annoying! Marji smiled at her but put a finger to her lips, then gestured for Daisy to follow her. Ellora was so tired lately and had been sleeping in regularly. Marji had begun to worry. Of course, staying up late reading was not helping. But it was summer, and they had recently been through so much.

Her thoughts drifted. This beautiful place was helping them all adjust to their new family—new surroundings meant they were all on even ground. As they descended the stairs, she glanced up at the ceiling fan. Was that a toy up in the rafters? She didn't recognize it, but perhaps it was one of Daisy's, tossed up by one of the boys. But as she turned away, she thought it moved! She tried to look harder. How could a toy move?

DREAMS

Ellora slept. She dreamed (or were they old memories?) of far off places and strange people speaking languages that sounded unfamiliar, and yet she could somehow understand them. She tossed and turned in her bed all morning, as if she had a fever. In her mind's eye she was handing something to a king dressed in fancy antique clothing. The item was heavy for its size and wrapped in silk. The king's face lit up with joy as a shining blue gem tumbled out of the wrapping and into his hands. He held it up to the sun, which poured in through stained glass windows.

The scene in the dream changed to somewhere underground, with a tap, tap, tap of metal upon glass as a piece of the larger blue gemstone tumbled onto the workbench and a child's hand snatched it up. An older person was there, speaking in archaic French. Ellora saw the child's hand slowly return the gemstone to the work surface.

The scene shifted again. This time she felt as if she were on top of some large animal, an elephant, riding slowly through a throng of people, and all of them yelling and waving, but the sounds were muted as if she were partially deaf. The elephant wore a royal headdress and when it raised its trunk to call out, Ellora could see another blue gemstone, more than double the size of the one given to the king, embedded in the head plate the animal was wearing. The people were smiling and cheering, except for one old man in the front of the crowd, wearing long rags, whose eyes drilled into Ellora so that she felt uncomfortable. Her head turned to keep eye contact with the old man as the elephant moved forward. When she turned her head away, she saw soldiers drag him away as the crowd parted to escape their lashing whips. One part of her felt so sorry for the old man, who had done nothing wrong as far as she knew. Another part of her felt satisfaction mixed with a tinge of worry. She had seen the man's lips moving; he was saying something as he was hauled away. Had it been a curse? she wondered.

The dream scene and scenery switched abruptly to one of a jungle with vines and a courtyard full of immense statues, nearly all with an animal face and a giant uncut gem in the middle of their foreheads. There were two elephants, a lion, an ibis, and a few humans, some with quarter-moon eyes and one like a Viking with many horns. There were nine in all. Ellora could feel all of their eyes looking right at her and passing through. They looked down upon the travelers—for Ellora sensed she was not alone—with stern but serene faces. Ellora began to sense that she was in something more than a dream and struggled to regain her own sense of identity. The Other in her mind was very strong and was trying to keep her here in this place, with these gods looking at her. One of the gods reached out to touch Ellora with its trunk. The giant blue gem briefly pulsed red, then faded back to blue as she pulled herself away. Some part of her told her this was dangerous!

In the real world, where she slept, Ellora cried out and tossed back and forth as Blouette watched her. Blou had learned that humans did irrational things in the short time she had come to know of them.

Luke dreamed too. He saw an old man in tatters removing a gemstone from a statue. He tentatively handed it to another traveler in medieval clothing. A small pouch of coins dropped into the older man's outstretched hands. His face turned from a smile to a scowl as he shouted and raised his fist.

The scene changed: another man, in an old leather apron, stood next to a study bench that held tools for gem cutting. He carefully set the giant uncut blue stone into a wire cradle above a burning lamp. Near his workspace was a huge, melting block of ice sitting in a puddle of water that had formed on the floor. The underground area was damp and cold. Luke shivered as if he truly felt it. The old man spoke to him and gestured, but Luke couldn't hear him clearly. The man repeated the gesture, then grasped his arm tightly to pull Luke forward. The old man held his other hand over the gem to test the heat, then quickly set the gem upon the ice. With another swift movement he smote the gem with a small but wide-headed hammer. A sound like nothing Luke could describe echoed in the cavern as the magik hammer struck the stone. A large piece of the gemstone fell to the floor.

Another man in the room uttered an oath: "Luck of the Goddess! Mon Dieu!" The man's face grew rigid with fear as he watched a wisp of blue smoke rise from the larger piece. It gathered itself slowly into a form. The entity looked past Luke with hazy eyes, its mouth trying to form a word.

"Master."

Luke woke up as this word was spoken. He felt afraid, but that feeling faded as he looked at his new surroundings. It was all right. He breathed deeply to settle his fears. He was in Grandpa's house, by the sea, in his own room that he now shared with his cousin and soon-to-be stepbrother Keevan. Luke did not think these things were strange at all. In fact, he had foreseen last year that this would happen. All the turmoil in his mother's mind this morning seeped into Luke, and he had to block it out. It was too painful. Her hurt had been the worst. Marcus would fix that, though, he told himself. He began to call the cat but stopped. Something new was in the house talking with Myster. Luke settled himself down to listen. After a few minutes he heard whispering but had to really concentrate to understand what was being said. As his friends had often teased him, Luke had "Vulcan hearing." He could hear what others were saying in other rooms, even with the doors shut. He didn't know that he had telepathic abilities; after all, he was only eight years old.

ANOTHER WIZARD?

Blou could sense the turmoil in the girl's mind. But it did not worry her. What did make her anxious was Myster the cat watching her. And also, somehow, she needed to release Raid from the red bottle, which was a prison. The larger red and tiny gold bottles were still on the mantle, along with some others. What was this? The word "Sprite" was printed in white on a thick green bottle and another was printed with the word "Moxie"! What was the meaning of this? She flew down to the fireplace to have a better look. Maybe she could lift the smaller bottle down to the hot coals. She decided to try.

The day went by. The adult woman hummed to herself as she made meals, baked some delicious smelling items, and talked on a small, slim box she held in her hand. No one paid any attention to the flying faerie as she struggled with the golden bottle. Two young boys came in and out of the house several times, slamming the screen door. They apparently were going fishing and then swimming, as if anyone would immerse themselves in water! Blou could hear their excited voices along with the barking of the dogs guarding the house. Blou had already made telepathic connection with the larger dog, who protected the older boy. But she was astounded as the younger boy looked up, sought her hiding place, and smiled. He sent her a telepathic greeting: *Good morning*!

Myster watched the sprite through lidded eyes, though he was actually fully awake. The young ginger cat, Kipper, lay curled with him on the hearth. But now, the day was growing hot, too hot, so Myster casually jumped down and, oh, so slowly, stretched. He knew that she knew that he knew that she was watching him from the rafters above. He felt that she was plotting something, so that made him nervous. He saw her on the mantle looking at the antique bottles up there. Then, something struck him urgently. What if Mother noticed one of the blue bottles was missing? His tail switched back and forth as he searched the sprite's mind to ask the question.

What are you planning to do with the golden bottle? Myster sent the thought to her. There was no response. He asked again, yelling this time.

There is no need to yell, Myster Cat Blou said *I simply am going to set whatever is trapped within free.*

Tonight, while they sleep?

Yes, with the aid of Ellora's magik and the fire we shall see what awakens. I know not what thou hast done but casting your spell may have ensnared one of my guard sisters, although none of them are this shade. I know the red bottle could be another of my kind. Raid is his name.

Why not set him free as well? Myster asked,.

Hast thou forgotten? Curses and spells are tricky and, at times, treacherous. We knowest not what will come forth. I would rather the smaller of the two than the large one. Red being a color of battle and all that. Raid, if that is who is trapped in there, will not come out willingly or in a friendly manner. I would rather be prepared with Ellora growing in power—

She is not for you to use Myster growled.

She knows not whom she is, does she? Nor does the mother, who is possibly a Guardian herself. The smaller girl has only a little power. Blou was tired of the telepathic link.

Myster continued the link as he strode into the kitchen and out the cat door. *No, but Ellora's younger brother has powers.*

Blou nearly fell from the rafters. Another wizard child? The one who bid her good morning? She nearly dropped the golden bottle she had struggled to bring up to the rafters to hide. She could barely see the etching on its surface, but it was of a pony or perhaps a foal. She didn't really think it was one of her sisters, but she wanted to keep that dratted cat off guard. She had to stop what she was doing as the two boys bounded down the stairs. The smaller one again looked up at her as she hid on the ceiling fan blade.

Meanwhile, Ellora decided to tell Luke and Daisy about Blou tonight. Keevan would not want to keep the secret. Luke would have no problem as long as they could keep his excitement down. He was a strange little boy, and sometimes odd things happened when he got excited.

"I was reading by the fire last night and a strange thing happened." Ellora lowered her voice, then waited to let that knowledge sink in. Luke was instantly curious. He thought had seen the faerie flying around in the open rafters of the family room. This was exciting. He wished he could tell his grampa about it. Tears swelled in his eyes each time he thought of the old man in his overalls, whistling while working in the boat shed. Luke's dad had been a boat builder as well, but he'd made loud, flashy, fast boats while Grampa Charles made elegant sailboats that spoke of grace and beauty. The last one Grampa had christened "Axoparia." Grampa said the name had come to him in a dream. He'd also told Luke he had put all of his love and soul into the sailboat.

"I have to tell you something that you cannot tell anyone—yet. Last night one of Gramma Charlotte's old glass bottles came to life after I put it in the fire," Ellora said quietly. "She is a faerie sprite named Blouette—"

"Blou thou may call me, guard sister to Princess Marigold, daughter of Queen Merritt and The King," the sprite interrupted. "I was wrongly cast by this cat, Myster, and held prisoner for a hundred moons or more!" She scathingly glanced at the cat., "I need your help to set free another of my kind, trapped within this golden glass!"

She dramatically spread her wings and gestured toward the bottle at her side. Once her wings were open, the two children gasped, but had very different reactions. Luke put his hands on his face to stifle a squeal. He kicked his heels rapidly on the carpeted floor in delight, then he stopped and simply stared at her.

Daisy reached out to touch Blouette's wings and received a slap for her efforts.

"Is it real? How does it talk? Can it fly?" Daisy asked all at once. Then she exclaimed, "Ouch!"

"Yes, yes, and yes!" Ellora and Blou answered together.

Now Blou took center stage, showing off, demonstrating how she could fly and hover. She crossed her arms and floated above the floor, moving slightly in the breeze of the ceiling fan, moving her eyes from person to person. They came to rest upon the deep bluish-purple eyes of the boy. Was there magik in the wilderness and barbarism of Maine? These humans are untrained, thus she would not be required to render service. She would have to be careful, she told herself. The cats were not to be trusted.

"This night, after the mother is in bed and the other boy is asleep, we shall put this bottle into the flames that set me free," Blou instructed. "We must be prepared for what comes forth!" She gestured dramatically. "Bring me flesh called 'ham,'" she ordered.

Luke and Daisy sat rooted to the floor. Blou gestured again, getting a slightly better response. Both children had been sitting cross-legged, but now sat up on the bed where Ellora had been stroking the cats.

"Should we do what she says?" asked Daisy fearfully. "I don't want to make Mom mad."

"We can do it if we keep this to ourselves," Ellora warned. "Keevan cannot be trusted yet, with this secret, so we will come down before midnight like I did last night."

It was hard to wait through dinner for the secret thing to happen. It was good that their mom was distracted, being busy with her cake and catering business. They were ushered to the living room to watch a movie together. The kids wanted another fire, so she got one going, then left the three of them to watch Japanese anime. Keevan didn't like anime, so he went upstairs to use his own screen. After the movie, Ellora got the two younger children to bed on time and whispered that she would not forget to wake them up for the event.

The fire burned bright in the dark house. The clock hands moved slowly toward midnight. The cat watched from the safety of the couch. Blou had brought the golden bottle down from the rafters to the hearth. Ellora had wakened her brother and cousin a few minutes before midnight. Sleepily, they all sat on the hearth rug. Ellora held the bottle with the fire tongs. When the clock showed midnight, she set it into the hottest part of the burning logs. Nothing happened. She turned the bottle around but still nothing happened. Daisy was devastated, but Blou asked Ellora what she had been thinking about last night.

"Last night I was reading a book and a note was scribbled in the margin telling me to put the bottle in the fire at midnight."

Ellora got the book to show her and thumbed through the pages to find the writing—but it had vanished! Luke looked through the book as well. When he got to the last page a faint bit of writing said, "Think of Charlotte."

"Oh, and I had been saying thank you to Grandma Charlotte so we could live here, but I was sad that she was gone." Tears welled up in her eyes as she also thought of her dad. Daisy was thinking of her Mom, who was also gone. A wail came from Kipper, who was intently staring into the darkness. Then a sound of breaking glass made them look at the fire again. The bottle was spinning and yowling!

"It's too hot!" screamed Blou. "Get it out of there!"

Ellora prodded the bottle to the side of the grate, where it cooled down enough to reveal a tiny four-legged creature with glass legs still stuck to one another. What could they do to help? The little muzzle lifted up and another yowl like screech came from it. The poor thing was in so much pain! Luke covered his ears against the sound and Daisy began to cry, covering her face with her hands.

The light in their mom's room came on and they heard a voice ask, "What on earth was that?"

"Only a screech owl, Mom. It's all right." Ellora answered. The light went out.

"I have an idea." Luke whispered. He ran to the kitchen to get some ice from the automatic ice maker. He brought a few pieces to place them on the legs of the tiny horse. Soon, they heard a pinging sound, and a crack appeared, freeing her back legs. Her tiny hooves scraped the bricks and she struggled to get up. Blou hovered excitedly near the golden animal. They all gazed in wonder at the beautiful horse as she reared up and then brought her front legs down to hit the bricks, separating them. She shook herself and her mane formed, made of splinters of golden glass. Blinking her large brown eyes, she reared up to touch the sprite hovering above her. Blou caught a tiny hoof and kissed it.

"What a beautiful little horse!" exclaimed Daisy.

Blou turned to her with a hushed voice. "Not a horse! A baby unicorn."

They spent a considerable amount of time trying to keep the unicorn quiet, until finally she settled down. Even Blou had been exhausted from the emotional effort of talking to the baby telepathically. It was hungry! But when she sipped some ice water she had a spasm, which scared them all. Finally, after eating a little bit of vanilla ice cream and nibbling on the green stems of carrots, the little unicorn calmed down. The baby, which they named Golden, fell asleep on a pile of pillows and afghan blankets. But after sleeping for only half an hour, she woke again to loudly call for food—demands they heard in their minds as well as in their stomachs. Ellora and Luke were very upset by this, though Daisy didn't seem to be affected. Golden did not have a nice, sonorous whinny. She sounded like chalk scraping a chalkboard combined with the sound a pterodactyl might have made! There was no calming Golden down until she had some more ice cream. She greedily licked her lips. When a curious Ellora looked in the baby unicorn's mouth, she was horrified to see sharp teeth instead of the blunt teeth of a horse. Golden was like a little lion and a horse combined. In fact, she looked like a long-legged lion with sharp little hooves and a face shaped like a pony's. Once her ferocious hunger was satisfied, she nuzzled Blou and snuggled in the soft bedding. Soon, they all fell asleep.

The next morning, Keevan stumbled out of bed from a night of tossing and turning. Descending the stairs, he found them all sprawled about the living room. He veered into the kitchen, rubbing one hand through his hair as he scraped the legs of a stool—to wake them up, but no one stirred. Only the coon cat was up, as if he were waiting for him. Keevan was certain Myster did not like him and felt his green cat eyes watched him as he got out some cereal and milk. Rats, there wasn't much milk left! He left everything out on the counter and went to snag some granola bars from the snack cabinet. He wished his dad would come home. He missed his mom, but she was gone—really gone now instead of just being away at work. He especially missed her guitar playing and had lain in bed listening to her latest platinum CD. Her voice sounded like a strangers, and he wasn't a huge fan of country music, but at last he could fall asleep. It was too quiet for him at night.

The screen door slammed as Keevan left the house with Myster following him. He went to feed the dogs, who were in the barn. He roughed up the shoulders and neck of the biggest one, his dog, Boris, who was so glad to see him. He was glad they had been able to bring him to the new house. The three dogs seemed to get along well. Maybe he could make a bedroom in the barn loft so he could sleep with Boris. Sharing a room with a weirdo eight-year-old who mumbled and talked in his sleep did not make Keevan happy. He wanted his own room, his own space in the new arrangements. Or maybe he could go live with Grandpa and Grandma Bradley, since they lived down the road?

THINGS ARE DISCOVERED

Marji came quietly downstairs. She could hear the three kids talking, but another voice was in the room too. She stopped on the last step as she saw Ellora feeding carrots to a tiny Palomino on the hearth rug. It seemed hungry. Where did they find it? Then a tinkling talking sound came from somewhere else, so she stopped to listen.

"...of course, we sprites are much fairer than pixies, gnatlanders, tinkers, or brownies. The gnatlanders are kin to the bees. Tinkers like metal and brownies are so wild and dirty they have forgotten they belong to Faerieland at all! They don't have wings, so they are never invited to celebrations or observations. Queen Merritt and the king are gifted with magik of the Faerieland, and have been since the beginning—"

"Are all the fairy tales true?" asked Luke. His eyes never left the sprite and, to tell the truth, she loved the attention. He was clearly enchanted by her.

"Of course, small-brother-of-Ellora-named-Luke. Thou must not interrupt!" she wiggled her fingers at him. "Our lands are full of stories and legends. We venture out at twining until the shining stars tell us 'tis time for sleep. Some nights we dance by the light of Luna and have merry times! When that cat recalls his wizard name, he can recant his spell to reverse the magik. Maybe then I can find my way out of Maine to my home, Balaktria in Faerieland."

Luke saw his Mom on the step. "Mom, look! Wait until I tell every-one on the bus about this!"

"I don't think you should tell anyone about her or the horse," she gravely told him.

"Golden is a unicorn, honorable one," Blou told her with a bow of courtesy. She knew to be as polite as possible to the Guardian. Even if she did not know who she was, it was not wise to make any mother angry. But if she did not know she was a Guardian and Ellora knew nothing of her own powers, then who knew what could happen? This might be quite a tale to tell by a glowing fire and the light of a midsummer's eve. All of her kin would be amazed and think she was not a truth teller! Imagine, a Blue Guardian and her seed, also a wielder of the blue magik and perhaps a rare wizard with the purple eyes spoken of in the prophecy! She clapped her wings together in delight.

They were all startled by a slam of the kitchen screen door, followed by Keevan bounding into the living room, as only a boy the age of thirteen can do, to announce, "Dad's home!"

All their attention shifted to Keevan, who was visibly happy about seeing his dad driving up their long driveway and being the first one to announce it. But also, he was clearly astonished at what he saw by the fireplace, a hovering blue creature with wings and a tinier, horse-like creature rearing up in response to his sudden presence. He rushed over to them to touch the horse, saying something about getting Luke another doll. At the same time, Ellora and Daisy tried to stop him. The unicorn dashed about, trying to hide under the couch, and Blou, furious, slashed at his outstretched hand, leaving a stinging cut. Marcus entered the house to a flurry of accusations, yelling, and a screeching neighing sound so high pitched it could break glass!

"What is going on?" Marcus hollered over all the commotion, looking around at this family that could never accurately be described as "normal."

"Dad! Luke scratched me with his new doll!" Keevan got his words out before anyone else could talk.

"I am not a doll, nor is Golden a pony. She is a baby unicorn and will grow. I am a Guardian sprite, so touch me at your peril, boy!" the sprite told him in a scathing tone, covering up the anxiety brought on by this new adult human. What would happen next? Things were getting out of control. She would need allies.

"I think we should all CALM down and get some answers!" scolded Marji, standing by Marcus as he put one arm around her shoulders. They faced the children, three of whom were in a semi-circle to keep anyone from hurting Golden. Blou could take care of herself.

Just in the nick of time, Myster dashed in through the cat door. He attempted to send thoughts of calm and reasoning through the chaos of emotions he felt. The next few minutes would be crucial to his plan. Those few minutes turned into an hour while they ate breakfast and asked so many questions! Marcus just kept shaking his head in disbelief. Keevan was beginning to get drowsy—he didn't know it, but Blou's tail had left behind a glistening drop of sleep venom when it had cut Keevan, and now it flowed through his body. When he nodded off over breakfast, everyone wanted to know what was wrong with him.

"'Tis only a mild sleeping potion. All Guardian faeries have this ability. I am a faerie sprite, so my venom is mild. A bite from a gnome or a troll can do more damage!" She did not want to add that Golden may also be able to inject venom, as the tiny fangs in her muzzle were slowly growing. Oh, well, they would soon know what the baby could or could not do. Magik was unpredictable in all matters. In fact, Blou was astounded that she could communicate with this human language so well. Magik must be helping. It had a way of giving you what you needed—but not what you wanted.

BELIEVABLE OR NOT

Marcus sighed. The story was so incredible. So unbelievable that he had many doubts at first. It took some extraordinary proof, provided by the pixie-faerie-thingy. She had made a potato with some sprouting heads grow into a vine that wound around his ankle at her command. She said there was magik in the house, and that Myster had explained there was strong magik in the family. All the things he had witnessed Luke do now all made sense, like his way with animals, wishing a thunderstorm would pass, or, more frighteningly, willing a storm to form. Ellora could take a potted plant that seemed dead and in a few days make it come alive, bloom, and grow out of its pot. Charles Dorr had hinted that his family was special, and he had a way with wood that everyone admired. Charlotte had a way with birds and animals. She'd nursed wounded creatures that always seemed to show up on her doorstep. She had a female shepherd named Molly that he swore could communicate with people. Molly brought Charlotte dying ducklings, hummingbirds, crows. Anything with a hint life, survived under Charlotte's care. It had all seemed like an elaborate game. But what did it all mean? What was going on? He had a feeling of foreboding that he couldn't shake. His family was different, sure. But how could they explain this? Right now, Keevan was the one he was worried about. He'd been asleep, still, when Marcus had checked him at midnight. He had half hoped that the magik hour of midnight would awaken him. But it didn't. Keevan snored on and the Pixie-thingy did not seem at all troubled. She said he would wake up when it was time. They all had a healthy appreciation for the little sprite's barbed tail now.

He turned over for the tenth time. A hand on his shoulder startled him. It was Marji. She also looked worried.

"I am sure Keevan will be fine. It's like he has taken a Benadryl. His heartbeat is steady, and his breathing is regular. It's as if he's in a deep dream state—his eyelashes are fluttering."

"If he's still asleep by late tomorrow, I'm taking him to the doctor."

She nodded in agreement and moved in to snuggle with him. It had been a strange day that she still could not believe, and yet, something within her did believe the crazy story the kids had told them.

"What do you think about ... all of it?" she asked him, needing to talk but rather dreading what he would say. She had known him longer than her deceased husband. Marcus had always been a good friend; she had known him since she was a child. Now he was more than a friend, and soon he would be her second husband.

"Well, I always knew your cat was weird. I always knew Luke was special in some way. I don't see anything bad in all of it, except the sleeping venom. I think we should cancel the kids going off to summer camp, though. I think we should all stay here ... stay home so we can—" his words trailed off and he couldn't think. He watched her face to see what she was thinking.

Marji began thoughtfully. "It's difficult to believe that I never saw any of this when I was growing up. I remember mom always told us that our family was special. She hinted at witches with empathy, energy vampires, and women with healing powers. The husbands allowed their wives to have their gifts and protected them from outsiders. I thought it was all a story. Now we are in the middle of something special and unique. The more we talk about it the better we will understand it. We are not doing anything wrong. We have been through something—something most people can't understand. Being here will help, somehow." Now it was her turn to grope for the adequate words and fail.

He hugged her tightly, feeling so thankful she was here to help him through this. He couldn't imagine dealing with it on his own.

"Hey, let's get married sooner than November!" he said in an excited whisper. "Let's get married in the rose garden, with my parents, your brother, and my sister as witnesses. Forget the fancy wedding—unless that's what you want?" He wasn't sure she would like this idea. But as he said it, it seemed like a great idea and would be less public, which was better, by his way of thinking.

"The girls want to be my bridesmaids and Luke wants to carry the ring on a pillow. We've rented the hall ... I don't know. ..." Her voice trailed off. "It would make things a heck of a lot easier this summer." Her own doubts were beginning to catch his excitement. "November is my busy month."

"Let's talk about it in the morning, okay? But let's decide soon"

These humans used the word "ok" for many things, Blou thought. She hadn't meant to listen in on their conversation. But her ears were better than most. Well, mostly everyone. She wondered what a "wedding" was. She clearly heard also that they had others in their family. Hmmm, she told herself, knowledge is power of a different sort. She tucked away the facts for use in the future. She flew on through the house, darting in and out and around their possessions, pausing to dip a finger into the icing on the beautiful cake that someone had forgotten to cover up— oh, chocolate was the best thing she had ever tasted! She left tiny claw marks in the frosting.

PRIVATE REFLECTIONS

The next day, in her grandmother's studio on the second story of the barn, Ellora held up the old mirror she had been given and softly called to Charlotte Drake Dorr. Ellora was a bit shaken up emotionally and wanted some alone time that she needed badly. The studio smelled wonderful. Memories clung to the old walls as if they had been painted on with oils or acrylic paint and the occasional sea mud mixture her grandmother had been fond of. This would be the first time Ellora would try to contact her with the mirror. In a letter, known only to Ellora, her grandma had described in detail some family secrets, left a rolled-up chart, this mirror, and a blue gemstone ring. It fit Ellora's finger exactly as if it were made for her. In fact, it had slid toward her as she reached for it in the cedar chest. Ellora had thought at the time it had been magnetic somehow. She felt mesmerized by the deep blue sapphire, or what she thought was a sapphire. The ring had some connection to Sir Francis Drake, their ancestor, but grandma had been unusually vague about how he came to have it. Ellora had read and re-read the letter to comb through its archaic wording and to see bits of her lovely relative within the stern words. Part of it had been written in a different hand—perhaps that was great grandmother's writing? The genealogy chart, faded in some areas, had for certain been filled in by many persons in the past. It was a very large and lengthy chart written on something other than paper; Ellora guessed it was papyrus. And it read from right to left—backwards, beginning with the very amazing name of Jasmine, seventh daughter of Eve! Other names popped out at her as she poured over at it; Queen Eleanor,

Queen Matilda, Katherine of Aragon. On the back, a shaky bit of writing said, "Kingdom of Navaratna." Some of the names were missing, and lines all over the chart led from one name to another in different ink colors. It looked like a weird map. She was having a tough time figuring it all out. She noticed another name was listed near Cynthia's: James Day White. Ellora wondered if the name was connected to the White family in Brunswick, who owned the bakery that her mom often used in her business. She sought an answer from her grandmother. As she held the old mirror, she said the magic words: Grandma has written that the mirror would not work unless a family member held it and spoke the words.

"We, the people of Navaratna, know our hearts are pure, our minds are our own. We seek the freedom and health of our souls and those of our descendants in perpetuity. So, say we all!"

At first she thought she had not spoken loudly enough, but soon the handle of the mirror grew cold. A frost formed upon the edges and clouded the face. She hurriedly wiped it with her sleeve, not wanting to miss anything. Faint images were forming like in her dreams. She could see people dressed in really old clothing as they walked or read from books. Occasionally, they would look up as if they'd heard her. One man actually took off his spectacles, frowning as he wiped them on his sleeve, and spoke to someone out of her view. He gestured to himself and mouthed something.

Oh! Ellora remembered: she had to put her finger on the chart in order to find the person with whom she wanted to speak. Her finger tapped on Charlotte Dorr Drake, and slowly the man faded while her grandmother came into view. She kissed the surface of the mirror and Charlotte recoiled.

"Good Gracious Ellora, what on earth are you doing?"

"Oh Grandma, it's so good to see you." Ellora's voice faltered as tears welled up in her eyes.

"Oh, it's so nice to hear your voice too. I see you found the letter, and did you find the ring?" she asked, sounding desperate.

"Yes, I have it on!" She held up her right hand and showed her the ring.

"Be careful of it, and do not let anyone else touch it—even your mom. The ring has powers of its own, in very subtle ways it can enhance your own talents. It can help you know the hearts of others and also give you strength when yours is failing. For me, it helped me find your grandpa—the love of my life—" She sighed as if she didn't know what else to say.

"Grandma, lots of things have been happening. Why can't I show people my ring?"

"Listen to me. You must go into the library and shut the door. Always remember to shut the door! There is a secret chamber through a small door to the left of the bathroom. To open it, you must lightly knock on the panel. When the door opens you must knock again to keep it closed. Otherwise, creatures will be able to follow you. They live in the library. I know this is a lot to believe. But if we wish to talk in private, you must do this. I will wait for you there." As she turned away from Ellora, who cried for her grandmother to wait, Charlotte's German shepherd came into the room. It always surprised her that Molly could climb the steep barn stairs. The other dogs would not, but Molly may have heard Charlotte's voice and responded to that. Molly searched the room as Ellora sat there, crying a few tears. She hugged the dog close, then stood up, gathering her things as she went to do as she was told. Outside, the maple tree was in the full bloom of summer, and full of very large crows! Silently they watched her. She didn't feel nervous at first, until one squawked, inviting the others to join in. The largest one leaned forward to Ellora, intently screeching at her. Molly barked back at them, which sent some of them airborne. She had to hold on to the dog's collar to keep her from taking off after them.

Myster came out of the house through the cat door, in a flurry and howling. The crows abruptly stopped. Luke also came out to see what was going on. This commotion of crows did not alarm him at all. To him it was "normal" for this family. Ellora unconsciously sent a telepathic message to her grandmother that she was coming. When she did that, Myster swung his head around to her, acting as if he wanted her to pick him up. But she brushed him off and hurried into the house, to the library. She forgot to shut the door.

⤜⤜⤝

"What was that all about?" Marji asked Marcus. They decided to leave Ellora alone and went back to reading their emails. The cat emerged through the little cat door, and the dog tried to follow but got stuck. This prompted some activity to get the dog unstuck, and then Daisy poked her head out of the loft to let them know that Keevan was awake. They all went upstairs to see him, except for the cat, who went to the library door and scratched to be let in. In all the commotion, none of the family saw that the hand that closed the door was not human but very faerie-like. Myster meowed his frustration.

Luke remained outside, listening to the crows. They seemed to be very agitated today. He realized there was a raven sitting among them. His awareness of his surroundings began to change and expand. He sat by the gate to the vegetable garden to the side of the house. The air had changed; he could feel it. He let his mind wander, as if he were day-dreaming, but it was more than that. The raven watched him intently. The sounds filtering to him were the faint calls of the Canadian geese nibbling grass down by the boatshed, and bees happily finding flowers. He could hear tinier sounds like salamanders wriggling under damp, dark objects for safety. A giant, quiet snail was also moving in one direction. They were all headed for the barn for some reason. Luke's senses picked up the feeling of urgency and expectation. He looked up. The raven bobbed its head at him, as if to say "yes." Luke squeezed his eyes shut and concentrated harder. Immediately his system was assailed by hundreds of clicks, buzzing, squeaking, and a stretching "pop"! The last sound was from the snail. Luke decided this creature would take so much time to reach the barn that it wouldn't make it. He gently picked it up, careful not to interrupt its equilibrium. The snail told him that it had to remain horizontal else it would become dizzy and sick. She also let it be known that she was thirsty, so Luke carefully dribbled some fresh water for her from the old-fashioned pump by the porch. The sound of the mechanism seemed extraordinarily loud to him, as if his hearing was one hundred times better than before. He would have to get earplugs if this kept up! After helping another, smaller snail and some June bugs, he decided to go inside to get a tray so he could carry more than a few at a time. That's when he heard Myster shout that he needed help!

MESSENGERS AND LOOKOUTS

The First Regiment of ravens flew ahead toward the island. One of their regiment had remained behind to watch the children who were now living in the magikal House. The First Regiment had worked hard to earn their names. They flew far and wide, keeping Dingley Island safe with knowledge of the happenings. New births, recent deaths, the return of the bears, the travels of the wolves—all could be seen by the Firsts.

Kassa was one that earned his name. He uttered three words "The children awaken!"

Kassa reported these words to his regiment commander. He knew there was one to whom these words mattered greatly: Rahven, the white raven.

Kassa was a grandson of their Commander, Taldassa. And he, in turn, was grandson of the great, Kaldassa. It was this raven who was called 'friend' by the original owner of the magikal house, Master Audran. Many tales were told of their adventures together. It had been many years since that wizard had been alive. Now it was Kassa's time to spread the word, and to guard the island with his mates. They flew high and proud each day. They reported all they saw to their commander.

IN THE LIBRARY AND THE CAVERN

Myster muttered to himself. Things were not going as planned. He was forgetting things that used to be so important to him. The humans considered him their pet- not the other way around the way as it should be! Ellora and Luke were his main concern, but now Keevan was waking and they were talking about taking him to see a doctor. Such a waste of precious time! Now Ellora had disappeared into the library, the door closing behind her. If she were in the secret passage, he would need help to find it. So far, as a cat, he had never been able to open it because the door would only respond to a human knocking. The crows told him that the ravens were coming with news, and he did not wish to miss that message either by lurking in the library. Drat, if he could only trust Kipper to do one of these jobs, but Kip, as much as he liked that cat, was not very magical. His awareness would not come for perhaps decades. Myster could not wait that long.

When Luke came up behind him, Myster sent him a telepathic message: *Quickly, into the library!*

Luke pushed open the heavy oak door and went in, the cat at his heels. Inside, the library was unlike any other room, for as you walked toward the north end, the room seemed to never come to an end—as if it grew longer. Myster hastily moved through the room, sniffing the floor like a dog. Ellora's faint smell grew stronger by the bathroom, as if she had halted her steps for a few seconds. Myster went over to the wall. He looked up expectantly at Luke, who in turn looked down at the cat.

Knock upon this wall and it will open! Myster commanded.

Luke looked behind him as he wondered if his mom would wonder where he was. She was upstairs with Keevan. A curious horsey face peaked into library—he had not closed the door after he and Myster went inside. Golden whinnied at him in her way, then Blou flew in. Luke went back to close the door. Myster impatiently clawed at the wall. When Luke returned, he tapped on it and a secret door opened slightly. He hesitated. Should he go through? What would happen?

Ellora isss in there and she might need usss! Myster exclaimed. Somehow, he knew this place was important! He had forgotten why but he must enter this new secret place.

Blou and Golden went through the secret door without any fear, so Luke followed, trailed by the cat. Myster stood up on hind legs to close the door behind them and told Luke to knock on it so it would remain locked until a human opened it up again. Little did he know how long that would take!

They were in a very large room with an arched stone roof and curved side walls with shelves dug into them. On the shelves were very old scrolls covered with cobwebs, old Christmas ornaments, some nicely made wooden sailing ships complete with tiny figures on them, very unusual dolls dressed in period clothing that Luke did not recognize, some other items that he could only guess what they were, and some old woodworking tools. The shelves went on and on into the back recesses of the cavern. There was a giant full-length mirror in a stand hewn from marble. It looked very clean in the dark, dank cave. Suddenly, they heard laughter and went to find the source. It was Ellora, seated on a beautiful wooden bench, holding an antique mirror that she put down in her lap as they approached.

"Who are you talking with?" Luke asked her. She motioned for him to sit next to her.

"We can talk to Grandma with this magic mirror! It's like she's not dead!" she said in an excited voice. "It's activated by a magic chant and a family member has to be holding it. If you tap your finger on someone listed on this genealogy chart, we can talk to them if they are in the sanctuary. Grandma said we cannot enter unless we have passed on in this life—so you and I cannot go in until we ...die."

"Oh" said Luke in a small voice. "Then I guess we can't come back either."

"No, honey bunny!" Grandma's voice came booming through the mirror into the cavern. "Luke, how are you?"

"I'm sad, Grandma. I miss you and Grampa," he said in a quiet voice. The echo in the room was unsettling.

"I know, honey, I miss you too. Grampa is around here somewhere. This place is a vast complex full of every sort of thing you can imagine, and there are a lot of people here working and learning. And you know Grampa, always learning something every day."

Both of Charlotte's grandchildren nodded their heads.

"And who is this, might I ask?"

"I am Blouette, elegant, honorable, Guardian," Blou said in the standard greeting with her hand on her heart, tail upright, wings beating ever so slowly, waiting for the greeting reply that should be coming.

"Greetings, fair one. I am glad of your presence. My grandchildren need you!" Charlotte replied as graciously as she could with her hand over her heart, fingers spread in the secret greeting she had been told about from someone special.

How did she know the secret sign? Blouette wondered. This Charlotte seemed to know her.

MEANWHILE

Marji and Marcus rushed over to Keevan, who sat up in bed. "Kee, are you okay?" his dad asked. "You've been asleep for quite a while."

"Yeah, I feel great! I'm hungry!" Keevan began to get out of bed, but his legs weren't quite ready for standing or walking and he slumped to the floor.

"I am going to get that sprite to ask her what's going on now!" Marji exclaimed, and she left the room, calling out for Blou.

Marcus asked his son, "What do you remember?"

"I remember seeing Luke with his new flying toy and another toy that looked like a horse. I don't feel very good all of a sudden." His voice trailed off as he tried to get up again. He, finally, simply sat on the bed. Marcus brought him a small glass of water. He gripped the glass tightly to steady his hand and sipped it.

"It isn't a toy, is it?" Keevan asked. "What is it?"

Marji came back up the stairs to report. "I can't find Blou or Golden, and the kids are also missing. They're not in the house. I'll try the barn!" And she left again.

"Well Kee, it's all kind of a crazy story that we don't understand. Apparently, this house has magic in it, our family can use magic, and it seems that Myster, the cat, can talk—or tries to at least. We're all just trying to ... believe it's really happening. The horse is a baby unicorn that acts like a cat or a lion sometimes. Oh, by the way, you should stay away from its horn and the tail of the sprite, too."

"It's not some kind of flying robot?" Kee asked.

"No, it's real," his dad replied. "The sprite stabbed you with a sleeping venom and you have been sleeping all day and night!"

"I have?" Kee asked. "I honestly feel fine, just hungry. But when I try to walk, I feel a little sick."

"How about I make you some toast and bring it up here?"

"Sure, Dad."

While Marcus made toast, he realized that he was hungry too. They hadn't eaten very much last night. He could hear Marji calling out as she searched for the kids. Then he also realized that Daisy was had disappeared since telling them Keevan was awake. A short search revealed she was fast asleep in her own bed. He tried to wake her up, but she only murmured and turned over. What the hell? Had that pixie thingy poked her with venom too? He shook her a little harder,

"Daisy wake up! *What* is going on?"

"Yes, what is going on?" Marji asked, coming up the stairs, a bit out of breath from running all over the yard and scouring the barn. "I can't find them anywhere!"

"Daisy is asleep like Keevan was. I think the sprite stabbed her too!"

"What?! Why would it do that?" Marji asked, not waiting for an answer. She yelled again, using a commanding voice that she did not like to use.

"Blou, get in here NOW!" The house shuddered in response, which itself was unnerving.

SOME ANSWERS BUT MORE QUESTIONS

The ravens of the First Regiment had settled all around the home unit of the cat who was in charge of the humans. They sensed a great deal of wild magik in the area, but none of it was evil. As one, they perched upon the house, the barn, the boatshed, even the sailboat in the cove. A few were on the clothesline, the vehicles parked in the driveway, even in the apple trees lining the walkway that led to the main house. Everywhere was being watched by many pairs of eyes. The waited for the cat to appear, but only three dogs were in the yard. Some humans were inside the house, the Guardian was calling out to her guardlings, or children, they were called, Kassa had learned from his teacher. One cat appeared from the smaller door in the side of the house, but he was young and could not speak to them. They waited in silence.

Down the road an amazing sight was slowly coming into view. If the ravens knew that their Rahven was coming, they gave no sign except for some ruffling of feathers and twitching. They'd been told to be silent and not one of them would break rank. Unless, of course, danger appeared. Then they would fight! There would be glory in the fight and in the telling afterward, but not before. The sight was a large white raven with blue eyes riding a bay mare.

Honey, the mare, had to step carefully, for when the bird lost its balance and it would use its talons to regain an upright position. She was tired. As she crossed over a low bridge connecting the island with another island, she came to the edge of a meadow filled with lush clover. She, halted, took one or two mouthfuls, then walked on, the goal in sight—the house. A few of the younger ravens squawked. A stern glance from their commander silenced them.

Rahven, for his part, trusted the mare completely. His eyesight was poor, and he had aged much in the past years. His one hope of finding the purple-eyed children of the prophecy was coming true. He'd heard the children had awakened, possibly making him the Rahven to fulfill the prophecy. He was the only white raven in this region. White animals or birds with the gift of magik lived in other parts of Terra. Was it... a gift? he asked himself. Sometimes he thought it was not such a gift. But of course, he should not think like this. What if the Others prevailed? What was it really that they wanted, that they had sought for thousands of moons? Magik, of course was stronger than plain magic, which sometimes was simply an illusion. Goddess magik had strength and tenacity, it was fluid and had its own knowledge. It gave you what you needed but not what you wanted. This he had known this ever since the Teacher had found him as a fledgling. The others in his flock had remained apart from him, and he was nearly dead from starvation. Two gentle hands picked him up and a kind voice told him that he would be okay, he was special. As he grew, he came to realize that possibly, he was the One named in the prophecy, the keeper of the history and the truth.

Honey stopped by the front porch, sniffing the dog bowl of water. She began to drink when, suddenly, a small dog came out of the house through the cat door, barking loudly. Polly did not like her water being drained by another. When the larger door opened, revealing the Blue Guardian and her mate, Honey bent down to allow Rahven to hop onto the porch railing. He gripped it with strong talons, waiting for the greeting. When it did not come, he croaked, "Greetings!" and then, telepathically, *I have come. The prophecy is coming true. I shall speak with the cat of this house.*

"The cat is not here right now. Myster is missing, along with my two children, and IF you know anything, you'd better tell me now!" Marji answered, using her "command voice," which seemed to fly through the air. The ravens scattered.

O Guardian, I know nothing of the missing children. The ravens tell me that there has been an awakening ... here. I seek the cat, Myster, who has been awaiting her coming of age. You tell me they are missing? The white bird was familiar with this house--he knew its former mistress and master. Now there were new humans in command, but they showed no knowledge of the courtesies to be spoken nor the magik within. He seemed outwardly composed, but in truth he was very nervous. The pulsing purple barrier of the barn was proof enough that there was still magik in the air, in the stones, in the very wood of the house and the forest nearby. The trees swayed to an ancient song, even though there was no wind. The stones in a straight wall following the path moved slightly and then undulated, and a few of them tumbled down off the top, hopping over one another as if playing a game. But much of the wall held.

The white bird sedately walked through the front door as if had been invited. There was a faint smell of burning in the air as the Rahven watched the male human put food in a metal box that burned it. A strange ritual thought Rahven. The man then used a blunt knife to spread some colors onto the food and place them on flat circle made of pottery. This he carried off to someone who called out that he was really hungry. Rahven could tell it was someone waking up from a sleeping spell; his speech was somewhat slurred. Rahven flew to the rafters to gain an outlook from above. As he peered around, he saw the house still had its view to all four directions through glass, which he could tap with his beak. He wondered if the construction could withstand an assault. The raven commander, Taldassa, thought yes. He squawked and some of the black ravens flew off toward the shoreline to survey the perimeter. The ancient salted water could be called upon as defense better than drinking water. Then he sensed the power in the fireplace and flew down for a look.

"*What?*" he croaked. "*What happened here?*"

"If you must know, my daughter, Ellora, woke up a captured pixie named Blou a few nights ago. Then other children, Luke and Daisy, helped her awaken a baby unicorn, which somehow stabbed my other son with a sleeping venom. Now Daisy is sleeping and won't wake up—I think that pixie stabbed her too! And I can't find any of them! Marcus, what are we going to do?" explained Marji.

"Awk!" croaked the Rahven. *Not a pixie. A sprite has the venom for sleep. Simple but powerful magik. This Blou is Blouette? Guard sister to Queen Marigold?*

"I suppose so, answered Marji crossly. Honestly, I just don't know what to make of all this and I am stressing out!" She realized that she had been speaking to the a that had flown up into the rafters of her home. Why did she understand what it was saying?

"*Certainly, search all you want, but the cat, a boy and a girl, along with the unicorn and the sprite, are within the library, which has mighty magik built into its wood and walls. The Brownies living there have told me thus.*"

Marcus and Marji looked at one another in amazement. Why were there Brownies were living in the library?

Marcus said, "I want to search the house and the barn myself, if that's okay." He bowed sarcastically to the bird, who took no offense, being glad one of the humans was using manners.

Rahven glided down to the library door and tapped on it gently. To their amazement, the door handle turned, and it opened. Just inside were two Brownies, who had clearly been standing one on top of the other. As the door opened, the top one tumbled off in a smooth acrobatic maneuver. The other, taller one, stood at attention, musty and sad looking, as they all entered. The whites of Brownies' eyes could be seen, but they were covered in all sorts of fabric, string, leaves, and dirt.

Marcus hadn't spent much time in the library, but Marjorie remembered it looking much different. The walls seemed taller now, and the room was longer.

The tall Brownie, looking chagrined and contrite, let them know his name was Gitchie and then he introduced his family; Abequa, Aisinwin, and Maemaegwin. Speaking rather well for a "dirty unkempt creature," he sang, "Gitchie tried, oh great Rahven, I called, but no one came to help me! The children who entered were magikal and the sprite told me to mind my own business! As if I were not! Minding my own business, I meant…" His lyrical voice was totally opposite his tattered attire.

Marji felt she could listen to him for hours. He had a sing-song voice—soprano, she thought, her mind wandering. She tried to focus. Marcus was looking dazed too, as the Brownie magik had settled upon them, making them forget what they were doing. They absently turned away from one another and fingered the edges of a few books before each choosing one to bring to the comfortable couch and chair nearby.

Rahven looked at them, looked at the Brownie and gave a command to stop sending his spell to them.

Stop! These humans are the parents of the magik ones. We seek them now. Two more children lay under a sleeping spell. Could you please, for the love of the Goddess, help them? We need their focus and minds to be sharp. There are changes coming and trouble is on the wing and the wind.

The master of the house requires us to guard the library and to not allow outsiders to enter. But mistress and master have been neither seen nor heard for quite a while—for over twelve moons passing, complained Gitchie.

Rahven assured him that he and his family had done a good service to the master and mistress. *But I believe that these two humans are in command now. The mistress is the daughter of Charlotte. He is a also descendant of the drake, and master of the house.*

Forsooth? Am I to make homage to these two? He scoffed and gestured to Marji, then Marcus. *They know not the secrets of this house nor of the magik within, and they have a sprite!* Gitchie continued in the less-than-polite tone he used when talking about lesser beings not in tune with the Goddess.

Perhaps thee can sing a ballad explaining it all to them? I am certain they would acknowledge your wisdom as caretakers of the library. But now, I have need of thee … please. And the bird gestured with its thick beak to the loft upstairs.

Not truly wanting to obey, the Brownie left the room to rush upstairs, for he was surprisingly quick and agile. Down he came almost immediately, riding the banister, letting out an undignified "WHOOP!" as he landed. From inside the library, his family, consisting of a mate and two littles, clapped in appreciation of the trick. One of the littles attempted to leave the doorway but was sternly halted by its mother. Rahven could not tell its gender but it seemed to have a determination to its face that made Rahven believe he or she would be the next caretaker.

It is done, oh Rahven. I did what I could, not having a true nicorn to cleanse the venom from their blood. But I used the mint of pepper to brighten their minds, the Brownie said proudly.

Well done and brightly performed, but linger, we have need of thee, replied Rahven. His attention switched to Marji and Marcus. The smell of peppermint filled the air and the spell was leaving them. They looked mildly embarrassed, questioning the books in their hands. Rahven decided to help them focus by shaming them ... a bit.

"Now is not the time for reading. Stories are for later when the mystery is solved. When did you last see your children?"

Kassa entered the room with a report. *The commander tells all that a storm approaches that is like no other in many moons. The villagers are preparing, and the eagle has left her nest. Many seek refuge within the barn.*

All the creatures including the Brownies looked expectantly at Marcus and Marji. But they had not understood the message, not being able to speak raven.

So Rahven had to explain and to translate. "Long ago this house was built by a master builder who was also a wizard. He was sought by the Others as their magik was waning. Within this fortress lie certain magikal artifacts that could be stolen, then drained of their magic. As the years went by each new master and mistress had a scroll of passwords and codes for maintaining Dingley and Eagle islands along with Feather and Bone Cove. This island was renamed for Dingley, son of Mistress Victoria and Master Isaac, who died fighting the Others. It is a sacred space and a magik place."

Upon hearing this name, the creatures in the room put their right hands over their hearts and bowed their heads, murmuring "Dingley" in tribute to the fallen hero.

Rahven looked expectantly at Marji and Marcus to see if they understood his explanation. They in turn were dumbfounded, still feeling abashed for their behavior, bewildered at the events unfolding, and annoyed at Keevan. He had appeared in the library and was now urgently saying he was still very hungry and that Daisy, too, needed something to eat.

Hopping up on a chair and then a desk that held a computer, Gitchie went online and turned on the weather tracker. The voice on the screen startled them all. News Weather Six was reporting a large Nor'easter headed for Casco Bay, Maine.

What would her Mother have done? Marji asked herself. Charlotte would have shooed them all to the barn and then begun cooking or harvesting food in the garden for everyone. Charles would have gone to check on his precious sailboat. Perhaps filling jugs of water would be a good task for Keevan and Daisy. Where were Ellora and Luke? Thinking of them lost made her very anxious.

Giving in to the absurdity of it all, she gave an order to the raven, she said, "Tell everyone that they are welcome to shelter in the barn for safety."

The raven gave a loud remark and flew off, with all the black birds following him. Good, that got him out of the house, and the rest of them off the porch. As she began to issue orders, Marji felt her sense of control returning. Rahven began exploring the library, for he knew they had another job to do—find the secret door. She went back to the kitchen, a room where she felt more naturally in charge. Marcus went out to the barn to see what was actually going on and came back a while later with an amazing report.

"You won't believe what I found in the barn!" Marcus said. "A badger, some skunks, a horse, all sorts of critters. The dogs are outdoors in the yard and Molly seems to be escorting animals to places inside the barn. Something—I think it was a huge raccoon—filled the water trough!"

"Please ask Keevan and Daisy to store water for us. If we lose power the pump won't work. There are plenty of clean jugs in the garden shed. I need to call the neighbor find out if we have his horse!"

The brownie came to give her the printed weather report, just as Marcus accessed it on his phone. "Kind Mistress and Master, this storm is a Nor'easter! Shall I activate the storm shield?"

"You have a printer? This house has a storm shield?" Marji asked incredulously. "What next?"

"Kind Mistress, the barn also has its own shield, which is automatic. That is why the forest animals and the woodland creatures have sought safety within. They know it will protect them. But the house shield has not been used in many moons. We missed the upgrade. I had no one to ask permission." His reply was contrite, yet it also sounded like a mild accusation.

"Henceforth, in the case of protecting the house and its grounds, you have permission to do upgrades as you see fit, as long ... as long as it does not interfere with or harm this family or our friends." She added, as a precaution, "and please continue to keep me and Marcus posted on critical events happening." She had a feeling that Gitchie and his mate, Abequa, knew about the all the amenities of the house but were very strictly following orders to say nothing because of an older command made by her father.

The worried brownie turned to Marcus. "The island locks on the bridges must be set free. The storm arrives on the high of the tide. None of the Others must access this island! It is necessary for the master to say the words. The shield will not activate because the magik will not heed my voice." Gitchie shrugged, and again his voice held a slight tone of accusation.

Marcus nodded. "What does it do? I mean, what do I say?"

The littlest brownie, Maemaegwin, bowed calmly and seriously stepped forward and handed Marcus an old scroll. As he unrolled it, Marcus read the words and let out a laugh. "Release ... the ... Kraken ... ha!" He laughed again. "Really? I have always wanted to say that!" He took a few seconds to compose himself, nodding to the brownies. Sternly and with composure he did not quite feel, he announced, "I am the Master, Release the Kraken!" Immediately a BOOM, BOOM! could be heard in the distance, causing the animals crossing the bridge to scatter, some jumping into the water to swim ashore. The locks on all eight ends of the two bridges exploded and came apart, leaving the island totally unattached to any other land. The massive stonework crumbled down like sand into the coming tide, its wake causing a tiny tsunami. A squeaking mother opossum began a terrified swim for the shore, her babies clinging to her for safety. One of them fell off in the swelling waters, but a raven swooped down to rescue it and also helped the mother to safety. A wild cat, looking very bedraggled, also made it to the shore with help from the same bird. The raven and cat eyed each other, but neither would break rank. Rescue was not the time for hunting. The raven flew back to report.

Gitchie had sent his son, Aisinwin, riding the smallest dog, Polly, out to inspect. He discovered the almost invisible storm shield was extending, slowly expanding, stopping along the shoreline, pulsing back and forth, undulating like a rippling wave. Aisinwin noted a stranded seal on the shore; she looked as if she were about to give birth. He urged his mount to run like the wind and whooped and hollered as he entered the yard for help. Polly added her quips and barks to the yelling. She was having a great time!

"There is a small Leviathan mother about to give birth!" he announced to the onlookers. "There on the shore, we must give her aid, or the baby may perish." His voice broke with tears at the thought of that happening.

Marcus got out the binoculars to take a look, while Kassa went to check out the situation.

"Indeed, commander, there is a mother seal about to give birth," the raven soon reported.

Aisinwin, mortified at his mistake, hung his head in shame while his father spoke stern but loving words of how he must learn the animals of the sea better than this!

Kassa's report went on: "I rescued an opossum family and gave aid to a wild cat. There are more animals on the opposing shore who dare not make the crossing."

What could they do? Marcus decided that the seal would be okay, as they typically give birth alone and outdoors, but he promised Aisinwin that they would check on her and maybe, just maybe, bring her a fish in the morning, if she were still there. He smiled reassuringly at the young brownie, whose countenance was not so sad anymore, for the master of the house had spoken to him! His chin came up with a little bit of pride.

The sky grew dark. Keevan, with Kassa balanced on his left arm, checked on the occupants of the barn. They found quite a menagerie. He spoke into a small round box as all the ears within the barn focused on him.

"Yeah, Dad, this walkie-talkie was a great idea. It looks like we are full up. Should I close the barn doors?"

Marcus flipped through the scroll, searching for the command that he was assured would be on channel sixteen.

"No, Kee, come back to the house. I have to speak the command. Hold up the walkie-talkie. Here it is: Close the pod bay doors, Hal!"

Keevan held it up as his Dad's voice came through loud and clear. He got out just in time. He watched from the yard as the enormous doors moved with creaks and groans as the mechanism within responded to the magik woven into its molecules. All the doors of the barn shut with a resounding thud, clang, click and whirls, and then the dust settled. The animals were in for the night. Good thing, because the wind was picking up, whipping the clothesline off its wooden posts. The scarecrow in the garden was spinning creepily around as the wind changed directions several times. The rain began to splatter on the yard and house. It was strange that the wind and rain would be able to enter the barrier, but not other things. Keevan had a hard time getting back to the house, as the wind buffeted him, snatching away his baseball cap. When he ran after his hat he stumbled across something in the rose garden. Astoundingly, a sword was stuck in the middle of the ground there. Keevan forgot all about his hat as he went over to the weapon. It did not look very special, having a plain hilt with nothing on it. He didn't remember ever having seen it before. As he grasped the hilt, the sword flashed blue then returned to normal. He pulled it from the ground with ease. There was no time to clean it or admire it as the rain and wind whipped him as if it were urging him towards the house. In all the commotion, he was able to take his newly found treasure up to his room without his parents noticing.

THE STORM AND THE BATTLE

Making homemade pizza was a great idea. It got Marji's mind off her worries for a moment. Rahven and Kassa, though, along with the brownies, thought the food was fine without the darkening of it in the fire. Daisy liked plain cheese, while Keevan ate the pepperoni with gusto. Marcus was looking out at the storm drinking tea. Abequa had made it for him and it was quite good. He was still worried about the kids, but more so about the village and the storm. The weather channel gave reports of power outages all over the Eastern seaboard. The eye of the storm was over the very town in Maine where they lived. That could not be a coincidence, he thought.

Marji was talking the raven's ear off, questioning over and over about what the kids could be doing behind the secret door. For all she knew, they were asleep somewhere. But where? Rahven assured her that if they were in the Sanctuary, they were fine—most likely speaking with the ancestors. Blou would watch out for them (to a certain extent, but Rahven didn't say this to the worried Guardian). Gitchie tried to help by finding journal entries made by past occupants of the house for her to read. She began to flip through the house journal hastily, because most of the entries noted births and deaths of the townspeople, who inherited what, what artifacts had been found. Wait a minute! Here was something interesting: notes of a weird dust storm appearing on the horizon at dusk, blotting out all sunlight, and accompanied by a wild thunderstorm that had killed some students:

The students who attended the School for the Gifted are no more. They did not survive being struck by lightning in the cruel thunderstorm. This is the lie we told the villagers. My husband, being the island coroner, was the one to sign their death certificates. After the battle, it was deemed necessary to erect better force fields all over the island, and to put in a power source to generate enough power to hold for several weeks. Dingley and his friends were buried on the hill overlooking the smaller bay and Bone Cove, it shall be known forever more.

Victoria Day Drake, Mistress of the House

Another entry caught Marji's eye, this one written by Katharine Drake, sister to Dingley:

This is my first entry, and one of many I am certain. More and more each day Father is drifting away from us in his search for Dingley's spirit. He sits atop the boulder, head in hands, meditating and listening. A white raven follows him, even into the house, but Mother shooed it out. It is quite an unusual bird, for it has blue eyes and so is not an albino.

Day two: Some villagers came to ask if we needed help with the yard work. The hired men were quick to cut up the wood into kindling. One of them aided Father's mare, Rose, in giving birth to her first foal, but the baby died within a few hours. They took this as a bad omen. Some of the men cursed the storm that had killed seven young people from their town. Many of them also cursed the schoolmaster, who has disappeared, leaving all his books and belongings in the schoolhouse. Mother agreed that the belongings of the missing headmaster, Mr. O'dran, could be brought here for safekeeping. The villagers wanted her to take up the task of guiding the younger students still at the school, but Mother shook her head no. The school will have to close. Sadly, the men all left after we fed them supper. Mother at least will eat. Father rarely sees anyone, having stormed into the library last night, locking the door behind him. The brownies have been forbidden to open it. Mother knocks softly on the door occasionally through the day. I miss my brother.

Katharine Victoria Drake, Assistant Mistress

As if in response to what Marji had read, a tremor went through the house, like a sob. The wind was really whipping through the trees and many branches had fallen. In amazement, Daisy saw parts of the stone wall tumble down, but the stones jumped right up and settled atop the wall repeatedly. She pointed this out to the others, who also watched in amazement.

"What's making them do that?" Daisy asked, munching on her second piece of pizza.

Rahven answered, with Gitchie chiming with an agreeable singsong phrase. "The stones will roll but never break, the crack will seal but never be healed."

Rahven motioned for the brownie to be silent. "There are eight cracks in the ledges under the ground. They were created by the Others to destroy the island. But Dingley prevailed and set the rifts with living volunteers, whose blood and bones forever keep out the Others. It is perhaps that they are attempting again to test the magik here. Since true magik of love is the strongest, it was Dingley's faithful friends who gave their lives in service to this house, this hill, this island. Each rift was met with the bones and blood of one of the eight warriors until even the ninth, Dingley himself, had died to forever seal the magik here. It is not known how he knew to do this. It broke his mother's heart, and after the funeral, she closed the journal and wrote never again. The seven friends came from the clans within the Village, six young men and one maiden, all from the village school. And not many know that Gitchie's own great grandsire was the eighth warrior to give his life."

The Brownie family stood in a row, heads bowed in a moment of remembrance. When they looked up, it was with sad pride.

Gitchie added, "My father was young. He wished to go to the battle site, but the house would not let him out. The library door sealed itself but with the aid of bino ... culars he watched as his father and young master joined with the very ground upon which they stood, staff in one hand and orb in the other. Ha! The Others were fooled! They conspired that he would throw the orb at them, but instead he thrust it into the dirt beneath his feet, and it seeped into the stones, rocks and sand, into the must and the dust…"

"Yes, yes," croaked Rahven. "We get the point." He hastily added, "All hail Dingley and his friends!"

As the solemn moment ended, the eye of the storm passed, and the wind blew again with renewed vigor. The lights in the distance flickered and went out, only to shine again a few moments later as the villager's generators came on. To conserve the energy of the solar power cells, a house generator came on. They could hear it power up behind the library.

Keevan spoke up for the first time in a long while. "I think you mean binoculars."

BUT NO ONE IS SUSPICIOUS

The barnies, or barn brownies, were happy as could be taking care of so many different animals. The honey-colored mare was their new favorite. She was a darling and loved the attention they were paying to her back, which had been scratched by Rahven's talons. The soothing herbal ointment she had requested from Abequa was carefully rubbed into her back. She waved her mane constantly, something she could not do when the bird was astride her back. Outdoors, the wind howled, and branches tumbled off the roof, which had a very steeply pitched roof and was the reason these branches did not linger upon the shield to cause a momentary surge in power. But Honey was not concerned with that. She knew she was safe inside the barn. She was now hungry and asking for meal. It came in a barrow wheeled by all the little barnies, who giggled and tossed her grass as high as they could so she could catch it. The neighbor's stallion in the next stall watched everything with much interest.

The chickens announced that eggs were coming, and sure enough, some white, light green and some brown eggs gently rolled down the ramps made especially for that purpose. The other animals were not particularly interested in chicken eggs, but they were very keen on the corn in the cargo hold. Someone, maybe the raccoon, had gotten into the storage bins, but the barnies did not stop him. As they saw it, it was good the animals were all being fed and watered. One of the older barnies climbed up into the storage above to cut the twine surrounding a bale of hay to give the animals clean, dry bedding. "Watch out below!" was the order given. They all watched the hay tumble to the floor. Then more barnies set to work distributing the hay. Once the lids had been replaced on the storage bins, they would magically refill. They did know not to overfeed the horses or allow the raccoons into the aging root beer. Once in a while, one of the bottles would blow and a good time was had by all! Perhaps, due to the storm, a bottle or two would burst this time too. Even the forest brownies would be pleased and come for a drop with their small tin cups. The storm did not seem too terrifying or suspicious.

THE MEMORY OF A MOUSE
A true account of the Battle of Dingley

Maemaegwin found another old scroll in the library. It was the testimony of Jeremy, the mouse who was a friend to the schoolmaster, O'dran. As Marji read it, she thought, hmm, the names Audran and O'dran are so similar. What if they are the same person?

Not many know the truth of the events leading to the deaths of Dingley and his companions. No one else knew there was a tenth participant with a fully-grown unicorn, Axoparia, up on the hill that night. What drew them to all be there that fateful night? In one word, love. The school-master, Mr. O'dran, was in truth, the ancient wizard Audran. His student, Dingley, convinced Axoparia to use her secret weapon against the Others. The nicorn, her horn, was a lightning rod with the ability to repel lightning. Also, upon the hill that night was the faithful brownie, Pilchie, sworn in allegiance to his master, Dr. Isaac Joseph Drake, who was Dingley's father. And one maiden, the fair Cassandra Drake, was one of the students also. The six young men were from families in the village, where they attended the School for the Gifted. (Wheldon, Billings, Rush, Lane, Dunbar, and Donovan families all lost one of their own that night.)

The love, and devotion they all had for the purple-eyed Dingley was what brought them together. The dark storm approached on the horizon. They could feel the unease in the unicorn as she reared up to fight an unseen adversary. Dingley, staff in hand, bid all but the wizard to stand in a circle around the white boulder, one on each mark of the compass. He spoke the spell words and an arc of blue flame began to slowly encircle the companions. They tried not to look at it. Once it had formed, the unicorn calmed down. But it was the calm before the storm.

The lightning strike came from the sky with a blow that bent them to their knees. They stood again and were hit again. They struggled to their feet. All but Pilchie, Dingley, Audran, and Cassandra had dropped their weapons. The brownie's chosen protection, a feather given freely from the eagle, held fast. Dingley's carved sea staff glowed blue. Audran's weapon was his mind and his own crystal staff, but in his pocket was also this witness. Cassandra had the very quill she had used to write a letter to her secret love. As the storm grew in power, Audran began to realize the folly of this—these were not fully trained wizards! How could he and Dingley think they could win this night? The onslaught came in wave upon wave until none of the youths stood but were arranged in ugly, deranged positions as the strike took their sanity. The boys screamed in pain, some calling out for their mothers.

Somehow the evil ones had blinded the unicorn. Audran had to control her so that she would not strike friends—her power was being used against them! Blind, she could not aim her horn to fend off the lightning. The quick-thinking brownie had leaped upon her head, holding on for dear life, singing to her in his native tongue.

"Hear me, Axoparia!" he sang.

It seemed to work because she stopped rearing up and striking out with her nicorn. Dingley brought forth all the magik he could bear into a sphere of glowing blue plasma he could barely control. The Others up in the clouds were taunting him by laughing and making his friends twitch on the ground near him. They sent another bolt at the unicorn, but the brownie had told her from whence it came. She sent it backwards toward them. A howl of anger flew around the hilltop. Audran, not having to control her, drove his staff into the ground with all his might. The ground ripped open as the shaft forced its way deep into a crevice in the ledge. Dingley saw him do it out of the corner of his eye.

It meant that Audran, the wizard, was grounding himself into Terra for a last stand.

"No!" screamed Dingley, which made the unicorn rear up, dislodging the brownie. He fell but quickly regained an upright position. The brave Pilchie did the same as the wizard. He quickly drove his feather upside down into the earth, allowing his little bit of magik to flow into it, then he collapsed upon the point, driving it into his heart.

Cassandra joined him. She had her quill pen, for she had learned in her short life span that "the pen is mightier than the sword." She spoke these words as she drove the pen into the ground in front of her. But their combined magik was not enough to quell the dance of darkness. Dingley was aware at some point that the battle was lost. But he was able to seal the cracks that had formed in the ground at their feet. He waited for one more bolt ... and one more came. He drew the plasma into himself, the intense pain making him nearly lose his mind! His last thought was to save Myster and the unicorn, who could return safely to a previous form. He thrust the magik sphere down into the ground at his feet. A stream of magik bounced outward and, capturing the wizard, blossomed as it returned him to his other magikal form, that of a cat. Axoparia was not so lucky—her nicorn tried to fend off the blue fire stream engulfing her. She spun around, then was suddenly gone—nothing left but a small golden bottle of glass. The magik traveled onward, out beyond the hill and down to the beach. Dingley had misjudged, or one of the Others had thrown another bolt—it simply is not clear but somehow the magik turned anything living thing in its path into glass bottles.

Somehow I survived. I lay in agony near a stunned kitten. We awoke to the sound of someone sobbing as if his heart was broken, for it was. Isaac Drake had found what was left of his son and the other youths. The disaster was told and retold everywhere, of how all but the one girl were charred almost beyond recognition in garish positions. A lump of what was left of a human was atop the large boulder. One finger had a gem ring on it so they could identify him, Dingley Isaac Drake. The others wore their school clothes, so it was difficult to determine their identities. They were buried on the hill in a small cemetery. The funeral procession was made up of most of the village. The sound of sobbing carried upon the wind past Eagle Island and onward into the woods.

A gift of history from Jeremy, the Field mouse, first witness to the Battle of Dingley Island, upon my honor what I have said 'tis a truth telling.

MEETING SOMEONE SPECIAL

Ellora and Luke were in a bit of a pickle. They were in a place where there was no food or water. Plus, they did not know how long they had been in the cavern. They'd been chatting away with their grandmother through the magik mirror. It was a good thing that the mirror was cold, because it became rather uncomfortably humid in the cavern. There was no light except what came from the mirror and some strange glowing twinkles high up in the roof. Luke had said they were luminous fungi or something like that. It seemed like their grandmother was going to talk forever. Ellora assumed that she missed them as much as they missed her. But now Ellora's stomach was grumbling and Luke was beginning to look around instead of paying attention to Grandma Charlotte. He was hungry too.

"Okay, you two, I can see that I have been prattling on and on. But it's so peaceful here and the light is exceptional, I do wish I had my paints," she complained. "Oh my, was that your stomach making that noise?"

Ellora grinned and was about to nod "yes" when a rumble sounded quite close to them. It was not her stomach! A feeling of fear gripped her so hard that she nearly dropped the mirror. What was going on? She looked for Luke as he had gotten up to walk around and look at all the things stored and stashed in the alcoves. There was a lot of stuff! Luke had said he was hungry, but his stomach wasn't making any noises.

"Grandma, did you know that your missing slippers were in here? And look, here's my train, and some of our old Christmas ornaments! That's Grampa's pair of old binoculars and his eyeglasses. Here's your

missing book, *The Last Unicorn,* which you accused *me* of taking Ellora!"
Luke was talking really fast now, and the sense of urgency and fear grew.

Ellora now could sense that it was not her fear, but someone else's.
Who could it be? Their eyes were not fully adjusted to the dark because
of the light from the mirror, so Ellora put it in her lap and really strained
to look about the cavern. The other, full-length mirror gave off a slight
luminous glow, which was weird and yet comforting at the same time.
She slowly got up to look at it closely and heard the rumbling sound
again. It sounded slightly cat-like. Luke looked at his sister and then
past her to where the sound came from, though it was a bit difficult to
figure out exactly where that was because of the echo quality of the giant
stones and the archways. The place looked and felt really old. Bidding
goodbye, for now, to their grandmother, they explored another cavern
tunnel, where they could hear Blou talking with Golden and Myster.

Sarisha knew who these children were and to whom they belonged,
but they knew her not. She had heard and seen the two of them in the
summers past when they came to visit. Those had been happy times
for the Mistress Charlotte! Sarisha was afraid they had come to take
her pretty things back, as the man had done once before. But she had
taken the eyepieces back again when he was not looking. She was fearful and excited at the same time. Her feelings were being felt by the
empathic wizard-girl; Sarisha could smell the power of the ring the girl
wore. The boy was a wizard too. Were they here to *play* with her? No,
they were talking to the mistress, whom they missed. She could feel
their sad and happy emotions. She missed Mistress Charlotte too, more
than she missed any other. There were many times Charlotte had given
her things, like the pretty pink slippers that smelled of the musty roses.
The Master had only given her things that were broken. But Charlotte
gave her things that were nice, pretty, and useful, to a point. There were
some items that had been tasty, being the burnt kind that she liked.
Once, a whole basket of cookies came flying through the doorway. The
basket was not so good, but the cookies were delicious! And meat, two

or three times a season, was given, the very good kind that she loved. When the master remembered that she would become quite thirsty and since he did not like finding a small but dusty dragon in his bathwater, he had given her a source of water all her own. It was a treasure! For she loved hearing the drip, drip, and knew it was the time of water falling from the sky, so it was the best time to forage. Most creatures were afraid of her. The house brownies and the forest tinkers were fearful she would eat them. Silly! She did not care for the taste of faerie, no matter what kind it was. But she did like chicken. The Mistress cooked a very large one for her once a year. That was a good feast! It was a long time, the waiting in between, but she was used to that. One of the earlier masters had been not kind to her. Those times were full of sadness and worry. She would simply sleep, her tail tip on guard. She also knew the house would alert her should something tremendously bad happen. The Others would never get her treasures if she had to eat everything and take it with her between worlds. She suddenly felt very protective of the two children and decided to open her eyes so that they may see her.

The beautiful eyes that popped open suddenly made Ellora gasp. Luke had been handling one of the ornaments and dropped it. Fortunately, it did not break. Sarisha unfolded herself, carefully so as not to alarm anyone, bent her long neck to pick up the ornament and gently place it within its nest of special things she had "borrowed" or simply taken because no one was looking after them. Lost things, forgotten items, were her specialty. She sometimes would leave pretty things for the large white bird who came to visit, but that had not happened for a very long time. She was beautiful and full of childlike grace. She blinked her eyes and settled back in her grotto. A bright expression on her face, she gently sniffed the children, immediately sensing the magik flowing through the girl and the boy at an enormous rate. She extended her tail in the standard greeting, upright to show her interest at making their acquaintance.

"Sarisha Chandi. I was named by the queen, my mother. Is there a new mistress and master? Do I smell ... cat?" was another question she politely asked the two standing in front of her with their mouths open.

That was the moment when Myster, Blou, and Golden returned from searching one of the cavern corridors. Sarisha was delighted; cats were fun to play with! She thought she knew the other smell, much like a nicorn, but not. Blouette instantly knew how to greet the dragon.

"Blouette. I was named by the queen, my mother. Art thou the caretaker of this cavern?" Her tail was also pointed upright in the standard greeting of happiness and joy (for she had only heard legends about dragons, never met one in person). Golden let out a howl-whinny that made the dragon's ears point backward in alarm.

"Caretaker, I am, collector and protector, as are thee," Sari replied politely, her tail upright. "Are you coming again to play with me?"

Myster was having trouble with his mind at this moment. He was suddenly remembering being much taller, somehow, somewhere. Myster shook his head and felt dizzy.

The dragon prodded him gently. "Thou does not remember me, friend? You and Dingley used to visit me in this place. We would go to the hill during the moon time when it filled the sky. You and I used to have long walks together."

"I am having some faint recollections and echoes of conversations." Myster told her, "But how can this be? Dingley perished generations ago. Am I that old?" he muttered to himself.

"Oh, Myster, poor old thing." Ellora tried to pet the cat, but he shied away from her.

"Let's play!" Sari said suddenly, and the lights within the cavern came on much stronger. She reached for a very old ball, one that was nearly worn through from so much love. She tossed it over to Golden, who quickly grabbed it and ran off, the dragon giving chase.

Later, after laughter and lots of play, they all sat back down for a rest. The mirror had gone dark, but the handle was still cold. Somehow nothing was broken! Ellora was truly hungry and thirsty now. Quick as a wink, Sarisha disappeared but came back immediately with a drink in each hand and a recently baked pepperoni pizza that they ate with gusto, even Blou tasting a tiny corner of it. Golden was busily munching and Myster chose to have only a little bit, with cheese please.

A tapping sound from the mirror gave them a start. Since it had not shut off, Ellora did not have to repeat the incantation, but she did wipe the surface again.

"Hey, anyone there?" their Grandpa Charles was asking in his jolly voice.

Both kids exclaimed, "Grandpa!"

"Hey, you may have already met the caretaker, Sarisha. Her job is to care for the magikal items hidden within the cavern. Some other jerks have tried to find their way in there to get the magikal things, but she heads them off each time. I think she has been in the cave for thousands of years. I don't think she is immortal, but she is totally a magikal creature who can pop in and out, so you have to lay down some rules for her. One time she surprised me in the bathtub!"

With this, the dragon's ears swooped downward, and she looked very contrite.

Grandpa continued. "But she was very thirsty and had been confined by the previous master to only the caverns, where there isn't enough water. So, I hooked up the hose for her that comes from the gutters around the house." His voice faded away, then came back. "I sure do miss you both."

"We miss you! Guess what! Mom is going to marry Marcus! That means Daisy and Keevan will be our sister and brother!" Luke said very excitedly. "And we met the brownies that live in the library! They have a computer! How come you never told us about them?"

"Well, Luken, that's a lot of information. Listen, when you're older you can read all the journals that explain everything. Just remember that Grandma and Grandpa love you forever. I have to go now. I feel something is wrong at the house, though. Could be nothing, but there's a white raven knocking on the door to the cavern. Remember, keep this place secret, Luke—don't tell anyone unless they are part of the family. And"—his voice faded—"remember to take care of the dragon. She likes to eat burnt things and she likes shiny objects. We used to toss her old toys and stuff we thought she'd like. Otherwise she gets sort of bored and goes off to get things herself."

Off in the distance and out of their sight, they heard their grandmother ask, "Did you tell them about the dragon and how she likes to eat burnt things? Ha, ha, ha! That's where all my burnt cakes, cookies, and meatloaf dinners went! What's this I hear about my daughter marrying Marcus? Did they both get a divorce?"

Ellora quietly told them the story. "No, about a year after you and Grandpa died, Dad and Aunt Cynthia died in a speedboat wreck. So, we are all living in your house and meeting all the wonderful things that live here! I found Blou and Golden were living beings cast into bottles, and somehow I was able to release them when I put them into the fire. I never knew I had magik talent!"

"Well, you'll find there are lots of things about yourself and the house that will surprise you. Like the barn, for instance. Whenever there's a storm, lots of critters will show up for shelter. The storage bins fill back up again when they're empty! One year a pair of goats, a badger, and a wayward circus elephant showed up and stayed one whole weekend!" Grampa chuckled and shook his head, remembering the event.

Sarisha nodded her head in agreement. She remembered the lovely time she had playing with the animals, the goats especially. The badger, though, had not been so playful.

"There's a large journal and a magik scroll that Grandpa wrote on— he jotted down all the passwords and codes. Marcus will need that. The brownies will help guide you but keep your eye on them! They *don't* understand sarcasm and will take you for your word when you answer questions. So, you have to be careful what you say to them. Sarisha here is a doll. We just loved her. She has a lovely but also a lonely heart. I used to let her curl up by the fire on winter nights. But she snores." Grandma whispered this last bit. "She knows about the ring. Keep it safe! Never let anyone else touch it." Someone behind her said something so she turned away for a moment to answer.

"Talk to me another time about the ring. There's a pair of magik earrings for Daisy, too," Grandma continued. "We did some research on it and have found out some interesting things. When you are wearing it, it cannot go to anyone else. It also increases your own special talents."

"And only you can take it off," Charlotte added. "Daisy's gems come from her mother. I think it's a pair of earrings; they are blue diamonds, too. Gotta go! Keep drinking your tea!"

Ellora and Luke somberly listened to this advice but didn't understand all of it. But they did hear their grandmother repeat herself which made them feel uneasy. Another, more urgent tapping on the secret door got their attention. Luke went over to open it and was greeted by one of the Brownies. That is when they saw the storm and heard the awful howling. They rushed out of the cavern, into the library, and into what could only be described as a battle scene.

THE SCARECROW AND THE ORIENTAL RUG

Some kind of wind creature was flying about the island like an angry black tornado. It could not get through the barrier that surrounded Dingley Island and the two smaller islands. One of the other islands was the home of a family of eagles that nested year after year in a tall pine tree. The force of the wind creature was too much for the ancient pine that stood very close to the edge of the barrier. The tree was the home for so many creatures. It tried to maintain its upright position, but it had grown so tall that it was too much strain to keep upright. The wind creature actually tried to go through the barrier as the tree, groaning, fell into the sea. In response, though, the ocean roared up to meet its enemy in a waterspout so strong that it cut the wind creature in half once when it shot up into the air and then again as the returning water dove downwards. Being cut into three segments meant the wind tornado lost its continuity. With its force spent, it vanished into the night. Before it left, however, it deposited the hooded figure of a man at the edge of the meadow on the opposing shore. No, the sea was not his friend at all. In fact, the ocean was one of the reasons they could not access the island fortress. They were ancient enemies.

When the storm ended there were hugs all around and questions flying. Marcus felt he had to put a stop to the hullabaloo by raising his voice and requesting that everyone calm down.

Luke said, "Wait, we left the dragon behind!" Sure enough, no one had shut the secret door and a sad but hopeful little dragon leaned in through the doorway. Luke gestured for her to join them. Ellora marveled at how she could fit into small spaces, then realized that Sarisha was most likely a shapeshifter, like a jinn or a genie. She made a mental note to ask her grandparents the next time she spoke with them. She hid the mirror behind her back, not wanting to explain about or share the precious thing.

"Can we keep her? Can we?" Luke asked.

Rahven spoke to them telepathically. *She may visit, but no one keeps a child of the dragon king. She is the anujan, the younger sister, Sarisha Chandi, a celestial being who chooses to be among mortals as a protector ... of a sort.* If Rahven could have smiled, he would have. Instead, he bobbed his head.

Ellora she smiled when she saw the Brownies, now dressed in doll clothing that did not quite fit properly. The pants were too short, and Daisy apparently had been able to find only one shoe for Abequa.

Golden was also wearing something new: a scarf. She snuggled up to the younger girl, which made Blou a bit jealous.

"Dear Daisy, methinks thou art too young to have a unicorn. And look upon Golden! She is more like a Lunicorn—part lion and part unicorn! She acts like no unicorn that I have ever seen."

Daisy made a face that was almost angry, and she stuck out her tongue at the sprite. Blou, sensing this might be a preamble to a fight, stuck her blue tongue out too, and made her hair stand on end, which to any faerie would be a warning sign. To Daisy it was simply funny. She giggled. Sarisha giggled along. This exchange was witnessed by the brownie family, who also smiled, thinking this was hilarious! The tension in the room vanished.

Sarisha and Golden went into the kitchen to devour the leftover pizza. The dragon upended a can of soda, which she abruptly dropped when she was finished. They were making a mess! Marcus and Marji looked at each other hopelessly. Blou flew up into the rafters to look down from above. She focused, for the first time, on the rug upon which everyone stood except the dragon and the Lunicorn. She noticed that neither of them would step foot on the Oriental carpet. She fluttered about looking at it, then let out a shriek that startled everyone!

"What evil is this? Get off that carpet from the Orient. There are markings of deceit and treachery woven throughout the design! Get off! Get it out of the house!"

Rahven squawked and lifted up into the air, settling on the mantelpiece, where he upset the bottles up there. Some of them fell to the floor. Myster hissed, then began to walk around and around the carpet to see what Blou was yelling about. It was difficult to see, so he jumped on to the banister post.

"Show us! Explain!" Myster demanded. In the quiet after the storm, Blou tentatively hovered, not daring to step on the carpet, showing them the marks and signs that were woven into the carpet design.

The brownies were on the job! They accessed the library computer database, while Marji and Marcus looked in the house journal for clues as to what to do. Rahven quietly conversed with the dragon and Golden thought it was all a new game as she playfully tried to reach the white bird and the cat, who were tantalizingly out of reach. So, she pawed at the bottle on the other rug by the fire, making it spin around. This brought another squawk from the sprite.

"No, must not, Raid is in the red bottle, I am certain!"

Golden's head drooped, showing her fright at being yelled at. Daisy came quickly to assure her darling that she was beautiful and lovely and smart. Never mind that pixie-thingy, as she had heard her father call Blouette. Aisinwin and Keevan began a mock battle, Keevan with his new sword and the little warrior riding Polly and foisting the small broom from the fire pit. A bit of soot from the broom landed on the rug and it promptly disappeared. Everyone carefully stepped off the rug after that.

"Here is something!" Marcus and Gitchie exclaimed at once. The brownie had found some ancient Sanskrit writing.

"Master, I believe the writing is not a dire as the sprite is telling (anything to get back at that wretched flying faerie). It says here the warnings are of fire and blood, wind and rain, earth and ... something else."

"Yes, but there are other markings written underneath that change them to a thing of deceit and desire, of tattlings and tellings! We must take it out of the house now!" Her fear gave her strength as she began to try to roll up the carpet on one end. Golden saw this as another game but whinnied as her snout touched the carpet.

Sarisha joined in to help but reported, "It burns. I like it not."

The carpet was heavy. Marcus and Keevan struggled to get it off the porch and into the yard. They looked around. There were downed branches everywhere, the clothesline was gone, pieces of fencing lay scattered, the rose garden benches were toppled, and the scarecrow in the cornfield was turned around and seemed to be looking at them.

Luke shuddered. He did not like clowns and the grin on the face of the scarecrow was really creepy. His mom began to explain that she'd bought the carpet and the scarecrow at an antique store in Seattle.

"What is this See-at-all?" demanded Blou. "It could be a place in league with the Others!"

Marji explained that she had gone to *Seattle* on a business trip two weeks ago. They all remembered; it had been an unplanned trip that she had not wanted to talk much about after she had returned home.

"There was a well-dressed man at the catering conference who sat across from me. I don't remember his name or where he was from. During a lunch break I went to a nearby antique barn. I was looking at these rugs, and kind of wanted one. He had come over to me, so we struck up a conversation. As we talked, he mentioned that a plusher rug would be best for the new little ones to come—Marcus, he knew I was pregnant before I did!"

At this new piece of information, the children gasped, but Marji continued: "I laughed it off, of course, and tried to move away from him. He grabbed my arm and insisted I listen to him. He offered me a job right there and then! He said he had heard of my work and needed a project manager! The high salary was amazing, but he made me so uncomfortable that I called over someone to help. He actually left a bruise on my arm!" She turned to the kids. "I am sorry you had to find out about the baby this way. I wasn't really certain until this morning." She pulled up her sleeve to reveal the mark on the back of her arm, and Blou gasped!

"It is the mark of the Others!" Something that looked like a letter 'O' crisscrossed with angry red lines.

Everyone came over to look at the oval-shaped mark more closely. Daisy said she thought it looked like a tattoo. Keevan asked what they were going to do about the rug, and to come look because it was moving! Sure enough, it had unrolled itself and its edges were rippling, even though there was no wind, like it was gathering strength. No one said a word as the rug began to hover in place. Above their heads they saw the eagle swoop down from the cupola of the barn, where she had been sitting with some of the other birds. She had seen the thing in the field turn around to stare at the house. The birds flew over toward the scarecrow and began to attack it. Sarisha, rumbling in her own language, flew over to investigate. As she grew near the meadow, the carpet gave a huge wave movement and leaped high into the air, then hovered above the yard! Was it going to attack the dragon? Over in the field, the scarecrow was appeared to have come alive! It was fighting off the birds by flinging itself around and around, its legs and arms flailing about.

A black hooded figure strode through the tall grass toward the birds, shooting some kind of yellow fire at them. Several ravens were struck. The thing aimed at Sarisha, but she fired her own blue flame, which met his, then engulfed it. The hooded figure stumbled backwards, and its flame went out. The eagle flew around behind it, grabbing the hood, revealing a pale human-like face with black circles for eyes. The birds backed off, wary of the Other's fire and not knowing what was going to happen.

Marcus remembered the chant from the journal and commanded, "I am the master! I command thee, go back, go away and come no more! Leave this house, this island, these shores! Your power is gone!"

These words had a very dramatic effect on the hooded figure. He gestured to the rug, which was truly a flying carpet. It rushed over, undulating in a beautiful but terrifying manner, like a gigantic manta ray. As it passed over the field, the scarecrow reached up, grabbed the edge and, somehow, flipped itself up and onto the carpet! It sat cross-legged while grinning back at them. The carpet lowered enough for the hooded figure to step up on it and sit down, and then flew off up into the clouds! They watched it disappear.

"I can't believe it worked!" shouted Marcus, and he and Keevan gave each other high fives. Everyone seemed excited for a minute. They were undecided as what to do next—maybe check the house for damage? But Gitchie told them the house would alert them if there were a problem.

Marcus said, "I need to go see about rebuilding the bridge." He brought Gitchie and the passcode book with him.

Quietly the rest went back into the house. Somehow knowing the rug and the scarecrow were being commanded by something so scary was really, really unsettling. Daisy sought the security of her friend, Golden. Blou sought the shoulder of the dragon and heard the words of the cat as she flew into the house.

"That was too easy," muttered Myster. "It went away without giving battle?"

"Perhaps the magik here is too strong?" asked Blou as they filed one by one past her. She had started to like the idea of being first anywhere they went, as if she were still a guard.

The dragon bugled to the eagle who was flying off, the regiment behind her as if lending her their protection.

Ellora, overtaken by the drama of the past hour, complained of being exhausted and flopped down on the couch in the library. Marji went over to her to feel her forehead. She was hot to the touch. Abequa began brewing tea by the fire. Golden and Sarisha were snuggling together by the hearth, so Blou settled down also. It was the calm after the storm. Marj busied herself in the kitchen, deciding what to tell everyone. In her memory, the antique dealer had seemed friendly and helpful when she insisted the stranger let go of her arm. In fact, the dealer had threatened to call security. Marji absently sipped the tea Abequa made for her. It was slightly like cinnamon and was very soothing. Yes, the expensive rug had been a sweet deal—too good a deal, she should have realized. But in her desire to thank the man for helping her, she had bought it. That was unsettling, to think she had been targeted by both men, whose agenda was still unclear. They wanted the magik items that were here in the house somewhere? How had they known about her?

AFTER THE STORM

Mr. and Mrs. Bradley slowly made their way up the dirt road, which was strewn with debris. "Are you sure their lines are down? My phone keeps ringing, but no one picks up," Mrs. Bradley said in a worried tone.

"Oh, the lines are down all over, even on the mainland. You should have seen Jacob and Fix-it Avenues. Both ends were blocked with downed trees hanging on the wires," her husband countered. His report did nothing to soften her anxiety. Soon they saw the top of the cupola of the barn, with its sailboat weathervane. The yard looked like a war zone: lawn furniture and fence boards were strewn everywhere, animals were milling about, and a goat happily munched on something that looked like pizza. The boys were out front playing baseball. When they saw Marcus's parents, they dropped their ball. Keevan let out a "whoop" which made the chickens scatter.

"Hey there, Kee, how're ya doin'?" asked his grandfather.

"Fine, grandfather! Did you lose any of your tall pine trees??" Keevan asked as his grandfather tousled his hair. "We lost a big one on Eagle Island."

Grandmother took notice of that as she hugged her favorite grandson, as she took notice of everything. It was odd that Keevan would be concerned about trees. But she smiled as she said hello to Luke and hugged him too. She noticed he had a sad smile, though anyone would be a bit sad after that awful storm. She looked about nervously. This house always made her feel a bit anxious, as if it were watching and listening. In the days when she was a child, many people thought the house, the forest, and the hilltop were haunted. The native tribe, the Abenaki, had stories about a creature that came out during rainstorms. They would find odd prints in the mud that belonged to some kind of bear or something. She had seen them herself, even photographed them, prints of a large animal with six toes left in the wet sand before the tide had erased them. Anyone she had shown the pictures to had told her they were faked. But she knew they weren't.

"Hey, where's the clothesline? Did the wind take your scarecrow, too?" she asked as they walked up on to the porch. "Is your dad home?"

Both boys answered "yes," and both grandparents gave each other a knowing look. It was so heartwarming to hear both of them considering Marcus to be their dad.

Inside the library, Ellora, who had only recently arisen, picked up on Luke's mental shout to get Golden out of the house. Suddenly, a screen door appeared in the wall which led to the rose garden! She was careful not to let the door slam shut behind her as she ushered the Lunicorn outside, followed by Blouette. Golden was now as large as Boris, their big collie dog, and was beginning to be a problem.

Blou flew on ahead briefly, then returned to let her know that "The coastal is clear."

Ellora smiled at her and replied, "The coast is clear, you mean."

This made Blou very annoyed. She snapped back, "Whatever!"

"Don't worry, you speak English very well. It's hard to learn our language. We haven't had a chance to talk since the other night. Was it two or three nights ago? I don't even know what day it is."

Blouette crossly told her, "I have a perfect memory and can tell you exactly what was said and when."

"You have an eidetic memory, but no, it's okay. I don't need to know everything, but please tell me about Raid. Was he your best friend?"

The sprite was hesitant at first, but as her words came spilling she seemed happy to talk. "In Balaktria, the queen rules with her king. Each time she chooses one of the males, he gives up his name and is simply known as the king. The queen is able to birth seven or eight babies at once, but the first-born girl is always the princess, who will become the next ruler. Her Guard sisters will always be near her, during the games, while hunting, during courtship. We are never away unless we are on stationed near the borders of Faerieland. Should there be any males born, they are taken away to be raised by the group. Any females that become Lemales go off to fight as well. They are always training, hunting, and learning about how to keep Balaktria safe. We are given guard duties by the Borderlands. This is where I met Raid. He was one of the fastest flyers! We would enter into contests to see who could hunt the best or who would dare fly highest! We grew to want one another in the manner of the Queen and her King—for only she can give permission to join together as a couple. I had thought—I had wished that Raid and I would be among the chosen few."

Ellora was confused. "What are 'Lemales'? And why were both of you on the hilltop the night of the storm?"

Blou's eyes narrowed in anger, but she hesitated before answering,

"Lemales are the females that choose not to mate, of course. Raid taunted me to follow him through the vortex, the doorway between this world and Faerieland. I should never have done that. I have dishonored myself and my sisters! Queen Merritt will never forgive me, and I will be banished."

Ellora asked, "But can you tell her about the battle and that it was Raid's idea for you to follow him?"

Blouette looked at her with incredulous loathing. "You know nothing! Honor is everything! We fly for the glory of the queen. It is a high honor to be Captain of the Guard. For it is my spirit that binds the sisters together and as one we aim our arrows!" Blou flew back into the library as Daisy held the door open. None of these Terrans could possibly understand her shame.

Ellora sighed. Everything with Blou was difficult. She took offense to any little thing that people outside of her world didn't understand. Ellora wondered what would become of Golden. She hoped the lunicorn would stop growing soon. So far as Ellora could tell, Golden was an omnivore. She loved nearly anything she was offered to eat. Right now, she was nibbling the roses. Maybe she should stop her? That was another thing she noticed about the creature. She did whatever she wanted and only Sarisha could really control her.

While Ellora was hiding in the garden, the rest of the family had been in the kitchen, talking while having cookies. Daisy was chatting about all the animals. Marji was afraid she would let the lunicorn out of the bag, so to speak, and tell about Golden. She was also afraid her soon-to-be in-laws would stay for dinner.

Finally, Mr. Bradley said to his wife, "Well, Mother, we'll need to be up early tomorrow to open the store."

Mrs. Bradley sighed. "There's so much more to talk about, the new wedding plans."

Marji quickly told her they would drive to town the next day and they could talk then. The elder Bradleys left. Luke quietly told his mom, "Grandmother Bradley doesn't like the house. She thinks it's haunted."

"Oh, Luke, she's really worried about what the townspeople will say about cancelling the wedding."

"But Grandfather is happy. He also wants to talk with you because someone was asking about you at the store. A dark man wearing a hood."

ONE GOOD OMISSION DESERVES ANOTHER

Myster was very troubled. He was having memory flashbacks that disturbed him. He was very much, still, a cat who was used to his humans doing odd things. But the events here recently were so strange. He had known about the prophecy and Ellora's coming of age at sixteen would be an important event. He'd never questioned that. But now he was questioning his role in all of this. What did it matter? Why? The dragon seemed to know him as someone different. She called him a friend. Who was he? Maybe the brownies could help. The sprite was no use right now. Earlier she had found one of the red bottles broken on the side of the fireplace where there was no rug to cushion its fall. She was holding the pieces, singing in her language while Daisy and Golden looked on very contritely, as if they had done the act. Myster thought the Rahven had done it with some deliberation, but it could have happened at any time.

Myster decided to ask the sprite anyway.

"Do you know me in a different form? As the dragon said, I was once a friend who walked with her in the moonlight."

"Stupid cat! Canst thou see I am in mourning? There will never be a sweet reunion with Raid now. He is gone. Gone!" she wailed. "The last time I saw him—Great Goddess! YOU were there the last time I saw Raid! We were—"

"I was there?" Myster asked, "How? When?"

"It was not my fault," Blou began. "But Raid was always being heroic, really stupidly so. How was I to know he had been sent by the queen? I—" She stopped suddenly, as if she were afraid to say any more.

"Go on, tell me, or shall I summon the Rahven? For none can be untruth tellers under his gaze."

"Yes, perhaps it was you," she began in her sly manner, not wanting to divulge she had figured out his human form. "I can tell you what I recall and no more! It is a matter for the queen. Raid, my—my friend, was always taunting me that as the captain of the Queen's Guard, I had not much else to do but fly around hunting dragonflies or play chase and capture among the toadstools. I told him that he knows nothing! Nothing I said would make him stop. Then he came close to me, saying he did not trust Audran the wizard, and that since Axoparia was heading off for some foolish quest, he was to follow them to Terra! Come with me, he taunted, if you can fly so well and aim your arrows better than I can!"

Myster could not tell if she was telling the truth or not. The admittance hurt her. Anyone leaving their post for no matter the reason would be banished from Faerieland! Why would Raid lie to her? Of course, Blou could have reported the incident. Oh, Myster realized that she loved him and wished to be his mate! That was the reason. Myster felt sorry for her now, as we all do things for love that are not wise at times. He let her finish her tale.

Her tail drooped more and more until its tip was on the floor and droplets of venom were soaking into the library rug.

"Raid and I entered the doorway betwixt these worlds. It is well known to us, but the humans hardly ever venture through it. That's all good, for they cannot fly as we do and crossing through doorway is, well, let's say it is not easy as cake. I saw Raid gathering his packing sack and knew in my heart he was going to join you on the stupid quest. This was the day after the gather. You were there, but you were Audran the wizard with your funny whiskers and hair. We laughed at you behind your back, my Guard sisters and me."

She said that to deliberately hurt me, Myster thought.

"Dingley was there too," Blou continued. "His words were so sweet, telling of his ancestors who fought the dark. He told of the magik house, truly a fortress with all its wonders—too wonderful for the evil ones to gain for they would seek to join its magik to their own. 'Well, it would be only a matter of time,' the queen laughed. 'All know that dark magik drains whilst light magik gains in strength. The balance will reinsert itself. We can wait.'

"That is when Axoparia entered the gather. She made it known that her mate's nicorn had been stolen by the Others and she wanted justice. Sweet revenge on those and rescue of her mate held captive by a Prince John of Ghent. Everyone shuddered at this name being said, for it was forbidden to say the cursed name, John. The queen answered the unicorn: 'We all grieve for thee, but it is folly for thee to leave Faerieland in this quest. Is it for thy heart's sake or for the sake of another? The wizard, perhaps, has colored your thoughts. What if you never return? Your beautiful magik will be lost and it will destroy the balance for eons.' Axoparia let it be known her belief that the queen's words were not for her. All gasped! What was this? The court unicorn would never go against her queen. It had never been done!"

Blou waited for her story to be acknowledged. Unknown to Blou, Ellora, Golden, and Sarisha were listening, too.

"It is a truth telling," Sari interjected. She gently nudged Myster, and said to him, "Before the battle of Dingley ended, you, my friend, were a human wizard of great kindness and wisdom. It was the young Dingley who convinced thee and the unicorn to use its nicorn to ward off the power of the Others."

They all hung their heads in tribute, except for the sprite. She added hotly, "If Dingley had not mixed his word with sweet agreement spells, this would not have happened! I would not be in this cursed land, Raid would be living and not made of broken glass, and Myster would not be a cat!"

"What happened?" asked Daisy, who had just arrived.

Ellora told her to hush. "I'll tell you all of it later."

"Truth can be measured from different points of a viewing," the dragon admonished. "We cannot bend the past to our needs. After the battle I rescued the first witness and brought him to safety. The ground was hot around him. His paws were burning. Axoparia was nowhere to be found, and the remains of the children were left for their human parents to find and to place under the ground on the hill."

Blou felt those words ended her story. She now wished to be left alone for a time. She flew up to the rafters to hide.

That night at a family meeting, Ellora began to unravel the mystery. She told everyone what she thought as she paced the floor of the room, where everyone had gathered. This time Daisy did not interrupt. Marcus had come in from the barn, then he and Marji had joined the conclave.

Keevan hung in the background, not knowing what to say, but seriously wanting to keep the new sword he had mysteriously found. When raised to fight, the sword turned blue. He thought the scarecrow had looked right at him, acknowledging the ancient weapon. Why had it come to him? He wondered if he had any powers or not. Recently he had begun to feel unimportant, with Luke and Ellora going off to secret places. Even the lunicorn seemed to like Daisy better. And there was going to be a baby in the family. He could tell his dad had been surprised at that news. How was all this going to change their lives?

"How does the magik doorway work" Keevan wanted to know.

Ellora shrugged then said, "This house has been here for a very long time. And our ancestors have always lived in it. There are secret things, doors and magical creatures that live in and around the house. A long time ago, an ancestor named Dingley Drake made it through the portal, with the wizard Audran"—she pointed to the cat —"and they met with all the rulers of Faerieland, convinced their court unicorn to join them on the quest. But a quest for what?"

Blou dropped down from the rafters to answer sullenly. "To rid Terra, this world, of the evil powers that live here, known as the Others. I don't know why Dingley thought he could defeat them, but Audran lost himself that day and our world lost its unicorn. For I believe somehow. that Golden is a combination of the unicorn known as Axoparia and the cat Myster. What I want to know is, why or how that did that magik spill over and turn me and Raid into glass bottles? Who found us and placed us in the house?" She eyed the dragon. Sarisha looked back at her with sadness.

"Not I," said the Dragon, "For I only rescued the first witness, Jeremy the mouse, who heard and saw the entire battle. His cries were heard by the crows, who would have savagely eaten him had I not intervened. Whenever a creature earns its own name, it is not to be eaten by crows."

Maemaegwin tugged on her father's shirt. He bent down to hear her whispers. "My daughter has an answer to one question," he said. "Dingley's sister, Katharine, was the one who found the bottles and brought them to the house. Over her lifetime, any bottle she found by the shore, she added to the collection."

Marcus continued the explanation, picking up where Ellora had stopped. "So, after this battle, and all those things happened, why this now? The storm and the creepy scarecrow—the guy who assaulted Marji. What is going on to make all of us gather here now?"

Myster now took on the task of telling. "There is a prophecy that tells of great things about to happen when a Rahven or white bird rides to find the purple-eyed children, a sister and brother. The mountains will shake, the magik gains, and—"

Blou interrupted. "And the queen's gem will turn blood red. How can a true-blue diamond become a ruby?"

"Well," said Marji, "we have seen the Rahven riding that lovely little mare—is she in the barn, Marcus?" She turned to look at him, really needing him to answer her without anger. He nodded, rubbed the back of her arm as if to erase the bruise, then put his arm around her shoulders,. She kissed his cheek.

Now it was Daisy's turn to ask something, "Golden is part unicorn and cat? If we get rid of the bad magic, will she turn back into herself again?" Daisy did not want that to happen at all. She was thrilled that the lunicorn seemed to like her better than anyone else, especially her brother. Oh, that's right, she had another brother now, too. And she was going to have another sibling! Aunt Marjorie was pregnant! She ran over and gently hugged Marji's belly. Marjorie smiled down at her.

It was Gitchie's turn to say something, and it wasn't good. He could not tell an untruth but left out much of the story of the prophecy because it was simply too hard to explain right now. He was not certain either, how much he should say. The past and the present often blurred together. He did not want Mistress Marji to change her mind about letting him make improvements and upgrades as he saw fit. This meant much to their survival, from his point of view.

"There is more to the prophecy than the cat recalls. But we can research that later. For now, we must be vigilant and trust only ourselves! For the Others were able to gain access to the house! We must make safeguards. This is bad, this is really bad. That thing was listening to us for two weeks! And who knows what the scarecrow saw. I ordered supplies, which should be arriving soon. The bridge was swept away by the tide. It will be rebuilt, but for now all deliveries will have to be brought in from the shore. Abequa tells me the Ravens' Council is over and Rahven wishes to speak with the dragon."

PLAN A AND PLAN B

Gitchie's Plan A, which he told them about at dinner that night, was to inspect everyone, and everything, that came into the house, no matter what. He surmised that because the new mistress and master had not been honorably and dutifully sworn in, the house had done nothing in response to the invasion. Or perhaps, he thought, the bad magik had not activated until the night of the storm. Or could it have flowered when Ellora had awakened the Sprite with her own magik? He was not certain of the abilities of the girl child or of the boy with blue-purple eyes. He felt good about the new mistress and master, or M&M as he referred to them in his own private journal (only to be read by his successor). The mistress would give birth in the Terran month of March, which meant the baby, or babies, as Abequa had assured him, would come in spring, in the season of the new moon. That could be tough because of Maine's cold climate. The children would be home from the schooling they were all required to attend. (Gitchie thought this was an unnecessary risk. He could train these wizards himself if they would allow it). Yes, he nodded to himself, it was time to use technology to their advantage. Some of the previous masters had not enjoyed new technology stuff. But this one did, and Gitchie was glad because then he could do his job correctly. Also, part of his plan was to fill out the state homeschooling forms. The education bureaucrats, seeing him on the webcam, would not know how small he was. He could fool them into accepting him as the children's teacher. Of course, he would have to clean himself up and wear a disguise. Luke was not opposed to this idea; neither was Daisy. Only the older two wished to attend the nasty place on the mainland, so full of germs and the children of the Others! Gitchie had told Abequa they could now have more children, a suggestion she did not take kindly to. The forest brownies were planning to bring more young ones into the world in order to aid the eagle and her two hatchlings. Imagine, the raven Kassa coming to the aid of the eagle. How honorable and good some creatures could be. With those thoughts in his mind and the good feeling they produced within him, Gitchie made his way to the dinner table to tap gently upon the glass goblet he had been given by the previous Mistress.

He announced, "After this dinner, we shall perform the ceremony that binds those of this house to the magik therein. The contract is then binding and can be broken only by entering the sanctuary."

Luke was confused. "Is the cavern the sanctuary?"

"No, young master, the cavern is the home of Sarisha Chandi, protector of Terra and collector of magikal items. She chooses to live here. The house welcomed her eons ago. Their agreement is their own pact, and none shall enter it. Sanctuary is accessed through the tall mirror gateway."

Gitchie hoped this would be the only question concerning the house contract with Sarisha, because Gitchie didn't really know what that was. He did not like not knowing everything. As chief aide to the M&Ms, he felt he should have total control. But he was learning that no one had total control over anything! Even one's own wife! For Abequa had not wanted to create more children, telling him that her studies were more important. More important than the care of the house? He had been astounded and was now quite sullen about it. She had ventured to suggest that perhaps some of the barn brownies could be cajoled into entering service to the house. He had to admit that was a good idea. One or two had honor and wit. But for now, he had to concentrate on his duties. He had to put many of his "check-ins" on automatic service via the library computer, which he swore was arguing with him and making unnecessary adjustments to his instructions. Thank goodness good magik could not be usurped by bad or he would think there was an invasion through the computer system.

Having satisfied Luke's question about the sanctuary, Gitchie continued explaining his plan to home school the younger children over the internet.

Marji seemed to like the idea. Marcus did too, adding that he had his hands full at the boathouse so he could not afford to take time off to help. He had a boat show that he was getting ready for, plus there were meeting with the lawyers over Jeremiah and Cynthia's estates. The sailboat, *Axoparia*, had to be readied for the season. Suddenly there was so much to do!

Gitchie nodded in agreement to all they said. In his own mind, he thought, Plan A had better work because Plan B would not be as fun. In order to keep the house safe, Gitchie did have the power to order a temporary lock down, which neither the master nor the mistress could overrule. But that was only under the direst circumstances. He had no power at all over the dragon, but she seemed to have her own agenda, one that was allied with the house, to keep the magikal objects from being stolen and used by the Others. This would ensure the safety of both worlds, Terra and Faerieland. He did not have any idea about the other worlds connected to this one; Chamavi, Palandine or Herstamonix. He had only heard of them in legends and stories. Gitchie wondered if the creatures who lived in those other worlds knew of the sacrifice given by this world each day for the safety of all.

APPROVAL

Rahven had invited all the animals to the gathering. "Everyone must know of the events that happened so we can all be watchful and wary," he had said.

After telling the story, he added, "The eagle has lost her aerie needs to build another. We shall aid her quest. Should her mate return, then he may take his position at her side." This news brought a multitude of voices, squawks, chittering, clicks, and other means of communicating. Rahven had the wisdom to allow this talk for a few clicks of time. But soon, he raised his voice.

"Who among you will join? Who among you will help her build a new aerie?"

Immediately, Kassa hopped forward. He had lived while several of his regiment had just been killed by the Others. His was the right!

Rahven asked, "Have you a mate?"

"Not yet," came the reply. "The Regiment requires much."

Rahven nodded, bobbing his head several times. "Commander Taldassa, have you a say in this matter?" The wise old bird knew that the commander would have to train another to take this one's place. He might refuse.

Taldassa replied, "Approval is not needed, but yes."

Kassa decided to build a nest in the very tall, old apple tree next to the barn. He would have liked to have the cupola, but an owl had recently acquired it. Kassa could fight for it, but he decided his watch should not begin with a battle. Peace is powerful, his mother had told him. It is our way. The eagle seemed to not mind the new location. Her mate was still missing.

Kassa said softly to himself, "And so it shall be."

LESSONS AND LOVE

About one month later, late in July, the air was very still. A slight rustling could be heard in the trees from the chipmunks that were chasing each other. Or was it something else climbing in and out of the branches? The little brownie children were learning the fine art of climbing trees, swinging from delicate branches out into the air, and then catching a leaf, dropping, doing a somersault, and catching another branch at the last moment. The quiet air had a stuffiness to it that meant the morning was going to become hotter and perhaps a storm would develop along the coast. The barnies' first watch had their hands full with the newest eaglet that had hatched. Now there were two baby eagles with big mouths to feed. The first eaglet had accidentally come out of her shell while Kassa was sitting upon it, so it partially imprinted upon him. She cried for him even when her mother was around. So, the first watch kept her occupied and diverted by jumping around the nest, staying out of her reach as she tried to catch them. Dangerous work, but someone had to do it!

Asa, as Aisinwin was now called by everyone except his father, had been accepted by the foresters as an apprentice. Their ways of foraging and metalworking would take years him to learn. One of the first lessons concerned mushrooms, the kind used for medicine, which his mother needed. Her supplies had run low, so he was eager to bring her what she needed. He missed his little sister. She had been saddened by the knowledge that she would not be allowed out of the house yet. She was still too small. He shuddered to think that a bird, perhaps a robin, would find her a tasty morsel. When his Mother, Abequa, ventured out into the wilderness of the garden, she wore armor. The house cat, Kipper, had been con-scripted to be watchful for birds, but he was easily distracted. His Father was afraid he would forget and pounce on her by mistake.

Asa listened to the laughter and whoops as the younglings frolicked in their dangerous game with the baby eagle. His ears had become attuned to the noises of the forest, which changed over the course of the day, he observed. His friendship with Keevan had stalled—they didn't see each other very much! The young master was taking karate lessons at Gideon's in town and was gone three days of the week. Then, if Gitchie approved, Keevan was allowed to have a friend over, but the sword had to be locked within the safe in the library. He had sulked at first, but then saw the wis-dom of this. How could they explain a boy being injured by the weapon? Sarisha had assured Keevan, in a rare display of affection and trust, that she could retrieve the weapon for him in an instant should the need arise. One delightful afternoon, the dragon had demonstrated her talents by shrinking down to a tiny size so that she could easily fit through the cat door that led out from the kitchen. And then she had gone up to the roof, where a thing called a widow's walk had formed overnight (the house was making upgrades again), to spread her wings to show them how large she could become. She was wonderful and frightening all at once to Asa. Maemaegwin was still too shy to speak in her presence.

Another sound filtered its way to Asa: Marcus's hammering, clank-ing, sawing, and sanding down at the boatshed. He was a good carpen-ter, but not in the same league as Charlie Dorr had been. The young brownie had shaken his head back and forth when he occasionally heard some words that had no meaning to him, though their tone had meant much. Marcus had wanted an apprentice of his own, but now was not a good time. As Asa searched for the right kind of mushroom, he heard birds chittering for the seeds left for them by Mistress Marji. They were never satisfied, he thought.

Daisy was baking with her soon-to-be stepmother. There was a lot more to baking than she'd ever thought. Her own mother had no interest in cooking. They'd had a nanny who prepared meals for them. When Cynthia was alive, they'd typically eaten out at the local restaurants on the mainland. Cook's Lobster house and Holbrook's were her favorite places to eat. Cynthia was rarely home due to her hectic schedule on the Country music circuit.

Marji was the opposite and had thousands of recipes stored up in her memory. But Daisy, so far, had only one, for very sweet lemonade. As always, Golden was also in the kitchen, eagerly waiting for bits to come her way. She was a never-ending source of hunger but also of delight for Daisy. She was very content to be anywhere Golden was, and vice-versa.

"Daisy?" questioned Marji, "are you paying attention? How many teaspoons of salt have you put in the cookie dough?"

"Oh, I don't know, Mom"—she was still getting used to saying this—"I was thinking about Golden. May we go for a swim? It's getting hot."

"We can go after all the chores are done. Your brother might want to come after biking back from town. I have some laundry to do, and you should do your own."

Daisy scowled at the mention of her brother Keevan. Then she brightened up and said, "I'll go find Luke. Maybe he'll want to come with us. Hey, we can have a picnic!"

She often had ideas that quickly escalated to include Luke instead of Keevan. Marji was a bit worried about how the children were dividing themselves up, often leaving Kee out of the balance. And Ellora was still sleeping so much and, when she was awake, was often daydreaming. Well, Marji thought, sighing, it was hard work being part of a magikal family that was featured in a prophecy.

"We can include your dad, too. I'm sure he will need a break soon."

They set themselves to finishing the cookies and making sandwiches for everyone. She sent Daisy down into the cellar to get a cooler.

"Is this okay?" asked Daisy, returning with a picnic basket she'd found.

"It's kind of old," said Marji, blowing on the basket and producing a cloud of dust that went swirling into a vent in the floor. The house apparently had its own cleaning system.

"I like it!" said the girl. She quickly hefted it up onto the counter.

Marji was surprised at how heavy it was. But once she looked inside, she discovered why. Carefully wrapped up within a length of cloth was a small bottle of private label wine, dating back many years. Too bad. The wine was probably vinegar now. Under the cloth was a length of hair tied with a red ribbon. At the bottom of the basket sat two small wooden dishes, and carefully folded and placed in between the dishes was a handwritten letter:

Dearest Cassandra,

Should you be able, pack a basket for us and leave it by the fir tree near the top of the hill. We may be there for a time and your biscuits are the best! I for my part shall bring some of Grandfather's sarsaparilla, enough for us all. Should you not be able to get away, please know that Pilchie will be with me, as will the wizard. I feel temerity writing this, for should my note be found it will be questions and trouble for us all! The fight will come with a storm, I fear. But we also have Axoparia with us. She has been hidden in the cave for nigh on a weeks' time. We could not stable her for fear of being seen in the moonlight.

I fear showing any feelings toward you because of your father's enmity towards my family. He will not understand the judgment of the house is as stone and cannot be put aside. As a judge himself, he should understand. But your mother is for us, I feel, is she not?

Please, my love, be careful. Should we not win the day, I can go to my grave knowing you will live on.

Truly yours,
Lee

Marji had tears in her eyes after reading it aloud. Daisy had a funny look on her face, not understanding the antiquated way of writing.

"Sarsaparilla? Is that like the wine in this bottle?" she asked. "Is Lee a shorter name for Dingley?"

"No, it's like root beer. And yes, it was written by Dingley two hundred years ago! It's been down in the cellar all this time." She carefully folded the letter and laid it on the counter with all the items she had taken out of the basket. She took the basket outdoors to clean it with the hose so they could get all the dust off. As she dumped out the crumbs and whatnots, another folded note fluttered to the ground. Golden snatched it, but Marji demanded she hand it over. She could still read it, despite the bite taken out of it.

Cassie, I will keep your secret. But I fear for you! I will be steadfast and true, even under your father's stern gaze. Our music group is having a picnic the day before. I shall bring two baskets and leave one where you ask. Mr. Dunbar will drive us in his wagon up to the row of trees where the ground becomes too rough for the horses. I know the place well. I love you like a sister, and hope to call you thus, one day.

Cat

Marjorie read this note and suddenly knew whose picnic basket this was: Katherine Drake's! She set it down to dry in the sunshine and went back in to finish making lunch. Later, when she heard Marcus coming up the road, she went outside to find the basket gone!

"Have you seen the large picnic basket with a red ribbon? I left it here to dry after cleaning it."

"No," Marcus replied, "but I'm going to town to pick up Keevan. Both tires on his bike went flat."

"Both of them? That's odd. Here, look what I found in the old picnic basket." She handed him the note she had put in her pocket. He read it with little emotion but had a question on his face when he handed it back to her. Was he so used to finding odd things in this house now, that this was commonplace? What was happening to them?

"So, who wrote it? You found it in a basket?"

"Yes, and here's another one. I think it was written by Katherine Drake! I sent Daisy down to the cellar to get a cooler and she came up with an old dusty basket. We were making a picnic lunch and were going to surprise you!" As she spoke, she put her hand over her tummy. Marcus was immediately concerned,

"Hey, you'd better sit down. I'll finish making the lunch. You look pale and worn out."

"No way, I'll be fine. Besides, you smell like turpentine." She wrinkled up her nose in dismay. That smell was making her nauseous.

Marcus backed away and went to wash his hands. Marji sighed and looked for Daisy. But she was not in the kitchen or the family room. She called upstairs. There was no answer. Except for Marcus running water in the bathroom downstairs, there wasn't a sound in the house. Feeling more than queasy, Marji slowly got up but then sat back down. The feeling of nausea grew worse.

Marcus, emerging with clean hands, told her, "You stay here, I'll go find her. Did she go down into the cellar?" He grabbed a flashlight and went down the old stairs that led to the cistern. To tell the truth, he was uneasy about this part of the house. He recalled Gitchie saying that there was ample storage down there for many people. Exactly what did that mean? He had a feeling he did not want to know the answer. On the bottom step, he found a large straw basket with a cover, but it was empty. He shined the light all around the immense room, which was filled with all sorts of paraphernalia. It was if someone had begun to make a World War II fall-out shelter down there. Large glass bins labeled "flour," "pickles," and "pasta," and then row after row of blankets, pillows still in their plastic coverings, luggage in racks, most likely filled with clothing, he thought. Cans and more cans filled shelf after shelf. And wine! Corked bottles placed carefully in their own wheeled rack on, some labeled with a year. Old root beer and apple wine most likely, Marcus mused. He saw small footprints in the dirt floor and followed them. He began to actually trot, with a feeling of dread filling him—the cistern! Would Daisy know to stay away from it? What if she'd fallen in? He found her way in the back, sitting on a bunk bed and looking at some old books. The room was lit by a tall candle. He sighed a huge sigh of relief. She was safe.

"Hey, kiddo, where have you been? Mom and I were worried about you!"

"I came back down here to find another basket since Mom washed the other one. Then I saw a light and followed it to this room. Isn't it fantastic?" her voice showed no anxiety or apprehension at being in a musty, dark place.

Marcus grinned at the use of this word, one that Ellora had been using a lot of late.

"None of these books are in the library." Daisy continued.

Marcus looked at some of the title covers. *The Other Brother Grimm, Tales and Tails, The Sisters Grimm, Disaster at Sea,* and another that looked even more horrifying, *Witches, Warlocks, and Wizards: How to Tell Them Apart.* It wasn't the title that was scary, but the very realistic lithograph of a creature wearing flowing robes and riding through the sky on a long, twisted stick. More of them were on the ground stuffing some poor thing that looked like a brownie into a large black cauldron. The picture seemed to slowly come to life. The creatures were all laughing and dancing, cackling and prancing, while the brownie was screaming! Marcus shook his head to come out of the vision.

Daisy tugged at his shirt. "Dad! Dad, the opera book sings and this one turns the pages all by itself!"

"We'd better bring these up to Gitchie so he can catalogue them in the computer." Marcus had a feeling they were not part of the required reading in the Victorian age—or any age, for that matter. He blew out the candle, then immediately regretting doing it. But there was faint light coming from the stairs, and the flashlight threw a strong spotlight. Marcus grabbed the basket before heading up. Behind him, as they went up to the kitchen landing, the candle relit itself. Its brief wisp of smoke swirled around the room before entering the vent in the wall.

Marji was still on the couch. She smiled at them. "You were down there for more than a few minutes. I was beginning to worry. Aren't you going to get Keevan?"

"Oh, yes, I forgot!" Marcus replied. "I thought I'd only been gone a few minutes. Guess what's down there? It's just what Gitchie said, a whole storeroom of stuff in case of emergencies. Blankets, barrels of food. Daisy found an area with wooden bunk beds, and she found these books, and she found your basket." He handed her the books as he searched for the car keys.

Marji was confused. This was not the same basket. It had a green ribbon. Before she could object, Daisy hastily wiped off the dust, which again swirled down through a vent in the floor.

Marcus got in the SUV and took off through the cloud of dust. It reminded Marji how dry the ground was. They needed rain soon. She was having some of Abequa's tea, which had miraculously appeared on the table next to her. She sent a mental "thank you" to Abequa. Daisy was reading out loud, but Marji wasn't really listening. Her mind was roving, and not concentrating on anything. She felt out of sorts. The smoke detector went off, bringing her out of her void with alarm! Smoke was filling the kitchen, but then it traveled like a mini tornado down through the floor vent. Soon the room was clear. Marji took the burnt cookies out of the oven, walked over to the library, knocked on the secret door, and then tossed them into the cavern. She hoped they weren't too hot for Sari. She sighed again and decided to save time by making the rest of the batter into blonde brownies instead of cookies. She decided to ask Abequa to help her bake them.

Gitchie, not leaving his laptop and new desk, told her over his shoulder, "No problem, Mistress, I will program the oven to shut off when they are done."

Marji smiled but gestured for Abequa to come closer so she could whisper. "Please wake me so I can take them out of the oven, so they won't overcook."

Abequa smiled and nodded happily. She was happy to help the mistress, especially since she was open to drinking her herbal teas. She had asked Aisinwin to gather some of the fungi she needed. Items such as toadstools, gomphids, and some agarics. No one but her son seemed to understand how powerful these were. She would also like him to ask the tusked suidae—the humans called them pigs—who lived near the pond to find her some truffles. But Asa had not checked in with her today. She would ask the suidae herself, but that would take time away from her important new duty of caring for the mistress and her unborn babies. Yes, Abequa knew, there were two.

A DISAPPEARANCE

Marcus had driven nearly to town when he found Keevan walking on the road. He rolled down his window as he came close to him.

"What happened to your bike?" yelled Marcus.

"You didn't come to get me, so I started walking." He told his Dad. "I left it at the shop on Fix-It Street. Not only were the tires flat, they were slashed."

"What? Do you have any idea who did it?"

"I have an idea, but no proof. My bike was fine before I went to karate. When I came out, I went over to the store for a drink, and I talked to Grandfather Bradley for a bit. When I walked back to the karate school, my tires were ripped! I looked around but didn't see anybody. I told Sensei Gideon, but he didn't see anybody, either," Keevan told him angrily.

"Do you want to keep going to class?"

"Yeah, but maybe I can drive the Jeep and earn my driver's permit? I'm turning fourteen soon."

"Sorry Kee, you gotta be fifteen before you can do that. But I can drive you. It's only three mornings a week and I need to use the town library. I want check the Job-bank so I can find an intern without Gitchie interfering."

"Oh, I don't know Dad. Gitchie won't like it, and he'll think I was lying to him too! No, forget it. I'll get my bike fixed and keep riding to class."

Marcus was surprised at how vehement Keevan was about not upsetting the house brownie. He grinned. It could be a good thing. He was concerned about how sullen Keevan had been lately. The only time he saw him laughing was when he and Luke were playing plasma ball. Showing some emotion was better than moping about like he had been doing. They headed back to the house for lunch.

Earlier, Asa had ridden into the yard on Polly, who went immediately for her water bowl. As she drank, Asa looked around but saw no one. The vehicle that Marcus drove was not in the yard. Asa yelled, but his small voice was not heard. He left a note scratched in the dirt that he was off to search the pond for the suidae, who could find the important truffles for his mother. The suidae leader was named Mother Sus; the family had been living in the pond for three or four generations. That was all the information his father could give him. Asa saw a wet, square basket on the ground, apparently forgotten. He needed something with which to gather the items for his mother, so he borrowed it without asking. He did not realize this simple action would have consequences. He held it over his head. If someone had seen them, and no humans did, it would appear that Polly had a basket on her back as she galloped, as only a chubby dachshund could, into the vast wood that led to the forest beyond, toward the pond.

Ellora, Luke, and Myster were in Charlotte's studio. Both Ellora and Myster were having an identity crisis. Ellora had felt her powers growing, but it made her feel strange. When she was alone, she tested her ability to move things with her mind. It was hard, but she could do it. Almost anything distracted her. This time it was a hummingbird flitting about. She wished she could step outside of herself and go back to being just Ellora. But truthfully, all her life she had known her family was different. All her life the villagers had treated her family like they were eccentric. Sometimes she would get angry, hearing them say things behind her back. Going to school for the past year had been tough, too, and she hated the bus ride. Sometimes she could ignore the other kids. But if they began to go after her little brother, she'd grown hot and reckless with her feelings. Luke always laughed at them—sometimes like a crazy person! One boy had begun to laugh with him, and then could not stop. He had to go to the nurse. It had been better when Keevan and Daisy had started to ride the Harpswell bus, but that was only for the last two months of school. Keevan was popular because he played sports. Daisy was popular because she was, simply, so sweet. Grandma Charlotte had told her before she died that the villagers were jealous, as if that excused them. Grandmother Addie had a different method of dealing with it, telling her to turn the other cheek. But, according to her experience, that just gave the bullies another cheek to slap.

Luke stared out the window at the stream of smoke coming out of the kitchen window. "Mom's burning the cookies," he reported.

Ellora got up to look herself. She knew that Gitchie would not let anything happen to the house, ever! But she grinned, thinking to herself that now they all had a friend who would eat anything burnt. She sat back down with a sigh. She had been sighing a lot lately, Luke noticed.

"Hey, Ell, it's going to be your birthday soon, and then right after, it will be Keevan's. What are you going to have for your birthday breakfast?"

"I was thinking of going to town for breakfast, or Holbrook's for lunch. They have some new items on the menu this season."

"Meaning that Mom hasn't been very good at cooking lately, huh?" Luke said that with a grin on his face. He plopped down on the daybed that Grandma had put in the studio for her afternoon naps. He stared up at the ceiling, then closed his eyes. He willed his mother to feel better. She had been nauseous every day and her other feelings of being unfocused were disturbing to him. She was usually very organized with her catering events. She had to outsource one of them already because she was too tired. He had a feeling that the twins were to blame. Two babies were simply taking more of her energy than her pregnancies with Ellora or himself. And these two were going to be magikal, that was certain.

There was simply too much magik swirling about, in the air, in the water, for them to escape it. The dreams were keeping Luke awake in the early hours of the morning. He wondered if his mom was dreaming, too.

"Are you dreaming at night?" he asked his sister, out of the blue.

She looked at him in surprise. "Yes, are you? What about?"

"Mostly about the ancient past, a huge blue gemstone that is super important. I'm riding an elephant and some old guy is really angry at me," Luke told her.

"This is weird. I'm having similar dreams! Always about a blue gem that people are trying to find. In some, I'm riding an elephant, too, and there are huge stone statues that come alive and look right through me. In the one last night I was flying, searching for a something, flying over the treetops and the shoreline."

"Maybe you were Sarisha, or seeing through her eyes?" Luke offered.

"Maybe. Hey, I'm hungry. We skipped breakfast, so let's go help make lunch."

Luke nodded. They left Myster in the studio, since he was asleep. After they left, the cat got up on the bench, where Ellora had been trying to get in touch with her grandmother again. Myster was hoping she had left the magical mirror turned on. Myster was trying to remember his life as a wizard, and was wondering why he could recall some things, like the prophecy, but could not remember any of the lives he had lived, including his life as a schoolteacher. Maybe Charlotte or Charlie could help him? But then he thought he should ask Dingley's father, Dr. Isaac. Myster cautiously poked the mirror with his front paws. Nothing happened. He grew impatient and pushed the thing off the bench and onto a pillow on the floor. It landed perfectly right side up and came on with a glare of blue light. Myster sat on the handle to peer into the shining face. Without warning, the face of the mirror became soft. As Myster pounced upon it, he fell through the mirror and disappeared!

The light was slightly purple on this side of the mirror. There seemed to be a faint ringing or singing sound. Myster looked about but could see only tall grass around him. So, he sat very quietly in order to decide what to do next. Then he heard someone humming a song that sounded familiar, so he went off in the direction of the song, "Frere Jacques."

When Ellora and Luke came into the kitchen, Marji let them know the plan for a picnic. "What kind of sandwich do you want?" she asked. "Oh, and Ellora, honey, I don't know if this will help, but that schoolteacher's things are in an old trunk in the attic."

"Where is the attic?" Ellora asked in a distracted sort of way as she got out the ingredients for a sandwich she would like peanut butter, sour pickles, and potato chips. But it had to be freshly made, because the bread would get soggy from the pickles.

"I don't know, but Gitchie told me he had the journals and books put in there because of the automatic shielding that's in the barn. So, I guess the attic is in the barn."

Luke said, "We just came from there and didn't see anything in the studio."

Ellora added, "But there's a set of stairs that look like they go up to nowhere. Maybe that's the attic."

Marcus and Keevan came home then and found the Lunicorn waiting for them on the porch with the dogs. But curiously, no one had seen Blou for some time.

"I wonder where she is. Maybe in the cavern?"

"No," answered Ellora. "She isn't human so she can't open the door."

Instead of taking the food somewhere for a picnic, they decided to just eat in the kitchen. Keevan realized he was starving and ate two sandwiches. He thanked Ellie for making them while Mom was on the couch, still not feeling well. They talked about their day so far. Marji asked all the kids if they had seen a basket in the front yard with a red ribbon.

"Are you sure the one I found down in the cellar isn't the same basket?" Marcus asked her.

"No! I am sure! The ribbon on your basket is green and it's all dirty. I washed mine with the hose and the ribbon was a bright shiny red," she replied irritably.

It didn't seem like a big deal, so Marcus decided to change the subject to tell them about what happened to Keevan's bike.

Gitchie came out to ask questions. Did Keevan register the bike? No? Then that must be done soon at the town office. Marcus could do that online, he told them. Should the sheriff be notified? Again, the answer was no. Marcus felt more and more that it was Gitchie, and not himself, who was the true master. He felt an urgency to get his own errand done, so he announced that they could all go to town the next day, with a list of things to do, and Marji could have the morning to herself.

It was nearly dark by the time Ellora remembered she had left the mirror on. She went up into the barn to fetch her prize possession. It had turned itself off. There was no light in the studio, but she had brought a flashlight. She searched, aiming the light here and there, looking beneath tables and furniture for any trunks or boxes. The barn looked so spooky in the dark. She went back down the three flights of stairs and into the house, where she noticed the kitchen door was no longer wooden but made of glass! The house has upgraded to a sliding door with a doggy door built into the side of the kitchen. It was still unsettling to her how fast the house could change, as if it was some sort of giant replicator or 3-D printer. What would it change next? It seemed to Ellora that the magik was getting stronger, somehow.

LIGHTS IN THE DARK

Far off in the distance someone had seen the light in the attic. He was so excited he hardly knew what to do! Imagine, his first watch and he saw the light! No one in hundreds of moons had seen any warning lights from the topmost window of the barn. No one in his lifetime, and not his grandsires, either. The raven assigned to him awakened in a grumpy manner.

"Squawk! What?" The old bird needed an explanation as to why he was awakened in this manner.

Oomy remembered his manners, and calmly said, "Please, sir, I saw the light in the uppermost part of the Barn. I am certain I saw three flashes!"

The old bird cocked his head. "Not the required number?"

"No. What does it mean?"

"I am not certain. We must tell the commander." The raven waited for the little forester to climb upon his back and grasp his back feathers. This always hurt, but it was necessary, for Oomy had no wings and would certainly get hurt if he fell. They waited to make certain there were no more flashes of light from the barn. None came, so they flew off toward camp.

The black bird silently settled into the clearing. The fire had reduced itself to coals within its bed of stones, with barely a wisp of smoke. There was one oldster sitting by it, waiting for his grandson to return from his first watch. Oomy had been so excited, and his parents had been so worried and anxious, but also proud. Their son had followed the steps, taken the test, and gained the right to join the watchers. Each night for generations, one of their clan had been silent witness to watch for the light. Euka wondered if any humans remembered their duty. No matter! The foresters would not break tradition. They had agreed to watch for the light, and that they would do. Euka had this argument with himself many, many times. He drifted asleep mumbling to himself. A hand on his arm woke him up, jingling the tiny bracelets he wore as a signal of his retirement. A voice whispered, "Grandsire! Grandsire, I saw the light!"

"What? It is your first watch! I never saw the light in all my nights! Is this truth?"

His question was also for the bird, who bobbed his head and squawked, which awakened the other sentry. Chitin came swiftly on silent feet into the clearing.

"What is the meaning of this?" Chitin asked in an irritated manner. "Your watch has hours to go, the sun set not long ago, Oomy, are you ill? Has something happened?"

Oomy could not find his voice in front of their best forester. He was doubting himself now. But he took a deep breath and said, "I saw the light in the topmost window of the barn, three flashes! What does it mean?"

"Only three? You are certain?" Her question was also for the bird, who again bobbed his head. "We must call a council." Raising the horn, she blew it once, then twice more to alert all the clan.

It took a long while, but all the forest brownies assembled, even the ones on watch by the shore.

"You all know Oomy and his clan. They are honorable and watchful. Euka has been a watcher all his life. They know the laws. They know tradition well," Chitin told the assembled, sleepy but becoming more awake with each word. They began to mutter and mumble.

"It is true!" said Oomy, defending himself. "But I saw only three flashes—no more, no less. My ride waited with me to see if there would be more. But there were none."

"Three? What does it mean?" many voices asked at one.

Chitin held up two fingers to her lips for silence. "We will trek to the barn with an emissary to ask. That is all we can do. Oomy must return to finish his watch. See you all in the new sun. Oomy, good work."

The little forest brownie smiled and mounted his ride. He thought the bird should earn his name for this night, even though he was old.

Naming ceremonies were always so much fun! They would dance and acrobat high in the air in honor of the animal that earned her or his name.

It was only nine o'clock. Keevan heard someone softly saying his name. It was Gitchie, standing on his bed, looking worried.

"Young master Keevan, I am apologizing for this bother. We have not heard from Aisinwin all day. He was to fetch fungi and mushrooms for his mother. Polly is also missing!"

Keevan immediately thought this was odd. His friend was usually really good at checking in and following rules.

"And my mom is missing a basket and my bike had slashed tires. No one has seen Myster or Blou for a while, either. I wonder if it's all connected." Keevan answered. "But what can we do at night?"

"Could you go to the barn and ask if he has been there today?"

"All right let me go tell Dad. By the way, why won't you call him by his nick-name?" Keevan asked him.

"Because a name that is nicked, is not a true name." came the short reply.

Dad was in the bathroom and Mom was asleep, so he went to see what the girls were doing. Daisy and Ellora were having a quiet talk. Keevan could tell it was about the house.

"Hi, Kee, we were just talking about the house and all the stuff going on," Ellora said to him. "What's up?"

"Gitchie says Asa hasn't checked in after mushroom hunting today, so with all the things missing I thought we should all, you know, watch out," He said quietly. "Mom's resting. Dad's in the bathroom."

Daisy said, "He likes taking showers at night. He says it helps him sleep."

Keevan said, "I'm going to the barn to ask if they've seen Asa. Polly might be there. That's all I can do until the morning. But if I'm gone in the morning, it's because I'm out looking for him."

Ellora touched his arm. "I'm sure he's okay. Luke would know if he was hurt, I think, and he hasn't said anything. What I think is weird is that Blou and Myster are also missing. Golden seems really sad. I haven't seen Sarisha for a while either. Maybe I'll go check in with our dragon friend."

"I want to come too!" Daisy added quickly. "I don't like being alone."

They quietly went downstairs to get flashlights, and Daisy brought an apple for Sarisha. The lights from Gitchie's computer screen and monitors were the only ones on in that room. Gitchie's technology now covered one area of a low wall in the library. Ellora wondered where Abequa had her dried herbs and teas stored.

Keevan asked, "When did we put in a screen door in the library?"

Ellora giggled, "It's been there since the day our grandparents arrived without notice. I didn't want them to see Golden and had no other way out. The house made a screen door right in front of me!"

"So cool," said Keevan. He now knew how he was going to get his own room in the barn. He would just ask the house! But he wasn't sure that he wanted his own room now. His little brother was turning out to be kind of okay.

Ellora whispered, "Be careful!" as she was careful to not let the screen door slam.

Kee waved his hand as he walked away from them.

Ellora let Daisy knock on the secret door. It opened suddenly, as if it were waiting for them. Out sprang Blou!

"I have been in this cavern for ages!" the angry sprite sputtered. "Did you only think of me now? I could have starved in there! The door can only be opened by human hands!"

"Then how did you get in?"

"The door was open, stupid." Blou stopped herself. Ellora was not stupid. "I apologize for that word. You and anujan Daisy are most kind for coming to free me from the cavern."

Before Ellora could stop her, Daisy tossed the apple in through the door as she said, "We were going to go ask Sarisha about what's been going on."

"What!? Has something happened to Golden?" demanded the sprite, instantly worried and upset.

"No, no, it's just that Asa and Polly haven't checked in, Mom is missing a special basket with a red ribbon, you were missing, Keevan's bike tires were slashed, and we haven't seen Myster in a while," Ellora explained.

"What is a 'bike tires'?"

"It's a thing you can ride on that has two wheels and gears." Ellora gestured as she answered. Then she peered into the cavern. "Is Sarisha in there?"

"No, she is not. I wished to ask her something about the past. I also wanted to know if she now knows where the terrible Others dwell. We might need that information in an answering strike."

Ellora thought about that while she shut the little door. "Wait a minute, how did the door shut after you went through it? Grandma Charlotte told me it has to be shut from the other side."

"As I have discovered, the door can be shut by anyone, not just a human. I shut it, not wanting the interfering brownie to spy on me."

That was understandable! Ellora had a sneaky feeling that Gitchie was spying on all of them by installing motion sensors—although Blou had called them 'emotion sensors,' which made everyone smile. Gitchie was so into 'techonicks'—also another Blouette-invented word—that his new clothing now included a special hat that sprouted its own light and an apron with all sorts of gadgets. She wondered how the home-schooling application was going. Ellora had a plan to get her driver's license so that she and Keevan wouldn't have to ride that awful bus to the mainland school.

"Okay," said Ellora. "Let's go make some popcorn and wait for Keevan to come back from the barn. Soon the smell of popcorn wafted up to the top floor. Marcus came down to get some.

"Where's Keevan?" he asked. He frowned when he got an answer. So many times, things had happened when they were separated. He wanted his family home at night and in the house! "Listen, I think your mom is having a bit of trouble with her pregnancy, so anything you can do for her will be great. I have been thinking of contacting her head chef to let him know what's going on."

"Does this mean the wedding plans are cancelled? Because, seriously, only Daisy wanted to be a flower girl. I ... I just want Mom to be happy. We can always have a celebration later, after the twins are born."

"Twins? Who said anything about twins?" Marcus nearly sputtered and spit out his tea.

"Abequa told me," Ellora said, "and she is usually right about things like that. I don't think that Luke or Keevan would mind cancelling the wedding, either. We could have a small ceremony in the rose garden, just family."

"You are so wise beyond your years, young lady! That's such a relief because your mom has told me she doesn't want to disappoint any of you. We need to make plans soon. Wow, this tea is really good," he said as he poured a cup for Marji. He went upstairs to see how she was doing. He found Luke sitting in their bedroom quietly reading with his mother.

"Hey, kiddo, how's your mom doing?"

They both smiled at him. She said, "Instead of me reading to him, Luke is telling me a good night story. He wrote down a dream he had that's full of intrigue and mystery."

"I love a good mystery. Let's hear it!" Marcus said.

As Luke read his story, Ellora and Daisy tiptoed upstairs to listen in the doorway. Daisy went into the room to curl up with Golden over by the window seat, her favorite place in the house. The youngest one of their family had a way with words. They were all spellbound, listening to Luke's complex story: thieves riding elephants, sailing in ships, stealing gems that were discovered to be rare diamonds. The thief got away with the giant gemstone, which he split open with a magikal hammer that was borrowed from a god. He found a jinn—or genie—trapped inside. It could fly and make people forget things. The thief lived on and on, adding his life to other people's as the centuries passed, traveling the world, discovering new and wondrous things—except happiness. Then he found out the huge mistake he had made by selling parts of the gem, for they were more precious than gold. During his search he found there were other thieves like himself. They banded together in search of any magical items, but they were not the best of friends and often fought each other. Once during a war, they did fight each other and one of them died. These thieves often hid themselves from the world, only to use their great wealth for themselves, to satisfy their lust for life. One thief, who captured other people's souls, was slowly going insane.

"And then one of their ships sank in a great storm, and another piece of the gem went missing. They tried diving for it, but with their outdated equipment they could not find it. So, they decided to sleep for one hundred years and awaken in another time to continue their search."

"Wow, that dream was like a movie!" said Marcus. "Maybe we should send it to a filmmaker."

"No" said Luke, "It would be unbelievable, but we should keep the manuscript because Gitchie took the time to print it for me."

"Ok, off to bed, kiddo!" He went over to pick up Daisy and winked at Ellora, who was yawning, too.

When Marcus came back into the bedroom, he said to his fiancé, "We need to talk."

Before Luke fell asleep, he felt his sister reach out telepathically to ask him a question: "That wasn't a dream, was it?"

"No," he answered through the same telepathic channel. "It was a vision. It is part of the story so far."

Keevan stood in the middle of the barn. He had never been there at night, alone. Boris was there but he was acting scared and whined at him, as if he wanted to leave. His flashlight seemed feeble in the immense building with its high-pitched roof. It was a hot night, and on the way over he had seen a lot of lightning bugs. Some of them were the biggest he had ever seen, as large as sparrows. He left the door open and those giant lightning bugs had followed him into the barn. He wasn't worried until they began to swirl around him in a creepy way. One by one they zoomed in near enough to pull his hair! What? He waved his arms about his head and ducked away from the fast, little buggers.

"Hey!" Keevan shouted, "stop it!"

"May we aid you in some way, young intruder?" A deep voice called up to him from the dusty, dirty floor. "Our apologies for the sentries. They are a bit bored."

"Bored? Why were they pulling my hair?"

"You have heard of counting coup? No? It is a customary challenge to touch or poke an adversary while on duty." the barnie replied.

"I am not an adversary! I live here!"

"My apologies," the deep voice said again.

"If you are truly sorry, then you have to stop doing the thing that ... Ouch! It's wrong! It doesn't matter if you keep saying sorry over and over without fixing the problem!" Keevan yelled and waved his flashlight around again, but he saw no one. There was nothing but row after row of old tools hanging on the walls. Inside the barn at night was kind of creepy, and he wished he could leave now, but he needed to ask if Asa was there.

"Look! I have been sent by Gitchie from the house. His son, Asa—Aisinwin—is missing along with the little dog, Polly."

Immediately some lights came on. "Polly? Missing? Why did you not say so? We adore that little one!" A barnie dressed in animal skins with a bird's nest for a hat stood on the last step of the stairs. "Give us details!" he demanded.

Keevan told them all he knew, along with his plan to set out at first light, with Molly, to search the forest. By the time he left the barn, some older barnies were scheduled for a search shift and were looking over very detailed maps of the island. They even had a plan.

FINDING THE PUPPIES

At dawn, all the brownies in the barn were shocked to see an emissary from the forest with news that one of the watchers had seen a light flash three times in the topmost window of the barn.

"But we made no such signal, and if we did send one, it would be the customary five flashes followed by seven with an extra-long flash should immediate help be required."

No one could fathom who had sent the signal.

"We wonder," asked Chitin, "we wonder if this has anything to do with the missing Aisinwin and Polly?"

"He is one of the brownies in service to the house and she is his mount," said Belle, the co-leader of the barnie clan. Her mate, Brayle, a tall brownie, nodded his head in agreement.

"What can we do? Shall we search the entire island?"

"Young master Keevan searches this morning-day. He has another tracker, Molly the shepherd. Aisinwin will be found. Yet, it would be good to be of service of the Mistress, and we need the practice."

An organized search set out from the barn, with the older barnies, Brass and Ket, riding the older goats while Grunge rode Jack, the rabbit. That was all they could spare for the morning. There was much to be done in the barn, chickens to be fed, a cow to be milked twice a day, stables to be cleaned out and a mare who needed looking after daily, now that she was with foal. Getting the goats out of the barn for a morning would be a relief! They would see this as a wonderful adventure. The two energetic baby goats, dressed in their pajamas, set out with their chaperones, along the well-known paths toward the middle of the island and the pond.

It was one day before Ellora's birthday and two days until Keevan's. But all he could think about was his little friend out there in the dark all night. One of them must be hurt—most likely Polly, because she would have found her way home if she were able to. He had not spoken with his parents this morning, so he counted on his sisters to tell Dad what he was doing. He was walking along the only path he knew that led to the pond on the western side of the island. He stopped to listen. Something was coming through the underbrush, hopping and leaping. Molly and Boris began to bark. The baby goats burst through the foliage, followed by a huge jack rabbit and one bigger goat. Keevan recognized the harnesses she wore- it was from the tack room in the barn. Molly stopped barking and sat down. Brass and Ket dismounted, while Grunge stayed on his mount, Jack.

"We are to be of service, Master Keevan. But you are on a human path to the pond. There are other ways of getting there," Brass told him in a deep voice. "Aisinwin would be using Forester trails unknown to thee."

Keevan agreed but had to ask, "How can I follow those? I'm too big."

"Ket will travel with thee, I shall take the littles, and Grunge will take Jack along another path. We shall meet on the eastern side of the pond. If Aisinwin is not found, then we shall cross the paths to the west. Lighting a fire by the shore will also help guide Aisinwin to us. If we do not find him by nightfall, you are to return to the house, and we shall camp." Brass's deep voice carried all the confidence in the world that his commands would be followed. Keevan did his best to look serious, but the darn baby goats were so cute, jumping around and on top of Molly. Ket gestured that they should begin. The dogs followed and Keevan brought up the rear guard.

What seemed like hours later, he resisted an impulse to ask what time it was, knowing he would get a cryptic answer like he should know from where the sun was in the sky or something like that. He was astonished when Grunge took a miniature pocket watch out of his shirt pouch. It was 7:30. They had been walking for over an hour this morning.

"We should be nearing the pond. I should not have to tell you to be silent. We need not let the fish hawk know we are near, nor the she eagle, who is also hunting to feed her young.

Keevan commented, "You don't think the eagle will get you, do you?"

"Mayhap not, since we have your company," Brass answered, Grunge nodding in agreement. "But Nishime has taken members of our clan in the past. And, certainly, the osprey will if she can get us near the water. In the bush and brush we are safer. When one's young are hungry, a parent does anything he or she can to feed them."

Except, Keevan thought to himself, when your mother was a famous country singer too busy to be home, missing birthdays and forgetting to call. Brass must have seen the scowl on his face, because he reached over to touch the tall young man's arm to reassure him, thinking he was worried that his friend had been eaten. Keevan smiled back, realizing he had new friends now.

Suddenly, Molly began to bark. They could hear a very faint little bark in response.

"Polly!" shouted Keevan. "Asa!"

They followed Asa's shouting until they found them in a tiny cave. Asa came out to greet his friend. Keevan grinned from ear to ear when he learned the reason they had not returned home: two little puppies were sleeping with their mother, Polly!

"Gosh! We thought she was just getting fat! Poor Polly, she must have been scared!"

"Yes, my friend, she gave birth without ease. One little one has died," Asa replied. "I buried it over by the shore. Polly was terrified then. I had nothing with which to light a fire—every twig and branch is wet here. I stayed awake all night to keep her little family safe."

Asa did look exhausted. Keevan bent over to pet the new mother and to look at the puppies. Grunge made a grunting sound and Ket nodded. They began to head back, but Brass remained behind.

"They will let Belle know of the birth. I do not believe she should be moved yet. Harm may come from the difficult journey."

But Keevan disagreed. "I can use this basket, and if I follow the human paths, I can be home in one hour. Can you ride ahead to let everyone know? Gitchie can tell my family what happened." Since the young man was son of the master of the house, Brass agreed, on one condition: that he accompany them on their way back. Brass thought, it will also give the baby goats more exercise!

Asa looked very sad at the new use of the basket. All his hard work—the mushrooms he had gathered—tumbled out on the ground as Keevan carefully placed the tiny dog family into it. Quietly, Brass filled his pouch with some of the fungi. Asa tucked one of the prized items into his sack. Keevan saw what they were doing and picked up the rest of the collection and put them into the sack that held his lunch. Together they all set off for home. They hadn't traveled very far when they heard a loud commotion coming toward them. A snorting sound and squealing came from a boar standing in the path. Keevan was alarmed at the size of its tusks. He had to think quickly but came up with no plan other than to try to put the loaded basket carefully up in a nearby pine tree. Help came in the form of the mother goat, ridden by Ket, who shouted and while she bleated her response to the challenge. The baby goats came bounding up behind, heedless of the danger. The boar lowered its head and scratched the dirt. Keevan thought it was going to charge. Brass must have thought so too, for he placed himself between the boy and the boar. Out of nowhere, up sprang Jack with Grunge brandishing his spear. He roared at the boar, which decided it had had enough. It turned and ran back into the forest. Jack followed close behind. They heard squealing and then silence.

"Come," Brass ordered, "we must hasten! Before more follow!" Keevan was glad to go with him. Ket gestured to Asa to climb up and hold on. Riding a goat was not at all comfortable or easy. The baby goats were just a big pain and not cute any longer. Keevan made a mental note to make sure the goats got more exercise. Maybe he could make them an obstacle course and that would keep them out of everyone's hair. He grinned because Grunge and Brass had no hair, but they did wear caps made of woven moss. Although Ket had a long braid down his back, he too wore a cap. Maybe Daisy would give them some of the colored feathers from her crafts basket. Daisy seemed to like decorating the faerie people. It was funny what you thought of when your life was on the line, he thought.

MEANWHILE

A bit later that same morning, Ellora was thinking about her birthday. She knew her mom was in no condition to make one of her fancy cakes, so she quietly asked Marcus if they could go to Pammy's Ice Cream Parlor. Daisy thought that idea was terrific!

Ellora told her parents that Keevan was out on a hike, searching for the missing faery and Mom's dog, Polly. They drove to the Village, stopping by the General Store to visit the Bradleys. Grandmother had seen them drive by and let her husband know they were in town. She was busy with the post office duties right now. The two younger kids went to pick out a cold drink. Luke he asked for some special jellybeans. He had told his brownie friends about them, and they simply could not believe him about all the different flavors. Grandfather Bradley, although not as jovial as their other Grandpa had been, still was a less serious person than his wife. He greeted all of them with a hearty hug. Luke told Grandfather about the upcoming birthdays, in case he had forgotten. Life seemed normal with the exception of all the little things that were suddenly missing; a basket, their dog and cat and their little faery friend.

Grandfather asked, "Where is Keevan? I didn't see him riding his bike to karate."

Marcus quickly answered before Daisy could say anything. "He's doing some sort of meditation in the forest. He'll be back in class tomorrow. I remember going off all day with friends when I was young. You and Mom never knew where we were."

"We knew you were on the island and it was different back then. Not so many strangers lurking about. That reminds me. Can we talk without little ears hearing?"

Ellora and Daisy knew exactly what that meant, so they went to the little bakery next door. But the adults didn't notice Luke, crouched behind the counter looking for jellybeans.

"A while back, a strange guy wearing sunglasses and a hood came asking about Island Catering. Said he had a big corporate shindig coming up and wanted to know if Island Catering could handle it. Before I could stop her, your mother told him that the owner has a permanent crew, hires workers as needed, and handled a two-hundred-person wedding reception this past April with no problems! She also gave him one of Marji's business cards. I didn't like the look of him. For one thing, he wouldn't take off his glasses to talk to me and he mumbled a lot. He seemed like one of those stalkers."

Marcus thought to himself, wow, a lot has changed. Two months ago, he would have said the guy was just eccentric. Now, he was suspicious of everything. Out loud he said, "We'll be on the lookout for someone matching that description. Should we tell the sheriff?"

His father looked at him, not knowing if he was being sarcastic or not, but added, "that's what your mother said after she saw how strange he was acting: We should tell the Sheriff!"

Marcus grinned and slapped his dad affectionately on his shoulder.

"Well, maybe we should tell Marjorie's crew that they might be needed soon. Can you also let James know, since you see him more than we do?"

"Sure, but Keevan sees him nearly every day at karate class too, you know," Jonathan replied.

"Yeah, but I think asking a fourteen-year-old to do that is too much. And the other students might think he's trying to get special treatment, or whatever they call it these days."

"Really, and you were only eleven when you first hiked around the island by yourself. You think Keevan can't get a message right?" He grinned while making this remark. "Hey, did you hear how much damage the storm caused? And they can't figure out why the bridge literally came apart the way it did. That'll cost half a million at least. Five houses and the med clinic were damaged too." He shook his head. "We'll have to have a lot of bean suppers to help pay for repairs."

Luke had heard their conversation from his spot behind the counter; his Vulcan hearing came in handy sometimes. He had been wondering how the hooded man had found them. Now he knew. It had been simple detective work on the man's part. They would have to have a big meeting at home about it and he had a feeling that his mom wasn't going to be happy. Luke agreed with Gitchie that they had to be much more careful. Twins were going to be born and that would also make the family more vulnerable. In ancient days a family could "circle the wagons," but in this day, anyone could find them through the internet. He giggled to himself, picturing his family in a covered wagon with the dragon sitting on top of it. For some reason, he made his decision right then to begin practicing his magik to find out what he could do. Ellora, too, would have to start. Where could they practice? Maybe Sarisha would have an idea as she would likely be their guide. Of course, Blou would be in on it, and Myster. But wait a minute; he hadn't seen the cat in a while, either! Too many things were missing! He hoped Keevan had found Polly and Asa. They were small but they had big hearts. He thought Polly had been looking fat lately. Luke sent a telepathic message to Ellora to come back. He smiled at his grandmother when she came in and spotted him. But she misread the reason he was behind the counter.

"If you eat all those jellybeans, you'll end up with a tummy ache," she said.

Not realizing the boy had been within earshot, both Marcus and grandfather looked guilty.

Daisy came back into the store. "I want to go home," she said. "I miss Golden."

"Who's Golden?" Grandmother asked.

Ellora said, "Our new pony. She showed up one day and hasn't gone home. We've been looking for her owner on Spacebook, but so far no one has claimed her." Ellora quickly took a bite of her chocolate croissant to hide her expression from her grandmother. Addie might not be magikal, but she had grandmother powers—she could tell when people were lying. Ellora thought, Well, it's not a big lie. We do have a new mare, but her name is Honey. Luke looked at her and grinned, giving her a thumbs up. They said their goodbyes and climbed into the SUV to go home.

Keevan had been home for about a half hour after his big adventure finding Asa. He left Polly in the barn where all the helpers fussed over her. He felt Blouette land on his shoulder. He didn't mind anymore. Golden tried to get through the cat door, but she was too big now, so he let her in through the new sliding kitchen door. Keevan wondered when it had been switched to a slider. He heard a twinkling sound and turned to see the head house brownie tapping on a glass to get his attention. Gitchie had begun doing that ever since he learned the custom.

"I sincerely thank you again for helping Aisinwin ...for helping Asa. His harvest of the necessary fungi was important to his mother."

"I'm worried about my family, too."

"Abequa assures me that Mistress is going to be fine. Her electrolytes are low, and she needs bed rest. Abequa has designed a special nutritional diet for her."

"My mom isn't the only one with new babies," Kee told him. "Polly wasn't just fat, she was carrying puppies! She gave birth last night and Asa stayed to protect her."

Gitchie was not surprised, having been told by the raven Kassa what had occurred. But he understood that it was important to Master Keevan to be the one to tell the tale.

"Birth is always a wonder and a special moment. I am glad you were the one to share it with Asa." Gitchie used the shortened name without hesitation this time.

Kee grinned, and asked, "Where is everyone?"

"They went into town to do some errands. Ellora told me that Luke wished to purchase something called beans of jelly."

A LOT TO SAY

It was decided they needed to have a family meeting. It went on and on. Daisy grew tired and soon fell asleep. They all had much to say and, more importantly, much to agree upon. Perhaps it was the recent events that made this conclave so important. All that was missing now was their cat. The basket with the red ribbon had been borrowed, not lost. The surprise of birth of the puppies as well as the growing need for help in the barn—for Keevan was adamant that he and the barnies could not get all the work done—were top on the list.

Gitchie was clear that no one else should come onto the property without clearance, but he did agree that Marcus needed an assistant with the boat building if his business were to thrive. Gitchie himself had the computer as an assistant, but he was careful to not say too much about that. He did not tell them he had installed security cameras and sensory devices all over the house and had enlisted Brayle in putting up more along the road and the shore and in the meadow. He bought them by accessing the Drake Foundation money that had been set aside for such things. Gitchie explained the Drake Foundation had been set up by a previous Master, and that it was to be used at the discretion of the family for emergencies. It had more than enough money for repairs to any village houses and the medical clinic also. He did not tell them that Brayle had refused to go up on the hilltop because he reported seeing a spriggan— He did explain why he was hesitant to venture down into the cellars. The recent find of books and baskets as well as a vast storage area that he knew nothing about had completely unnerved him. One book in particular was so unsettling and creepy, a term he had recently learned and begun to use often, that he could not look at it. However, his daughter, Maemaegwin, seemed fascinated by the pictures that came alive the longer you looked at them. In fact, the library alarm had gone off when they tried to put the three new books on a shelf. For now, the books were on the fireplace hearth, where there was just enough magik to keep them in control and closed.

Another report came in from the barn with some new information, also. One of the foresters had arrived to let them know that a watcher had seen the light. When no one, including Gitchie, knew what that was about, they invited the forester to come personally to tell them. Kassa was sent to the barn with the message.

After that they all agreed to tell everything they knew about the island and the house—anything that more than one person needed to have knowledge of was important. This is when Ellora made the decision to tell all she knew about the magik mirror. Of course, they all wanted to see it. She had a hard time sharing it for some reason. Keevan, also, told them about the sword that had magically appeared in the rose garden the day of the attack.

"This meeting has been needed for some time," Marcus said. "We need to react logically and make a plan for survival and to keep our way of life safe and somewhat normal. We must tell each other about any odd things happening."

"I believe we all need to say what's on our minds," Marji added. "And we all need to tell what we know about all the events. Gitchie will be adding what he knows, and we will record this, too." She pressed "record" on her laptop computer.

Gitchie, not singing this time, began: "I believe a history of the house is in order. Many centuries ago this island was known to be the site of a doorway between worlds of Terra, Chamavi, Faerieland, Herstamonix, and Palandine. Faerieland is a green world teeming with life that is not known to Terrans. Winged creatures are the dominant life form. There, Queen Merritt rules the Queendom of Balaktria. There are other places of wilderness that none explore because no one ever returns. The Court of Merritt had a unicorn named Axoparia; with the aid of her magik, Balaktria thrived. Terra has other doorways in other places, and we can research that another time. The first Master was a wizard, known to us as Audran Capuchin, began building the fortress here on the island, which was then called Indian Island and later called Bateman Island. Audran was powerful and wise. He made the fortress nearly impregnable to the Others who search for magikal items to add to their own power. One day the Others attacked and there was great loss of life. After the battle, the island was renamed in Dingley's honor. I believe that Audran's journals can be a valuable source of information, but someone needs to read them." Here he paused to see if there were questions. When no one asked him anything he continued.

"When my people, known to you as brownies, made the choice to leave Faerieland, we journeyed through the portal to Terra, and found this house. The master gave us refuge here. As time went by, we separated ourselves into clans that lived in various places. My family became house brownies, entrusted with the survival of the house and the security of the master and mistress and their family. The barnies made the decision to live in the barn and the foresters inhabit all other areas of the island. All of us can use simple magik. I must tell you that, should I deem it necessary, I can call a lock-down, which will close the island completely. Should this action be needed, it will supersede any orders made by either of you." He looked directly at Marcus and Marji.

"How long is a lockdown?" Marcus asked.

"As long as needed. Anyone within the house will be in suspended time as will anything within the barn or the boatshed. I believe this has never been used, and I do not know if it includes the cavern and the sanctuary. Time will be suspended until the lock-down ends." Gitchie answered. He did not add that doing this would take all of his effort, indeed his very essence. He would not survive the event.

"What I want to know is why the Others are trying—or have been trying for centuries—to get onto the island and into the house?" Marji asked.

Abequa answered this time. "Honorable Mistress, there are things here that lie dormant until they are needed. Special things that could be drained of their magik. Some of these things are jewelry, some are books. One item was used by Cassandra to write her love poem to Dingley. I have been brewing your tea in a magik teapot that seems to know exactly what kind of tea is needed. The house itself is magikal and changes to meet the needs of those within."

Marcus added, "Now things are starting to make sense. The house is like a replicator, like a magikal 3-D printer! But what's the connection with Sarisha being here, and why did that hooded guy leave without battling? I don't know about you, but I would like to drive to the mainland without worrying we were being watched."

After hesitating, he continued. "I have some news from the lawyers, too. Guess what? We inherited some money from your parents, Marji! Enough money that you can continue your catering business and I can help out here at home."

Marji took his hand and squeezed it, knowing how much the boat building meant to him. But he still lacked the knowledge and special skills of her dad. He needed an assistant.

Keevan said, "Sweet! That's great news!"

"There's more, but the estate has not settled yet. Your famous mom, Keevan, left a huge legacy also, which will go to you and Daisy when you turn twenty-one."

"What? How much?" Keevan was really excited now.

"We'll get back to that. Also, Jere left a fund for Ellora and Luke, when they turn twenty-one."

Funny, Luke thought to Ellora. *I feel like they are leaving out something, don't you?*

Marji said, "And there's more. We are going to have a private ceremony in the rose garden with family and very close friends instead of having a huge, expensive wedding. We want to have the ceremony soon, maybe in three weeks. We have to contact family first to make certain they can come on such short notice. Plus, we need to allow time for Gitchie to prepare the house and the grounds for an influx of people for the day. We are going to ask the catering crew to come in and help. Gitchie, I will supply you with their information."

Gitchie nodded in agreement, or perhaps simply to indicate that he had heard her.

"There's more." She looked at Marcus for support. "I am pretty certain that I am having twins. I am going to also try to give birth here at home. I will be getting a doula for help before and after—"

Marcus began to say something, but he was cut short by a loud shout.

"Hello to the house! Anyone home?" came a bellow from the front porch. It was the forester Chitin, who had come to join their meeting.

They all sat around the dining room table in silence. Gitchie had given Chitin the floor, but she stood in silence. Finally, Marcus spoke. "We are honored that you made the trip here from your homeland."

Chitin bowed slightly. "I am honored, Master. I am here because one of our watchers has seen the light from the topmost window of the barn. In the past—the long past, before the Battle of Dingley—a pact was agreed upon that should the house have need of us, five flashes followed by seven shall be the sign. Two nights past a signal of three flashes was seen. We have need of explanation."

Ellora made a gasp, and then said, "Oh, it was probably me! I was looking for something up in the studio. I had a flashlight and they saw me—my flashing light, I mean."

Marji told Chitin, "We are sorry we didn't know about this pact. We have much to learn about the house. May we offer you some tea?" she said, with a nod to Abequa.

"I am honored, but no, I must return with this news, and we may cancel the special search shifts. Should our pact need to be altered, please send an emissary, the one named Aisinwin, to the forest." She turned to leave with a bow.

No sooner had he left than they heard another "Hello to the house!" It was James and the catering crew!

FRIENDS AND FAMILY

It was such a pleasure for Marji to see her crew: James, Bethany, Gayle, and Fern. They had managed to find a boat ride from the mainland because the bridge was still not repaired, but there was a plan to rebuild. The Village, with help from the state, was building a replacement causeway using quarried granite blocks. It would allow the tide to flow through the bridge. It would take more time, but the resulting bridge would last longer than one built on pilings. After the excitement died down and everyone settled in, they began to talk about the upcoming wedding. The girls were very excited, and James had already gotten on the phone to order all the supplies they needed. To his surprise, bundles showed up that evening with a note to check in at the General Store for the refrigerated items. It seems that some of the order had already been made by someone else. James wondered who.

The meeting was adjourned the instant the newcomers showed up, Gitchie and his family disappeared into the Library. He could not fathom how they had not tripped the alarms. He personally would check what Brayle had installed as soon as possible.

"We are so happy to be here," Gayle told them.

"Happy that you're pregnant, too!" said Bethany, Gayle's twin. They had a habit of finishing each other's sentences.

"Can we bunk down here in the family room for now? We can put up a yurt tent tomorrow for the summer," said Gayle excitedly. "You'll need us for the banquet in September, and the Christmas season begins soon after."

"We've got cool new recipes, and we've made a new friend who has a fresh oyster farm in Yarmouth," Bethany said. "He puts diamond chips into the baby oysters to make diamond-pearls! He wants to add another farm in Brunswick, too. So, we'll have a good supplier."

"Oh, you like him, that's why," Gayle teased her sister.

Marji began to laugh. It was hard to know which twin was talking. Their honest energy was exhausting, though. She sighed, which they immediately reacted to.

"Oh, we'll be no trouble. We brought an air mattress," Bethany promised her.

"Breakfast in the morning! My treat!" Gayle said merrily. "Gosh, the air smells good here."

Marji recognized the aroma of Abequa's tea simmering in her pot. She wondered how they would react in the morning to the house. Or would the house even let them stay?

STILL LOST

Myster peered around. He could neither see anyone nor hear anything. The silence was unnerving. He sat down again. A small breeze came up, so he decided to follow it. He felt the air had a slight scent of the ocean. He recognized that he was walking uphill, and when he came to the crest, he jumped up on a white rock to look around. Astonishingly, he saw the house behind him, but it had no dormers and no widow's walk. He started back the way he came at a trot and then a full run. He rounded the corner of the house and ran to the front door, an old-fashioned-style entryway with an enormous door knocker in the shape of an anchor. He scratched to be let in. No one answered. He scratched again and the door was opened by a young woman who had a sweet expression on her face.

"Why you look just like the little kitten my father found yesterday!" the woman said. "Father, look!" She turned away from Myster, so he snuck in and ran between her legs to the library, nearly tripping her. She followed him and tried to scoop him up, but he twisted out of her grasp.

"Look, Father, he looks just like the kitten I found, only a lot older."

The elderly man sitting at the antique desk had his head in his hands. Myster looked at him through a haze of memories.

He finally knew who he had been as a human. "Master Isaac, it is I, Audran."

The master of the house looked up then, anger written on his face.

"How have you come here and why now?" he roared. "My son is dead! Because of your scheme! Because he listened to you!" He swiftly moved from behind his desk.

Myster realized how vulnerable he was at that moment. This grief-stricken man could possibly kill him. He lowered his head and sent one more message, telepathically. *I have more sorrow than you know. Do with me what you will.*

Katherine was able to pick up the cat then. She cuddled Myster as her father stood in front of her, boiling with fury.

"Father, too many have died," she said softly. "Let us find out what happened before making a hasty decision in a moment of emotion."

Her father turned away from her. The room was silent. They heard a squeak from the box by the hearth. The little face of Jeremy the mouse peeked out from under a blanket.

"Master, may I speak of the Battle of Dingley? I was first witness to the sad night. I heard what happened. It will be hard for thee to learn the truth, but I will forswear upon my life that Audran tried to save your son. It was Dingley that led the charge. It was Dingley that made the choice."

"I never condoned what they did, and I will never forgive!" Master Isaac said.

"Please bring the truth candle. I will dictate my sworn testimony for all to hear," the little mouse told them.

As the truth candle burned and the scroll was written magically, Jeremy spoke the words that Katherine would never forget. His detailed explanation did nothing to soften their grief. But it did convince Master Isaac that Audran/Myster, although not completely free of guilt, had tried to thrust his magik staff into the ground to stop the fighting. When he did that, his human form was vulnerable to any kind of magik. As everyone knows, wizards have two or, sometimes, three lives. The man known as Aaron and then as Audran was now on his last life as a cat. But how was he to get back to Ellora and Luke? They would need him!

"We should ask the dragon what to do with this cat." Katherine's voice broke the silence. There had been so much silence of late. She needed to talk with someone, anyone who was not broken with grief. Her father was not himself, nor was he thinking clearly. She was sad, but not to the point that she could not function. Her father strode out of the house after Jeremy began to cough and shake from the effort of conversation.

Katherine was worried about his burns, but she had treated them with a plantain poultice. His poor little feet would never be the same.

She knocked upon the secret door. As she stepped through, she felt the cat slip past her and into the dark cavern that was home to her friend, a wonderful magik dragon named Sarisha Chandi.

THE OTHERS ON DRAKE'S ISLAND,
UNITED KINGDOM

While the family living on the magical island, in Maine, was searching for answers and trying to live normal lives, another sort of family made up of a group of brothers were attempting the same thing, on another island in the United Kingdom. One of this group, named Jean Fayen was writing in his blog, as he did every week. This time his entry concerned the origins of a simple song that was known worldwide; Frère Jacques, frère Jacques, are you sleeping? Are you sleeping, Brother John? Morning bells are ringing, morning bells are ringing, ding ding dong, ding ding dong. Fayen wrote; Although there is not clear evidence, there is a theory that this age-old rhyming song was attributed to the famous composer Jean Philippe Rameau, born in 1683 and baptized the same day (which is unusual). He was a highly secretive man. His early years were very obscure, although it is known that his father's name was also Jean. He was educated at Godrans in Dijon, France, by Jesuit priests. He became a master of the harpsichord. There were stories in that region that he was the seventh son of a seventh son. But even his wife did not know anything about his early life. There are also rumors that the song, "Frère Jacques," was simply committed to paper in 1720, but composed much earlier. It is, possibly, much, much older. As for me, this song is often stuck in my head.

He continued, in our culture, there is an inordinate number of references to the names John and Jack: Jack and Jill, Jack and the Beanstalk, Diddle Diddle Dumpling, my son John, the boy with one shoe off and one shoe on, John Jacob Jingleheimer Schmidt, Jack Be Nimble, Jack Sprat, Jack o' Nory, jack-o'-lanterns, John Doe, and, last but not least, Dear John. It has been one of the most popular names throughout history. In my story, all of the Others are named John, or *Jean*, or a form of this given name. For them, it has a significance attributed not only to Christianity, but to honor one of their own who lost his head very long ago. At this time in history, the Others are waning. Their strength and ability to survive for centuries stems from sleeping in their magikal sarcophagi. But due to circumstances beyond their control (or perhaps because of their interference with humans), they have been forced to seek energy from different sources. Our leader, John of Gaunt, lies regenerating in his chamber, hidden under the sands of Egypt. No one knows why he chose that place to lie for one hundred years. There are other places around the earth where we hide while sleeping. Before resting he told his followers that he had read an old Akkadian scroll that hinted that the blood of a unicorn would stem the flow of time. He and his best friend, John Chaumeau led an expedition to Herstamonix, one of five worlds connected to this one through a vortex portal. They captured the unicorn then used dark magic to trap it within an Egyptian obelisk. They would have traveled to Chamavi, but that world was protected by its King to prevent such a crime. (The connected worlds are; Terra, Herstamonix, Chamavi, Faeryland and Palandine.)

Gaunt told his followers, the Others, "Time is changing. I feel in my bones that the blue magik is strong in the West of Terra. You must take great care, and yet you must gamble if you wish to live—if we are to survive."

But their plan failed due to the efforts of a young foundling boy named Aaron. (Details will be forthcoming my blog friends, in another story.) If only Gaunt had known the truth in his words, perhaps he would have waited to go to sleep. Here Fayen closed his laptop in irritation. He could hear the conversation in the next room through the web-voice machine. It interrupted his flow of thought.

One of the latest members of this group of brothers, the new Earl of Lancaster, Lord Tavernier, was bellowing at his Secretary, again. Fayen found this man quite tiresome yet they needed his island as a base of operation, so he was tolerated, for now.

"Did the girl's package arrive?" yelled Lord Tavernier.

"Yes, my Lord," the last two words emphasized by a low drawl.

"Good," said the *nearly* immortal Tavernier. Hundreds of years ago he had begun life as Jean-Baptiste Tavernier, but through the magic of his jinn, he had continued his life to this day by taking the lives of many others. Right now, he was an English Lord. "What took you so long to report?" he rudely demanded.

"I was at the Seattle exhibition. The Hope diamond is too heavily guarded. I then had a problem, dealt with it, and was forced to use an airplane, like a human, to return here."

"There is more—" The jinn hesitated to continue, but after receiving a scathing look, went on. "The Dingley island people have a dragon."

"What! I thought you said dragons only lived in Herstamonix! How could this happen? A dragon! Then this means—"

"It means that we must combine our talent." Fayen's disembodied voice entered into the conversation. "We must join our forces. Your Jinn has lost much of his power because of your wasteful conjoining of people!"

The voice commanding him through the web-voice machine was startling and also annoying as hell. "My jinn is no concern of yours!" bellowed the Earl. How had they accessed his personal internet? This deal was not working well for him. He strode over to the machine and smashed it with his fist. This not only hurt like hell, it did not destroy the talking black box as he had wished. But it no longer spoke. He then decided to really smash it with a hammer. In a few minutes of acting like a crazy person, he hurled his entire desktop all over the office. He could see the shocked face of his newest assistant through the clear glass doorway. The jinn watched passively.

"Get the queen. Maybe she will give us answers!" he demanded.

"My Lord." The jinn bowed before exiting the room. Inside, he seethed, because he'd had to use the door like a human. In order to save his power, he had to conserve it now almost one hundred percent. Thus, no more flying about, no more opening doors with a wave of his hand. The trip to the island fortress had taxed him beyond belief. Instead of gaining any power from simply being near a magikal place, he had been drained. The ocean demon had been a big surprise. But he thought it had been the blast from the dragon that drained him. Another thing was worrying him: the last conjoining of his master had become twisted, then stuck to him instead of Lord Tavernier. So, jinn had taken on the human form of Richard Lambert, the secretary of the richest men in the world. (At least the police would not be investigating another dead body). The emotion of worry was something very new to him. He was also beginning to enjoy human food. His footsteps sounded loud to his new ears. His attention wandered as he followed the old tunnel to the dungeon below. He rounded the doorway to the queen's cell to find the door was open, again! Alarmed, he ran into the stable area. Aborath was gone as well! After a quick search he found them by the willow fountain. The "unfortunates" were together in their misery. The unicorn had become accustomed to afternoons bathing in the warm waters while his miniature queen tended him. As ancient as the unicorn was, the queen was just as old, but she looked as young as a middle-aged dwarf. As usual, her crown was atop her head. She was never without it. He seethed again. If only he could get his hands on the jewel within, he could take its powers. But she would have to give it completely of her own accord. They had threatened to kill the unicorn if she would not hand it over, but she had merely shrugged, answering, "He is already dead."

Richard had come to believe that was merely a bluff but said nothing as he laughed inwardly. He was truly learning much from the humans. His lord loved the late-night poker games of chance and lies. It seemed to be the only thing that brought him joy any longer. In another lifetime, Lord Tavernier used to love travel and meeting new cultures. But after becoming so many different humans, he was growing insane. He was having huge lapses in his memory. His great wealth was a buffer to being persecuted by the law of many lands. He had his fingers in so many pies; so many famous and great people owed him huge favors. But nothing would stop death from coming now, he thought with much pleasure. Soon he would be without the master. His phone vibrated. He looked at the message with disgust.

It read: Never mind the queen. I want to enact my plan to become president. Call the Others for a meeting!

MEANWHILE, THE CAT RETURNS WITH NEWS

Myster was somehow back in the past. He knew he needed help. He ran past Katherine into the cavern, expecting Sarisha to know him as Audran. It took her a minute of sniffing and looking deeply into his eyes to finally say, "Friend, I have missed thee. The battle did not go as planned and Dingley is no more. I have other news for thee." She paused. "Two of the Others gained entrance to Faerieland with help of a traitor! I fear the worst has happened."

Katherine interrupted. "Is it safe for him to be within the cavern?" she asked. "Right now, his younger self is in the library."

Sarisha thought about this for a minute. "I have news for thee. Tell me what occurred, please."

Katherine explained finding the kitten this morning. Myster told them how he became a cat that jumped through Ellora's mirror to find himself in the meadow. But that was in the future!

Sarisha continued her report of what had happened next. "I was told that one of the Others, John of Gaunt, battled the Balaktrian king and killed him with a shooting sword. He reached the queen before her guards could intervene, taking her to somewhere, here, in time. When I reached the Battle of Dingley Hill, I could hear Jeremy the mouse crying out for help. The crows were advancing so I rescued him. I did not see thee, dear friend."

"I picked up grandfather's cloak and the kitten was underneath," Katherine told her. "I am *so* glad that you saved Jeremy! Now we know what truly happened." She laid her hand on top of the dragon's, then put her head down, unable to stem the flow of tears. She missed her brother, but also missed her cousin and the other boys—her life before the battle.

"Father is petitioning the town to rename Bateman Island in Dingley's honor. Some of the villagers are opposed. Mother cares not for the name. As if it matters, what the island is named." Her gentle sobbing echoed in the cavern.

Myster gently asked, "How am I to return to the other time? We are about to upgrade the house fortress and choose what to do next. The Others attempted to enter the island during a storm. You came, Sarisha, spouting blue fire, helping to defeat them! The Others have spied upon the house. Oh, I should explain that Marji Drake married Jeremiah Donovan, and Marcus Bradley married Cynthia Hamilton. Then Jeremiah and Cynthia died. A year later, Marcus and Marji are to be married. They are the master and mistress. Gitchie, grandson of Pilchie, is the house brownie."

"They must be very old now," Katherine said.

"Charles Dorr and Charlotte Drake were the previous master and mistress," Myster told her, then regretted his choice of words. He must not interfere with the timeline of events. But then, simply by coming here he had accidentally done that!

"Who is to be my husband then, a Mr. Drake?" the young girl asked him.

"No, Isaac was not a Drake, but I should not be telling you any of this! You do marry and have at least one child. Your cousins also marry and have children, which is very common within this great family. Doing so helps keep their special powers. The Others are still intent upon defeating the fortress."

"Have you forgotten so much?" Sarisha asked. "It was you that built this fortress to protect the doorway. The other connected worlds, Chamavi and Herstamonix have their own protection. But Faerieland and Palandine must also remain free!"

"I must return. I fear for Luke and Ellora, and their mother, Marji, is to give birth to twins. There is so much going on!"

"I will help thee, old friend. Have no fear and follow my words." Sarisha took him in her arms. "When you hear sounds, do not look around but go straight ahead through the fog. It is made of crystals, so do not touch it or it will shatter. Heed my words! Do not answer anyone calling to you or you will be lost in time. There are shadows caught between time—ghosts, the humans call them. They are the shadow people in Faerieland. You may see great beasts or tiny faeries. Let no one hamper your steps forward! I will be watching you from here, but I dare not enter. The mirror gateway is not for me. Follow the silver thread back through. Once you are there, I will be in the sanctuary to greet thee."

"Why can't you just carry me in your arms and take me there?" asked the cat, mystified at what she could do.

"You would disintegrate, my friend. You would fade into nothing in my arms," Sarisha told him gently and looked very, very sad. He wondered if she knew about such disintegration firsthand.

He rubbed up against Katherine. He felt it was time to go. She picked up the giant cat and hugged him gently. She smelled much like Ellora.

"Please tell Dingley's father that I did not mean for his son to die. I tried to save everyone! I meant only for myself to perish in the battle. We, in the future, honor his name and the island will be called Dingley and Bone Cove. The house maintains itself far into the future for hundreds of years."

Katherine quietly closed the door behind her. She held in her hand a special mirror that Sarisha had given her. It came from the originators, the builders, she had told her. It was made by Malavisch herself. She also had the magikal incantation that she planned to use to awaken the mirror. She saw her father sleeping at his desk, head in his arms. She was glad he slept. Her mother came into the room, and Katharine put her fingers to her lips, in the certain way members of her family did, two fingers pressed to the lips. Her mom gestured for her to follow. Once out of the library she gave her mom a hug.

"What is this for?" her mom, Victoria, wearily asked her.

"Just because," her daughter said. "I think we need to tell each other in case something happens, and we don't have the chance."

Later that evening, after dinner, Kat excused herself and went upstairs to her bedroom, latching the door quietly so as to not allow them to hear. She had practiced the incantation repeatedly. Sarisha had told her to use feeling and urgency to awaken it. The mirror will become ice, but do not drop it. Kat thought to use her mittens. The dragon had told her, "Touch the name of the person to whom you wish to speak and they, if they are able, will emerge in the mirror. It is the magik of love so it would be harder to communicate with someone you do not know or have no feelings for. Katherine wished to find her friend, Cassandra. She did not think she could find her brother, and it would hurt too much to try. Kat was ready. The magik hour neared midnight. The moon was full—another helpful agent of good magik. She sat in the moonlight, spoke the words, and tapped the name Cassandra on the scroll while saying "We the People of Navaratan—"

FINDING A WAY BACK

Myster was very glad that Sarisha Chandi was his friend, and that she gave him advice to help him on his journey back to the reality. She told him others had become lost attempting to return in this manner. Perhaps being a cat was of great help. Many of the ghostly apparitions he came across gave him passage with nary any trouble. One young girl who saw him gave a ghostly squeal of delight, but he ran past her, always following the silver string, which was hard to find in the fog. Then the string ran out. He had a moment of panic. What had happened? Sarisha had told him to follow it to the end and said she would be waiting for him! He leaped forward into the fog, which turned black around him. He lightly touched down, feeling the sandy floor of the cavern, where he did indeed find her waiting for him. In fact, the entire family was glad to have him back when they let him back through the door.

Back at the castle of the Earl:

"Shh," Queen Merritt cautioned the old friend she was casually massaging. "He has seen us." In response, the weakened unicorn moved his tail. His eyes fluttered open. Her small but strong fingers urged his head to remain on the pillow. She began to hum, which she knew annoyed the jinn enormously. She sang softly: "When the Kee Van returns from finding the blue sphere hidden in the tower, we shall flee this miserable place and return to my homeland. There, I hope to find a way to heal your nicorn and heal your heart." In her own thoughts she was careful to not show any emotion that the jinn might notice. In truth, her heart was beating fast and feelings of anxiety were threatening to overwhelm her. But she was a queen, she reminded herself. That thought calmed her down, so she was able to remain composed. Still, after so many years, rescuers were here!

Blouette waited with her queen, keeping up the pretense that, of course, she knew the queen was here, why else make the journey? In Merritt's memory, Blouette was still captain of her guard, able to shoot stinging arrows from her tail to vanquish enemies. While she waited, Myster searched for the tower where he used to live as the boy Aaron. He was not certain if the tower was still standing. From his cat's perspective, everything seemed different. It might even be a stack of rubble. He did not have the power to send out a telepathic message, but Sarisha did.

"Blue fire, beautiful fire, Aaron seeks thee."

Keevan watched the cat climb into the tower. He felt uneasy as well as astounded at this turn of events. He had only dreamed of going on a quest and now was on one! Truthfully, he was beginning to believe that they might not be as fun as they looked in the movies. Just an hour earlier he had been home in Maine. He had been astonished when his parents had awakened him. As he sat waiting for the cat, he went over what had happened that morning. Marcus had hustled him downstairs. It was early in the morning on a Saturday, he had said, what was going on?

"Sarisha has an idea. Ellora found something in a journal—a clue as to where the mysterious hooded figure came from. We may be able to find Golden's mate! The dragon has asked for you and Myster to aid her. Go ahead, Ellora, explain it to us again." Marcus urged.

"I found the answers to some questions. They're here in Audran's journal."

He asked sleepily, "Isn't Myster really the wizard Audran?"

"Yes, but he has lost his memory. I read Audran's old journal. It translated itself when Myster placed his paw on it! I've been up most of the night reading."

AARON AUDRAN'S JOURNAL ENTRIES
Read aloud by Ellora ...

Weeks later...

I do have a talent for learning languages and can speak with relative ease now in Portuguese, French, and English, as well as my own native tongue, Finnish. Brother Fayen, being the youngest monk, seems to be friendly with me and it is nice to have a friend. I am suspicious of the others who have "taken me under their wing" as they have said. Fayen whispered to me to watch my back, which I have taken to heart. I have a plan to sneak away should anything happen. I found a silver coin in my wanderings among the gardens. Someone dropped it, apparently, but my blue light is afraid of it, so I tossed it away. I have some other coins hidden but not enough to make a living on my own...yet.

The entries continued, describing a voyage, the arrival in Alexandria. One name jumped out from the pages. Blou took on the task of reading to give Ellora a rest.

Aborath! I have translated the name of the creature held within, known to Europeans as a unicorn, with the name of Aborath. He is magnificent! How the Egyptian priests captured him within the obelisk, I shall never know. But I will use everything within my powers to free him.

The journal seemed to end there. Blou turned a few pages until she reached a scribbled passage written at an angle and not at all like any other of his writing.

I know not how much time has progressed. Much more than a day, perhaps half a week. I awoke to find myself in chains in the hold of a ship. I closed my eyes, wanting to ease the feeling of nausea. Near me is the body of Aborath. In the weak light I can only make out a bit of color. I dread the answer. What had happened, I know not. I feel my sack behind me and the hardness of my journal. Relief floods me that my hard work of writing has not been lost. I have tried to recall any memory of recent events. I briefly remember the moonlight flooding the temple theater, bathing the image of the unicorn carved within the granite of the Obelisk. Then a sharp pain and all went black. Now a feeling of sharp, burning betrayal entered my heart. My beloved master had been the one to drag me into the temple. I had felt fear before, but not this kind of dread. I was to be used to kill such a magnificent creature! But I refused. Why had they spared my life? The answer was simple—I was to be used for further magik of the darkest kind.

Here the entries in this journal ended.

ANOTHER BATTLE TO SAVE A BROTHER

After reading the journal entries at breakfast, Ellora had exclaimed, "So this is why Axoparia was so angry at them—they stole her mate Aborath! He has been a prisoner all this time. It's been centuries now, but Sarisha told me that he may still be alive. Myster assures us that the blue sphere could still be in its hidden spot way up in the tower where he used to live..." Her voice faded as she fell deep into thought.

Sarisha added her own assurances. "I will need Keevan to help me with this rescue. Myster may not be able to find the sphere. If I have one warrior to aid me, we can win this quest. But you must be ready for recriminations! The Others may strike!" she told Marcus.

She had then turned to Keevan. "Bring thy sword!" she commanded. It was hard to say no to a dragon.

Myster said he remembered where he, in human form, had hidden the sphere in the old Capuchin Convent in Italy. Ellora had also read that Sir Francis Drake had made an island into a fortress citadel, naming it Drake's Island. Today, it was seemingly abandoned, but it was the perfect place to hide something like a unicorn from the outside world. They looked up the island on Google Earth. It was located in Plymouth Sound in the United Kingdom. Gitchie gave Sarisha the coordinates. Then, Keevan had gotten dressed and fetched his sword, attaching it with a carabiner to his belt. He wore his riding gloves. His Dad, and Marji, each gave him a hug. She held on to him longer and began to have doubts, "Wait—"

Sarisha quickly said, "No more waiting. Time is passing. I would not put him in extreme danger, but I cannot carry a heavier human. The unicorn will be heavy enough, and I may have to do battle. Keevan can defend himself. I watched him hitting the balls of fire with great accuracy. That is what he must do if they fire at him. Luke must remain here—he has another destiny, as does Ellora. Sir Brownie, please make certain Golden is in the barn and ready. Everyone must be on guard. They have sent the spy device, so have you all given the Others false information?"

Everyone nodded. That had been fun—it had been like putting on a show for the listening device Gitchie had found inserted into the necklace given to Daisy by her mother. Before she had died, Cynthia had taken the blue sapphire earrings to be made into a necklace for her. Recently it had arrived in a small package, sitting atop the supplies that Gitchie had ordered. Grandma Charlotte had been right. The blue sapphires were truly rare blue diamonds! The dragon had told them the necklace emanated power. The jeweler had written a note to Cynthia, not knowing she was deceased, saying he hoped that she enjoyed the new setting and he would be happy to work on any of her Other items. Other items? Why was the letter "O" capitalized? Blouette had thought it was a clue that the Others were involved. Truly, the diamonds in their new setting had flashed red when Luke touched them. So, very carefully, Ellora had also touched them and the same thing happened. Myster and Rahven then decided the gems were part of the prophecy somehow. Marcus had been against the plan of Keevan joining in the rescue. Gitchie had quietly set a charm upon him without anyone knowing so that Marcus would stop arguing. Marji, still had reservations but then she suddenly agreed. Everyone wanted justice for the unicorn. But what would be the cost?

They all gathered in the garden for a last hug. At the last instant, Blouette joined them. She had decided she must go on this quest. It had been Blou's idea to check on Aborath first to make certain the unicorn was alive. It was time to go. Myster agreed. Blouette held on to Keevan's shirt collar. The trip had only taken a few seconds. They arrived in the morning in a clearing on Drake's Island that had a fountain by a weeping willow tree. Keevan could not believe their luck! Sarisha indicated there was blue power here and her senses led them right to the spot. The unicorn they found bore a very small rider wearing a crown: the queen.

Queen Merritt heard the dragon before she could see her, as the rumble of the air was divided by the telekinetic jump. If the jinn had been at hand he would have heard the shockwave also. Blouette had made the necessary and correct introductions, then quickly told them of the plans. Merritt had commanded that Blouette remain with her while they searched for the gem. It seemed like forever as Blou hid herself among the leaves of the willow tree. She grew more fearful as the minutes went by. She'd been shocked to find Queen Merritt with the unicorn! How had this come to pass? The queen should be in Faerieland! Blou looked down from her perch to see the jinn enter the fountain garden, look at a black box in his hand, then swiftly turn around and climb back up the stairs. Merritt winked at her captain of the guard, Blouette, and continued her quiet singing. The only other movement was the swishing tail of the unicorn.

The Capuchin tower was rubble, but one side was still erect. Perhaps it was held together by the very existence of the hidden sphere? Keevan dismounted cautiously. The fortress museum was not open so no one was about, but that did not mean he could be reckless. Myster jumped off his lap and hurried to the spot. Sarisha had sent her message. She could hear a faint ringing bell, but the boy could not hear it. Myster heard it, too, and quickly climbed the wall up to where he used to live. The cat clawed at the wax cover he had made in another lifetime as the human Aaron. Thankfully no one had walked these stairs in hundreds of years. He removed the covering and saw the sparkle of the blue sphere. It was ringing and shot out of its hiding place. It hovered in front of the cat, who reached up to touch it. The sphere flew on to where the dragon stood at the base of the old tower. She was very glad to see it as it snuggled into the fur on her forehead. She gestured for Keevan to climb back on. They waited for the cat. Myster leaped from the wall onto the back of the dragon and they all transported back to where Blou, Merritt, and Aborath waited for them. But something else was there as well. Sarisha teleported back to the spot where the queen lay with the unicorn. She snuggled up next to him, to encourage him to rise on his knees, then looked up to the willow tree. Blouette flew down to sit on her back. The dragon was frowning though—something was not right. Even the cat was looking around, growling. Out of the shadows strode Richard. He was drawn to the power emanating from the blue sphere. Sarisha Chandi stood up and made herself larger. In her anger, her enormous wings expanded, dislodging Keevan and the cat. She did not wish to transport the jinn with them—he had to be made to go far enough away. Keevan jumped out, gesturing for them to back off. He unlocked his light sword from his belt and pressed the switch to turn it on. The adversary backed off, not knowing what this young man was wielding. Keevan, in his mind, was going to fake it and act like he was a swordsman, so he added some karate moves. All they had to do was make the jinn back up a few feet and Sari could transport them all. Now the unicorn was wide awake, rearing up, the queen upon his back. Keevan waved the sword as it made its singsong noise. Richard did indeed take two steps back.

Keevan made a lunge forward and Richard backed up again. Sarisha roared "Now!" He spun around to leap aboard but slipped in the morning dew. Richard grabbed his ankle. Keevan grabbed the outstretched hand of the dragon, and they all transported back to Maine. In the blink of an eye they were all in the peaceful meadow.

Since Richard had been brought by the dragon, the house did not activate but the barn's shield came on. Once the dragon dropped her helpers, she transported the unicorn into the barn, but she could not leave due to the safety shielding! She roared in anger and frustration. A deadly foe was on the grounds because of her! All the barnies armed themselves with whatever weapon they could find. The Bradley family ran to the magik meadow. Marcus had his crossbow in hand, aiming at the jinn, who had Keevan in a headlock, a knife to his neck.

Queen Merritt was the first to speak. "Halt!" she commanded. "Everyone stop. Let us speak to Richard."

He gruffly replied, "You know what I want!"

The queen answered, "And as I have told you, the jewels of the Goddess are not for you!"

"I will slit his throat and his life will end before the crossbow can touch me!" shouted Richard to Marcus. Richard reminded himself that the bow was probably magikal or, at least, "magic bound" to find its mark. So, the crossbow aimed by the father of the boy would also be aimed with love and would at the very least strike him. The boy must be very good, some sort of young ninja, else they would not have sent him. All this fluttered through his mind as he calculated his next step. But that decision was made for him.

As she walked forward, Ellora spoke next. "I figured out that you want part of the jewel that was your prison. I know not what you plan to do, but this I do know. If I trade my brother's life for the jewel, how will we know you will not betray us all?"

He laughed. "You have my word. Upon my life, I will not strike any of you in this meadow, nor on the grounds of the fortress."

Queen Merritt spoke. "Have a care, human, it is not in the nature of the jinn Richard to be truthful. More often than not, the words can have another meaning in another time!"

Ellora, not taking her eyes off the jinn, stepped even closer. She could hear Keevan's breathing, it was strained, and his eyes were wild. She was afraid he would attempt something to save her. His eyes moved up and down as he kept looking at the light sword lying at his feet. It was glowing blue still.

Myster came forth to put himself between the jinn and his beloved Ellora. For his part, he was worried the jinn would kidnap her. So, the scene like in a play, unfolded in the charmed peaceful meadow, the giant coon cat an arm's length from the evil one, who was slowly strangling the boy in his arms. Keevan was trying to tell his sister with his eyes to send him the light sword. Ellora stood, calmly fingering her grandmother's ring. She wished she could trust the evil thing that held all their attention. An angry rumbling could be heard in the distance.

A storm was coming. Luke was summoning the clouds and the wind was picking up.

"My brethren are coming," Richard said, trying to bluff them. "You had better make a choice."

It was Ellora's turn to laugh. "*My* brother summons this storm, you pathetic thing. Your force is nearly spent, and you have no family. Hear me! The only thing keeping you alive is my compassion. But, I believe peace is powerful. So, I offer this ring as the token of peace betwixt *and* between me and thee. Should you ever harm anyone upon this island and these shores, you will die a horrible death. I also speak to the evil ones, the Others. We have only to wait, and you too shall have no power. For you have angered the dragon and she does have brethren."

Richard nodded in agreement. "I shall comply, and I shall agree, from this day forward."

Blouette interrupted. "No, for all of time, make him *swear* it, Ellora!"

This made him angry, for his loophole had been discovered by a fairy! Suddenly Rahven, fluttered down next to them, and Richard felt compelled to tell the truth.

"For all of time, from this day forward and this day back, I shall comply and agree to never cause death or dismemberment or memory loss to this family, living or dead upon this island and including these shores and anyplace under the domain Terra."

The queen interrupted him, "Or Faerieland, Chamavi or Herstamonix."

Seeing Ellora frowning, Richard continued, "Including Palandine also."

Queen Merritt added, "Nor to prevent any joining, natural or otherwise."

"Forsooth, all these true words I will swear!" said the Jinn. His hold relaxed on the boy, who twisted out of his grasp to grab his light sword, which he held out at the adversary. Blouette landed on Keevan's shoulder, her tiny tail-sword paralleling his.

Richard put his hands on his hips in frustration and declared, "I have forsworn peace!"

Ellora again took another step closer to be by Keevan's side.

Keevan asked, "Are you sure, Ellora?"

In her hand was the ring. She had picked it up with invisible fingers as she could now teleport small things. Richard reached for the ring, but it vanished!

"What!" he roared angrily.

Ellora calmly said, "Just a hint of what life will be like without it." The ring reappeared.

He snatched it out of the air and stuck it on his pinky finger, for the ring would not change to accommodate his larger ones. No matter, he could already feel some power seeping back into his bones.

Luke angrily strode forward, "And now you will leave!" His arm whipped the storm around and then pointed at the jinn. A microburst obeyed his command. Richard was thrown backwards past the broken bridge, far down the road on the opposite shore. The wind whipped up again to go after him as he swept his hooded cloak about him. He turned into a column of black smoke just as it hit him. He disappeared. At this, the barn released its hold on the dragon, which it had barely been able to keep. She burst out roaring and went after the jinn!

Marji and Marcus ran up to the group on the shore, enveloping their children in a group hug, laughing and chatting. Wow, what an ending! After, Luke stood for a while on the shore as the others trooped back to the house. In his mind's eye, he was watching the jinn in a battle with Sarisha when a strange thing began to happen. Richard was trying to defend himself in the courtyard of the Drake castle. He was growing feeble, then as the dragon sent a burst of blue flame at him, Richard collapsed. Sarisha returned to the house because she was not a murderer. But instead of going to her sanctuary, she went to the barn. Luke's vision of Drake's castle vanished. His attention returned to his island.

A little voice in Luke's ear said, "Let us eat pizza, celebrate with beer of the root and make s'mores by the fire!" Blouette tone was one of asking, not command. "Have no fear, for I stabbed the jinn with my venom right before your wizard wind struck him. He shall sleep, and it will give us time to plan."

Luke, with Blou on his shoulder, walked slowly back to the house. The wind died down and became a slight breeze. As he went across the yard, he could hear the barnies cheering and clapping! He had a good idea why they were celebrating. But he wanted to be with his family. Marcus met him on the porch, put his arm around him then ushered them inside the house.

OTHER PLANS

Lord Tavernier was beside himself with anger. Not only had his jinn taken off without permission, but it was obvious he'd lost the battle! His unicorn was gone. He had paid millions for use of the creature in stud fees—how dare they take it? A whoosh of air told him some sort of floating craft had landed on the roof. Couldn't they use a helicopter like normal people? He whipped the side of the fountain with his crop, not daring to whip the jinn. He wasn't certain what had transpired, but the sleeping face of his "secretary" wore a grimace. The unicorn and the queen were gone. But Richard slept on, even on through the short meeting outside with the Others. Finally, another servant announced that cocktails were being served, and would the gentlemen wish to join everyone on the terrace?

"What about your secretary?" one of them asked.

"Leave him. He'll sleep it off," Tavernier replied, trying to make it seem like the man had been drunk.

"Jis laimejo musi," said Du Temps in a voice that sounded like he had been a smoker.

The Other laughed and looked at the man on the ground. In his thick Lithuanian accent, he replied, "He won neither the battle nor the war. He is lucky to be alive at all."

The earl scowled, not knowing Lithuanian but also not liking that the other man had guessed the truth of the recent events. Well, he was the only one with a genie who could do magical things. The unicorn's descendants were running in an important race today, and he would make millions in stud fees if either horse won. It was not called the sport of kings for nothing. When he received word that both horses had won, he laughed out loud! Unknown to him, the Others standing around were linked telepathically and had been talking among themselves:

This very rich man is quite an idiot. But he would be a useful tool, thought Jean Chardin.

Unpredictable, argued another named Jean Fayen. *We must find something to hold over him to keep him in control. His mood swings are unsettling in the very least.*

He brings a certainty that no one will be watching us while he makes a fool of himself, thought Jean Chaumeau.

I feel he brings nothing to the table and is too unstable. I vote NO, thought Jean Du Temps.

Still, the devil you know is the devil you can control, replied Chaumeau.

The jinn cannot be under anyone's command except the idiots. It makes him too much a risk. Yet, if the world watches him, they won't be watching us. We can accomplish much, agreed Jean Leclerc.

Because all of them bore the first name of John or Jean, they all knew one another by their surnames. They were all ancient beings, with knowledge of how to extend life. Once, they'd all slumbered while the humans ran their wars and explorations. Upon awakening they were astounded at how many humans had actually survived the plagues they'd caused. Each one hundred years or so they had to return to their sarcophagi within the deepest tombs and catacombs to enter into the healing sleep—to awaken in the future and command much of the world. But they feared that while they slumbered, they would be discovered. They needed new sources of energy or they might not survive.

Humans are too curious and not subservient enough in this century, complained Chardin.

True, answered Chaumeau. *We must be more skilled in scrying to find out what lies in the future. We need assurances.*

Du Temps retorted. *We must own technology in order to survive, and we must own the law so that our sarcophagi are not disturbed.*

Leclerc snorted. *I still say the idiot will serve, although he knows it not. Let us control him and we control the jinn. Then perhaps we can regenerate in safety.*

The wine was delicious, of course, imbued with the blood of the unicorn. They had taken as much as they dared. The blood of the racehorse that had recently shot to fame by winning was not good enough. There was something in its blood that was too much like its dam: not enough of the unicorn. So, new plans had to be made for obtaining their energy drink.

"So, my lord, Lord Tavernier, since when do we need titles among us?" Chaumeau asked out loud.

"Since I have been knighted by the witch," laughed the earl.

Du Temps set his glass down with a bit too much force and the stem broke. He swore an oath and turned to his host with malice in his voice. "You will not disparage the queen in our presence. We tolerate much from you but not this! When culture and custom are abolished, then what do we have? Barbarism and chaos." He handed his broken glass to the butler, who appeared at his elbow with a new wineglass. "Therefore, you will have courtesy, or we will teach it to you." He let his voice drop. It was time to get this idiot under control.

"How dare you talk to me like that?" Lord Tavernier sputtered and then began to choke. Since he could not utter a word, his jinn would not come to his rescue. His eyes bulged and he banged his fist on a plate to get some attention, but only the butler came. Fayen made a signal and Du Temps nodded.

Fayen said coldly, "It would seem, my lord, that you need to learn manners. Now, on to more important matters."

The meeting went on with no more incidents, but the 'idiot' was quiet, too quiet, and very sullen, observed Chaumeau. He gave a mental signal to Chardin to begin taking Tavernier under his wing in a pretense of friendship, Chardin being the least disgusted by the rich man's presence.

"So, did your horse win today, my lord?" The words tripped easily off Chardin's tongue, whereas the others had difficulty calling the him "my lord," having lived many lifetimes with kings, popes, earls, and a few blacksmiths that had more claim to a title than the current host. He didn't even know which fork to use for salad! His constant interplay with the media was, at best, quarrelsome, and at worst inflammatory. And now he was planning on becoming president?

"Yes, both horses won—one placed and the other took the title. I will make millions!"

"I am sure you will. My lord, may I inquire, where is the dear little queen this evening? And the unicorn, is he in good health?"

Lord Tavernier looked at the John asking him these questions. He was hesitant to tell them, but the wine was having an effect on him. What the hell. He hated the blood wine and the queen was annoying and condescending. "I don't know where they are. When Richard feels better, I am sure I will learn all I need to know. I'll send a chopper to fetch them back. I am sure you will love having the blood wine from the beast. Me, I hate it!"

"My lord, having been airborne earlier today, I saw, when flying over your island, some sort of ninja landing in the garden, with a trained cat and another tiny faerie warrior, perhaps the queen's own guard? Then, somehow, they disappeared in the wink of an eye! I would not have believed my pilot if I had not witnessed it myself." Du Temps told him.

All of them were looking at him now, with varying expressions on their faces. He realized that most of them hated him. That was fine. He was used to the hate and used it for his own purposes. It was the silent John Surhon who troubled him. Surhon never spoke but was included in everything they talked about. Someone who never talked made him nervous. Tavernier felt like he had to fill in the silence.

Suddenly, the butler opened the door and Richard entered the room. His master gestured and made a sarcastic quip about how nice it was for him to join them. The second course was just being served. Richard sat down. He did not feel like talking, but the command to come to this dinner could not be ignored. The battle he was in today was still a whirlwind in his mind. The effect the ring was having on him was not at all what he thought it would be. He had been summoned by the silent one who was, in fact, another type of jinn who was more powerful, known as an infrit.

"Tell me, should I call you by your human name?" Chaumeau politely asked. A jinn could not lie but could still twist the words.

"Ask my lord which he would prefer." The sullen tone came through loud and clear.

"His name is Richard Lambert," answered Tavernier dismissively.

Chaumeau turned back to the somber jinn and said softly, "Richard, tell me what transpired this day, in the fountain garden, two hours past."

The jinn turned to him. "Because I was in the office talking with the master about the upcoming presidency and not at my usual post, a young ninja entered, in a magikal manner, the fountain garden in the presence of Queen Merritt and Aborath. He had three companions with him, a large cat, another faerie who was also armed, and a dragon. They flew under the radar, landed, and I gave chase. Upon my return I battled with their dragon, who must have cast me with a sleeping spell because I could not stay awake. I collapsed in the garden, where I remained until awakening a few minutes ago."

Everyone accepted this news, hiding the alarm some of them felt. After pausing, Richard continued, "I am not feeling well. The sleeping charm affected me more than anything I have ever encountered. I wish to go to my quarters and sleep until needed, of course."

"Certainly, my dear Richard, if that is what your master wishes," Chaumeau replied.

For the first time, Surhon spoke, which astonished them all. "First, I command thee, take off the ring. It is why you feel sick. Second, the faerie must have slashed you and injected her sleeping venom, which takes many hours to sleep off. I am surprised you are awake now. Third, where is the dragon's den? For she must also sleep after battle. And the fourth, final question: Who sent you back to Drake's Island? Do not lie! For I know a wizard's wind when I hear it. A powerful one he must be to send you clear across the Atlantic Ocean."

The silence in the room was tangible. The very air was full of query and caution as Richard chose words to speak that would neither infuriate his master nor anger Surhon, who could hurt him. He also did not want to answer any more questions tonight. He had much to linger on. Who were the boy and girl? It was clear now the Others had old information about the sitting master of the house. They needed to know what was going on. What did the cat have to do with anything, and where was his scarecrow? He needed to go over the data it had recorded.

To answer Surhon, Richard told him, "I am not certain who sent me back."

Fayen interjected. "Perhaps, good sirs, we should adjourn after dining to a more secure area. I am certain we all have much to ask and much to add. Their chairs made no sound as they all stood up to exit the terrace. Tavernier sat dumbfounded in his seat. Richard, groaning, stood up in a shaky manner. He looked as if he were about to pass out. Tavernier snapped his fingers at his butler and wait staff.

"Take him to the green room." Then, more quietly, he said to the butler, "Lock the door." The butler nodded subserviently, but thought, *as if that will keep a jinn from leaving.*

Once they were in the secure area, Chaumeau said quietly to Surhon, "You picked a fine time to talk!"

Surhon answered, "I talk when there is something important to say. This is what I know; I recently was at the Seattle exhibition of the Hope Diamond. The Johnsonian agent is traveling with it in order to raise money for operations. They are also increasing their security system to keep the diamond safe. It is emitting some sort of radio frequency, or waves of some kind. Richard became embroiled in following a Blue Guardian around the city. In fact, he inserted a tracking device within her purchases so that he might find where she lived. I read these thoughts in his mind as I tracked him myself. Having learned where she lived, he followed a storm that enhanced his strength, only to find she is a guardian in the fortress that guards the entrance to Faerieland. It is where Prince John of Gaunt abducted Queen Merritt during the Great Battle. That is not where we obtained the Unicorn—we went to Herstamonix to get it. Prince John was actually the one who put that plan into motion. He was a genius, not like the idiot we have to deal with today. He was also the one who told our order to stagger our sleep. He is scheduled to be awakened in twenty years' time. I wonder what will happen to Tavernier then?"

Fayen said, in a worried tone, "They have a dragon. Are they in league with Herstamonix? This changes everything. The prince will have a lot to take care of when he awakens. I myself will be happy to sleep. This century has changed far too much for me."

Chaumeau advised, "Let us gather facts, then deal with this presidency idea. I know a rich and well-connected someone who will be a good candidate for conjoining with Tavernier. I can also help that process so that it does not become twisted or fail. But for now, I shall go check on the prince's resting chamber. I saw a news story about a new sarcophagus that has been found in Luxor. I leave for Egypt soon."

A TRAGEDY IN EGYPTIAN STONE

Chaumeau was too late. The excitement of the discovery team was tangible as the Egyptologists opened the sarcophagus. How long ago had this person been put in the stone box the experts wondered. One person in the crowd knew. He knew all there was to know about this person, as much as the great John of Gaunt had allowed anyone to learn about himself. He had had taken many secrets with him into hibernation. All the deeds he had done, all the plans he had made were just words on a scroll that Chaumeau had found it in the ancient secret library. There had been many men named John of Gaunt or Ghent, but only one who committed so many horrible deeds; he imprisoned a unicorn, slayed a faerie king, capture its queen, then arrived safely through the vortex back in this world. He was the head of their order. Chaumeau was soon to hibernate himself. Would he suffer the same fate as his mentor? Who would be their leader? He wanted to scream, tear out his remaining hair! He wanted revenge on these puny humans! Instead, he watched and held up his camera to take pictures as if this site would not be forever engrained upon his memory. The reddish-brown sludge that was in the sarcophagus was vile, disgusting, and unspeakable! He had to turn away, tears welling up in his eyes. He had to leave. He went into a part of the temple complex where no one could see him. He gathered his robes, twirled, and disappeared in a column of sooty black smoke.

Back with the Others, he had to ask himself, was he becoming too human? No, he told himself. Allow for the mourning and then the revenge. Who had done this? The templars? Who had been on his journey with him? Tavernier? Could he have damaged the time link somehow and killed his friend? Why would he do such a thing? No, it was not to his advantage. It must be someone else. He shouted in his mind to his brethren. *We have a new enemy. Something has destroyed our master from within. John of Gaunt is no more!* After reviewing the news and watching it on the screen, the Others stood in silent prayer, for want of a better word. To anyone outside of the group, it would seem as if they were praying. Dressed in bishops' garb or like visiting ambassadors or other dignitaries, they stood in a semi-circle, heads bowed. Turmoil could best describe how this group felt, learning their leader, who had survived for tens of thousands of years, was now, essentially, dead. Never to resurrect again.

We need a new leader. We need safety during our slumber. Our numbers have depleted so drastically. If only one is to be awake while the Others hibernate, what then? asked a worried Chardin.

We shall do something we did in the far past. We shall each take a wife and live as a human, teaching our children's children to care for us as the ancients did. All is not lost, advised Du Temps.

What of revenge? This question came from the infrit, Surhon. He was very good at revenge-seeking.

NO! That is a human emotion that serves no purpose. We have done things that make some hate us. We have survived holocausts, wars, famine, regime downfalls. We shall survive raising children.

"So, it will be written, so it shall be done!" these last words were spoken aloud by all present save Surhon. He would never take such a vow. Their end had begun and they could not see it. They must try one more time to acquire the blue gems in this world and slake their energy within. How could they abandon that task?

No, Surhon, we have not abandoned that task. We shall leave it to thee. Take the little ring if you want it, since it is of no use to us, said Chaumeau, taking off his robes. *We have new horizons to conquer.*

Surhon, with Richard by his side, studied the little ring as it sat upon a circular plate of silver and clear quartz. All their attempts at handling it once he had taken it off were of no avail. The ring simply moved away from each of them. Fayen didn't even try. But after asking the Butler to pick it up, which he did with no problem, they put it where it was right now. Instead of seething, as he was wont to do, Surhon searched his mind for any clue as to how to withdraw the energy from the blue gem without losing it to the Universe.

"Sir, may I suggest," asked the butler, "that you command a simple crystal singer to do your bidding?"

The infrit took the advice. Later that day, a small woman claiming to be a crystal healer was brought via helicopter to the island Fortress of Drake. Once there, she was treated like a royal guest, with a terribly extravagant luncheon with some of the Others, including Surhon. They spoke of many things concerning crystal energy and how stones could hold power, even secrets, if one knew the correct incantations.

"Simply speaking, madam, we have brought you here to engage you in a special event. We wish you to unlock the powers within this ring that has been in my family for generations. I wish it to bring me longevity, as the family legends say." Said Chaumeau.

The old madam, knowing a lie when she heard one, replied back, "I am a singer as well as a healer. I know how. But it is not a simple ceremony and requires a secret place to enact the ancient methods."

Her quiet words struck the jinn as too willing, too easily tripping off her tongue, but he remained silent. She did not know with whom she was dealing—or did she? He kept his thoughts to himself, but Surhon turned to look at him. Jinn looked away and found his gaze being sought by the butler, who was looking concerned about something. The man actually moved away from the table and looked nervously toward the door, fingering a crystal pendant around his neck.

The old crystal singer, Obashra, kept her thoughts to herself but could not quell the surge of exultation she felt as this strange request. She must be ever so careful right now. All her years of hiding among these humans and the disgust she felt at being so near beings such as these nearly made her vomit. Be cool, be happy, she told herself. Your time is at hand. No need to rush this. She actually began to hum the song, "Don't Worry, Be Happy." She made a pretense of examining the ring with her monocle. She felt the ring belonged to someone young, and very likely a girl. It was so small.

"Oh!" she gasped. As she looked at it, it gave off a sparkle of light and actually grew larger right before her eyes. Her surprise was genuine. The light of blue magik was trapped within the gemstone. No wonder they wanted its little bit of power.

Surhon began to intently watch what she was doing, so she closed her eyes and waved her right hand, and then the left one, palms down, just inches above the ring. She repeated the gesture and the ring moved toward her!

Now she had the attention of everyone at the table. Still humming the silly little ditty, she opened her eyes, raised both hands up to the sky, and mumbled an ancient Sanskrit rhyme (hoping no one there could understand the ancient language). One of the Others rose to his feet. Apparently, he did know ancient Sanskrit!

"What is the meaning of this?" Chaumeau roared. But her magik had already ensnared them all. She had suspended time within the dining room. Quietly but quickly she rose, but instead of walking away, she climbed up onto the table. She bent down to the ring, holding out her hand. It hopped into her palm and she closed her hand around it. Giving one nod to the butler, her friend, safely standing in the hallway, she gathered her robes about her, twirled once, and disappeared! He made the immediate decision to also leave, knowing they would blame him for this. He knew the old secret ways out of the building, using his keys to unlock a pantry door that led down a long tunnel. He saw a strange and creepy scarecrow tucked into a corner by the entrance. As he ran past it, unknown to the butler, its eyes followed him. He held on to his crystal pendant as he ran, his breath coming in gasps. He was terribly afraid the infrit would find him and tear him to pieces. Finally, he made it down to the shore, where he had hidden a motorboat loaded with supplies. He was well on his way when the spell faded from their minds.

When time reasserted itself, the Others were astounded. There was no sign of the ring, the crone or the butler. They'd been had!

A CELEBRATION BACK AT THE ISLAND

The smell of marshmallows melting and burning filled the air. Also, on the menu were burnt hot dogs, corn on the cob, potato and other salads, and blueberry cake as well as strawberry shortcake (the family recipe, in fact). Everyone seemed in good spirits, as if they had just won a game. Perhaps, Ellora mused, they had won a game, an ancient one that might not have an ending, like the Lost Boys and Captain Hook. Chatter and laughter of the barnies mingled with Keevan's voice re-telling the tale. It would not be long until the full moon would enable them all to see the full beauty of Aborath's magikal nicorn. Ellora wondered what Daisy thought about Golden's mate being returned. She also wondered what Blouette thought about seeing her queen—they were all waiting for her to tell her tale, but she had said she would wait. Her mom and Marcus—no, her mom *and* dad—looked happy. Soon they would have their wedding ceremony in the rose garden.

While they were celebrating, people in the village were beginning to suspect something was amiss. Strange things were happening on the island again. Sinclair Bruce, an old shaman who had witnessed things with no explanation recently. He began telling the old stories once more so the truth would not be forgotten ... again.

AUDRAN'S JOURNAL

I wonder if this is not happenstance, but a way to make us aware of something ... something so secret, yet it is "in front of our faces." We need only to look in a different direction to find the truth. The writing within the journals shall be the truth of my life, so help me Goddess.

Aaron Audran Capuchin

I was told I was found by the Friars of Capuchin at the age of seven or eight, apparently after a shipwreck off the coast of Italy, with a head wound. No others survived and no one came forth to claim me. I was brought to the Capuchin Convent, where under the tutelage of Master Jean Chaumeau, I learned to read and write several languages. I have many fond memories of my dear teacher. He was, at first, very kind although strict. He allowed me movement around the convent that not all the other boys had. Master Chaumeau was quick with the rod when catching me daydreaming. I learned quickly to mask my emotions, finding a way to complete my chores while my mind wandered. In time I found some of these daydreams were visions. It was whilst I was gathering fresh eggs for the morning meal that I had my first true vision.

I saw the wreck of a ship with the name Marigold. I heard men crying out to God for their lives. A strange green-gray roaring wind surrounded the ship as it foundered. It seemed that all hands were lost until I saw one rowboat with huddled men aboard.

As I was telling my master this strange dream, I saw, for the first time, a wicked gleam enter his stern eyes. I was advised not to tell a soul, for they would take me for a witch! I was terrified at the thought of this. It made me very careful with my journal as well (hence it is written in several languages).

I am learning many other languages from all the wonderful translations in the library of the monastery. Some of the books are forbidden, yet I find the door unlocked many evenings.

One week later…

There is a sly and quick-witted merchant, named Tavernier, here at the convent with his entourage. I do not like the look of him. He looks at everyone and everything with the lust of commerce and gold. His guard is a man who is always hooded and rarely speaks. He has a piercing glare that makes one shiver and shudder.

Through a peek hole I observed, and witnessed thus; A strange, dark-hooded figure entered the old man Pittan's workshop. He seemed to be sniffing the air! I held my breath, remembering I had not scraped my teeth that morning.

He bent down to look underneath the bench by the wall. Master Tavernier entered the doorway demanding, "Did you find it?"

"Yes Master, "the man all but growled a reply, his voice had a deep grating edge to it.

"You are certain, a piece of the gemstone lies here?"

Again, "Yes Master."

"Then retrieve it and let's be on our way!"

"I cannot, it will burn me." the hooded man answered.

"Must I do everything?" Tavernier retorted, not waiting for an answer, he bent down in a surprisingly agile fashion for an older man. As he reached for something it scurried out of his reach of it's own accord! It was a beautiful thing! Tavernier tried again, but it flew in the opposite direction right for my peephole in the stone wall! I could not react in time, and it entered my mouth! Not wanting to swallow, but knowing the men would come after me, I backed out and down from my perch. Following a secret back way to my solitary room, I ran as fast as I could, hoping to not encounter anyone. I rushed into my room, having left it as it was in case someone did enter to find me gone. I had just covered myself when my door burst open, three persons were in the doorway, their faces masked as the light was behind them. But I could tell by their smell that it was my own beloved Master with the Tavernier merchant who smelled of wine, and the silent hooded man. I sleepily looked frightened, and cowered in my bed clothes, as my Master told me to do- but that is another story.

"See, he has been here since midnight, as per my orders. Come boy, they repast is awaiting thee." Master Chaumeau gently commanded. When I hesitated, he motioned to the men to leave, and for me to join him in the corridor. Whether it was to protect me or to see what I had been truly up to, I will never know because his arm went around me protectively. The two men turned, and one followed the other down the winding stone corridor to the place where all the monks were eating. If they were surprised at being joined by such as us, they gave no sign. One table was nearly full, the tallest of them stood to beckon to the Master. His hand held me tightly as he bid me sit next to him.

"Young Aaron had been up late tending the lamps," Master Chaumeau told them, "He needs a bit of fattening up, don't you agree, Du Temps?"

"More the like he has been reading in the library, since you gave him permission!" retorted the other master.

"When there is skill, and dare I say, talent, it should not be wasted among the muck." Shot back my master.

I hung my head, almost embarrassed at being the center of attention among such honored monks. But they looked at me with new respect.

"Talent you say?" asked another one, "Is it with languages also?"

My master merely nodded, as if to quell any more discussion on the matter, but also to absolve me and hopefully to keep anyone from giving me a whipping later when the master was not about. One of them winked at me. I hung my head even more, wondering how in heaven was I to eat with a blue sparking sphere in my mouth? So, I began to cry silently, hoping that I would be excused. It worked. I was gruffly, but not unkindly given a meat roll and a mug to take back to my room.

"Please escort young Aaron to his room, Fayen. I have need of him later and do not wish him to become among the missing." Chaumeau glanced at the high table where an angry Tavernier was skulking, talking low with his nephew

Six months later…

I have been told that I am too old to be at the convent. I may be older than they surmised. Now with regular meals and care, I have grown. I have been told I am to join a caravan that is traveling to far-off Egypt. Part of the journey shall be on the sailing ship Porpoise—not the Marigold, for I inquired. I am excited and worried too. I must hide the gem here in the tower. The blue pulsing gem greets me during the break of day after hiding all night. I worry for her sake. I shall make a hiding place for her in the topmost tower, in a small crevice in the stone wall. I hope she waits for me to return.

The spice guild merchant that has acquired me is very generous. I am told that a small purse of silver has purchased my services as scribe. I am to be treated better than a cabin boy, but still I dine with the crew. My bunk is near the cook. He is a jovial man who likes to sing. I shall enjoy that, I hope. My journal I have had to hide. None of the crew can write. Somehow they believe that I am good luck. The ship's cook often winks at me and rubs my head.

We have taken on five survivors from the wrecked ship, Marigold, as I had foreseen in the vision. Tavernier, and his friends had been on board, yet somehow survived the wreck. His hooded servant is still solemn as ever. When he saw me, the merchant exclaimed, "Well met, young Aaron!" Yet his eyes held no warmth. We encountered a smaller fishing vessel trying to rescue the same men. A well-dressed lord named de Norville took charge of the survivors. He is the Lord of a great castle to whence they were taken.

At last, land…We have reached Alexandria, having out-sailed the pirate ship following us. Walking down the gangway seemed nearly impossible, but I was afraid if I fell into the water, no one would rescue me. Everyone is sullen and hungry. We took more time to reach the ancient city than planned and the cook was murdered in his sleep. I was assigned with the task of preparing meals. I used every bit of knowledge I could muster, recalling my favorite meals at Capuchin. What I had to work with was very limited, but no one complained, at least to my ears. Thank goodness I was only employed thusly for a few days.

Alexandria is wonderful! The ancient ruins of the temple on Pharos Island are not visited by many. We headed for the citadel, built by Sultan Al-Ashraf Sayf al-Din Qa'it Bay. I am to learn much here. I am in wonder of the obelisk. Something draws me to it. I actually found it while wandering by myself. As I stood there, admiring the Egyptian glyphs, I found myself reading the words out loud. I stopped myself once I felt someone watching me. It was my master, Chameau. How had he come to be here? He must have taken a different ship or made his way overland.

That night at dinner, Master Chaumeau asked me, point blank, to translate the writings on the obelisk. I nodded my head in agreement. I wished to say that I had already done some of the work, but instead hung my head as usual and watched their expressions. The other men at the table were named Jean or John. They all seemed rather pleased with themselves. I feel I am in danger and need a plan of escape. I have made friends with the stable boy, yet again I must be careful.

Aborath! I have translated the name of the creature held within the enormous obelisk, known to Europeans as a unicorn. His name is Aborath. He is magnificent! How the Egyptian priests captured him within the obelisk, I shall never know. But I will use everything within my powers to free him.

Later...

I know not how much time has progressed—more than a day perhaps. I awakened to find myself in chains in the hold of a ship. I was able to write even though I was chained. To ease the feeling of nausea I pulled myself into wakefulness. Near me was the body of the unicorn. In the weak light I could make out only a bit of color. I dreaded the answer. Of what happened to me I know nothing. I felt my sack behind me and knew my journal was still in it. Relief flooded me that my hard work, months of writing, were not lost. I have tried recalling any memory of what happened to me. I briefly remember moonlight flooding the temple theater, bathing the image of the unicorn carved within the granite carvings. I read the words upon the obelisk, then felt a sharp pain, and all went black.

I vow vengeance. But escape must come first. The voyage to the coast of England was miserable. The sudden jolt as they ran the ship aground was a surprise. In order to walk the unicorn down the ramp, they scuttled the ship. I am still tethered to him. He is not feeling well, it is plain. He barely raises his head. I speak softly to him to encourage him to live. "Revenge will be so sweet," I whispered to Aborath. I have not even told them his true name. I made up something that sounded honorable. Since none can read my journal I felt safe revealing his name amidst the charmed pages. Still, it would not be wise to tempt the fates.My heart breaks for Aborath. My mind worries all day and night for how to free my friend. He and I have discovered we can speak together in ancient Sanskrit. He tells me his mate's name is Axoparia. She lives with the queen and king of Faerieland, a world connected to Terra by a spinning vortex of wind and energy. He imbued me with some of his magik by touching me with his nicorn. He told me he could have stabbed me with it, but he wished me to live. In fact, he asked me to find Axoparia. There is a part of Terra where the wild people live. If I can find the vortex I can find help. I told him about the shining blue sphere, about my life at the convent and of having abilities with languages. He thought for a time and then told me that I am a wizard! He assured me that my powers will grow now that I have some of his power. I have told him I would die for him, but he shook his mane. No, you must survive, he told me. You must escape and find Axoparia, tell her of my true love and where I have been chained. I swore I would. I will.

One week later…

My powers have indeed grown in ways that I had not imagined. I can understand the language of the birds. I can read people's lips as they speak. Animal conversations are also known to me if I concentrate hard enough. Then, right before Aborath's eyes, I transformed myself into a cat! He told me it meant my original form, in the ancient path my spirit had taken, was a feline. He said he feels the Others are planning something and I will need to leave. He did not wish that my blood be spilled during the ceremony they were planning. He told me that my escape will save his life because instead of drinking my blood, they will need his and will keep him alive to do so. What form of vampire are they?

When he feels strong enough he tells me about the Others. He said they are worst kind. They prey on the energy of magikal beings, then after living a great long time, sleep within stone sarcophagi for a century to rejuvenate. Tonight, you must leave, he told me. If I had known what they were about to do, I would have stayed to fight.

Two months later…

I have left behind my name of Aaron and have chosen to be called Audran. The last time I saw Aborath I transformed into a cat to escape the chains, then changed back to a human to fetch my sack and the precious journal. I gave my friend one last hug. He again touched me with his nicorn as much as he dared. He said he wished to drain it so it would be of no use to them, but he still wished to live. We both knew of whom he spoke. If I have any strength within me I will accomplish the task he has set for me. I invoked the name of the Goddess, as he instructed. I felt a surge of power and a clarity of mind. I wished with all my heart I could take him with me. But he said his pathway was to travel sadness for a time, but he would, indeed, be rescued by Axoparia. He had faith in his mate. I gave one last look at the magnificent being, He had tossed his mane then turned away, for some noise had caught his attention.

"Hurry!" he had urged me. "They are coming!"

January, Mongolia…a new year

My grief and guilt at leaving Aborath is with me constantly. Yet it may be giving me the strength to go on. The long walk to the Tibetan monastery left me weakened, but after two weeks living at the high altitude, I feel better. The monks believe I have a broken heart. I cannot tell them about the Others or the unicorn, but I feel I must, somehow, find someone to talk with, someone who will listen to my story. The air is so thin, but it is clear and without malice. At times, I recall finding the air at Capuchin full of negative energy, which probably came from the hooded man with his disease of character. Here among these honorable men I am learning herb lore, meditation as a method of healing, Tibetan throat singing, and the ways of the wind. They believe that news travels first upon the air currents of the world. They may be correct.

My studies continue and I have discovered that I am nearly six feet tall! Amazing for someone who began life so small. The monks smile when I enter any room. They have a private name for me, I am certain. I have exchanged my European clothing for their very comfortable hoods and wraps. Blue is my color of choice. It took some time for the cloth dye to arrive, but a deep indigo is now the color of my robes. I discovered that if I meditate I can bring up glimpses of my early childhood. These images of a golden-red-haired woman, a race to save us, and a storm that wrecked their ship. But nothing of a certainty, as if there is a fog in my memory, placed upon me to make me forget.

Four years hence…

I apologize to myself for the seeming abandonment of my journal. My studies as a monk, and using my hidden abilities, have taken me away to far off places in my mind. These journeys leave me exhausted and weak. If not for the kindness and care of the monks, I fear I could not continue.

Another year gone by…

Within this house of the Buddha there are many secrets. I have found a friend in the Ganden Tripa Monastery with whom I have confided nearly everything. His countenance was clouded, but I felt neither fear nor repulsion from him.

"In this world there are many kinds of people. Most follow a path unknown to them, one that unravels as their life flows out to its end. You have shown us that you are above such as live upon this earth," Shatra explained one evening. "Your story is one that a Buddha would tell! There is one among us such as you. We never allow outsiders within the secret temple, but perhaps he would like to meet thee," Shatra, one of the monks, told me.

The next moon cycle...I have been granted an audience with the holiest of their order at Gandan Tripa. It is such an honor that the monks would not sup with me, but kept me to myself within a special room, to cleanse my aura. Truthfully I am nervous! This monk is so holy that he will become a statue to be worshipped as he becomes mummified. But now he wishes to speak with me. The monks were horrified when he rang his bell and spoke slowly his wishes to talk with the European dressed in blue robes, with the name of Audran. The old man spoke in a low tone. There was a sense of urgency in his voice. I will try to recall his every word.

"There is beautiful blue magik in this world that is very ancient. It came when this world was formed by the creators. The first temple at Gobekli Tepi honors those who came from the stars. Your spirit is one from such a place. As the colonists ventured forth, the magik followed and flowed throughout the land. Terra, or Earth, is bound by magik that is enhanced by the love all of us have for one another. Magikal things take on power, and more so if made by a child. The flow of love when a child is born follows that child, if not taken by the Others. These beings of darkness, which are all over this world, also came from the stars. The Others feed upon magik. They need it to continue. Otherwise their powers diminish. They seek their sarcophagi to hibernate. These granite chambers are imbued with magik, thus enabling them to rejuvenate. The priests of many religions were their caretakers. The priestesses refused. The Others are creatures full of dark magik but are not always evil. They simply wish to live. This information I must give thee, for you will encounter these powerful beings. There are other peaceful warriors, male and female, upon this world who can be of service to thee. They will be able to feel your power. But there is a secret signal I will show thee that all these warriors know."

With this, the holy man put two middle fingers of his left hand to his lips, then placed his right hand, fingers splayed open, over his heart with his head pointed downward. After a few moments, he did not move. I sensed panic in my own mind, as well as in those in the tower. The holy man had passed to the other side, before my eyes. I could not leave the room, wishing and wanting him to speak again. I had so many questions and could not even ask one. When it was proper, I rushed to my room to write down what he had told me.

I read it over and over again, hoping to glean every bit of wisdom within the words. Should I show this to Shatra?

One moon later...

I am to leave the monastery. Reports have come in from afar that reveal the Turks will be invading soon. The monks do not fear for their lives, but tell me my life's journey, my katra, lies in a new world. I wonder at their words. Does this mean I am to leave Terra? Upon speaking with a traveler named Polo Bragadin, I was given hints of lands free of Europeans with a people tall and darker of skin, but full of honor for the land. If I were to go there, I would be free to continue my search for a way to help Aborath. Perhaps there are more of my kind? The holy man told me there were. With the help of Polo, I was able to purchase European garb with a bit of the flavor of the Orient. He assured me this was what all the wealthy were wearing. The clothing is so strange, after wearing my robes. I kept the outer, dark robe for travel in the wetter regions of Holland and land of the Scots. Polo tells me religious fever and fervor are rampant in Europe. If I tell all that I am a doctor or surgeon I will gain passage more easily. I did not tell him I have a scroll that I imbued so any reader believes anything I tell them. As I set off on my journey, my friends Shatra and Polo were waiting for me by the large rock that juts out to the sea. Each man solemn but serene. They had for me two bundles wrapped in sailcloth. Each knew they would never see me again. Shatra, had plans to go build another monastery in a far-off land. And Polo, a descendant of that famous traveler for whom he is named, I had a vision that he would not meet a glorious fate but would simply live his life until old age. What they had given me was precious beyond gold. One wrapping contained another journal, blank, waiting for my words to fill it, and a copy of *The Marvels of the World*, signed by its author. The other bundle held a Fra Mauro map. Oh, Polo, what a gift you have given me! I sent a word of thanks along the wind.

I know not the date, but the moon has passed twice since I left. Strange how I mark my life as before and after leaving that wonderful place. A sense of security came over me, one that I never had before, when I stepped upon the first stone up to the terrace. And each stone step brought me closer to a group of brethren who took me in, guided me, and provided my curious mind with such rich lore and wisdom. I owe them much. Sitting in this cave, another pilgrim tells me in broken Italian that many have perished along this route. It is full of religious people on a dark, dismal road of a kind of slavery, yet they consider themselves to be Christians and profess God's love is bestowed upon them. I see it not. Many of them are simply ignorant of the truth and are guided by the Others because they cannot read. They are, as I was, seeking refuge of the soul. Only I was lucky. These poor people are simply being used by the leaders of their religion. For what, I dare not tell, but I see many of them in a vision being slaughtered by knights wearing white with a red cross. I, myself, met some of these stern, hard men one morning as they roughly demanded who I was and where I was traveling. Had I news of the holy land? For they took me for a Friar. I replied in French, lying easily to them, letting it be known I had come from a vast land and barely escaped with my life. I had news for the cardinal alone. This news, along with a glimpse of my scroll giving me safe passage, convinced them to let me go. Dangerous times are ahead, I fear.

It is the new year again and I am astonished at the growth of my beard. It had begun when I left Italy. Now I look the part—an old Franciscan friar, dressed oddly in a blue robe. I have acquired a page, who is also dressed in robes, but of brown. I am teaching him to read and to write in Italian and French. His mind is very curious, and he sees the details in every living thing. He has begun his own journals. I feel blessed to have met one such as he.

My page has left me, but I care not. I hope his status as a bastard will not impinge his life's work, for in a vision, I saw him on his back, painting a vast, colorful depiction of man greeting his creator.

Basque country...
My favorite people so far are this curious group that care not for outsiders. I was not allowed in until I showed them my books and sketches. They were intrigued. I also was able to heal a sick child, and so they allowed me safe passage into their mountains. Here it is peaceful, but I can understand why they mistrust outsiders. The religious persecution I hear of throughout the lands of Spain fills me with such fear. I must retreat to a safe land where people can be free.

Until then, I must hide myself. I must move around, not staying anywhere for more than a year at a time. It seems that

I do not age. That in itself would have me hanged for a witch. But I can also tell a bit of their future. I advised these wonderful, freedom loving, musical, and colorful people to hide themselves, too. For a great calamity was coming, not soon, but within some of their lifetimes. I feel also that I need a benefactor of great wealth in order to get to the New World, a vast land to the west. The Basques trade with some of the Portuguese, and tales have been retold by passing minstrels of the lands to the west and the noble people there.

New journal, a new world passage…

I have booked passage as physician A. Audran on a ship called the Roselyn out of Cornwall, England, owned by Prince Henry Sinclair, another descendant of a Sinclair of the past. We were well met at an inn in Brittany, where the main fare was shellfish. Being unused to such foods, I became unwell, which is how I met Sinclair. For he, too, was unwell, and we were both nursed by the innkeeper's daughters. As we talked, I learned of his thirst for exploring the shores of North America, having been told many secrets by his forebears. The excitement he felt shone in his eyes as he told me, "There is a Southern America also! The bards sing of great riches to be found there, along with a fountain of perpetual youth!" He then told me of the chapel built by his namesake called Roselyn, hence the name of his own sailboat. How we will sail past the pirates and warships of France and Britain is unclear. But he was very happy to learn how many languages I could speak. (I have added to Basque to my repertoire.) He has yet to learn that I can also write legal documents as well as genealogy charts. His boat sails in a fortnight. I plan to be aboard.

Postscript: Sinclair has given passage to both of the innkeeper's daughters. They have kin in Boston and will be taken in by them. I wonder what will become of them.

This small caravel ship is very quick. We have outmaneuvered two British warships, Sinclair having hoisted the flags bearing the colors of a cartel ship so we would not be subject to capture. I am very glad, not wishing to be conscripted into the Royal Navy. We set sail for the waters of the Lobster Coast and the Cape of Cod. Having tasted the wonderful creature that turns red when boiled, I am certain to eat as many as I am able (even with my sensitive stomach).

We land in a busy port...

I am professing myself to be of a legal mind, being able to read and converse in many languages. This is of use to merchants, and I have found my time here in Boston to be fruitful.

There is much unrest in the colonies. Britain's rule of New England is strict and in many ways unforgiving. Most subjects of the king have no knowledge of the hardships the colonists endure. Henry, I am afraid, will be taken any day now. He has been sending messages and documents that I have drafted to the Continental Congress. I have no fear for my life, as the documents are penned under a false name. But Henry is reckless at times! He also cannot ride very well. There is something innately wrong with him as he becomes seasick at odd times. I am curious as to the cause. Summer in Boston is miserable! I am fleeing for parts along the northern Coast called Maine.

This is the place!

I will use the remaining pages in my journal to write of the magikal place I found. I was led here, following my heart, as I was told to do so long ago. The island is large, but I need only half of it. There is blue magik here. I can feel it humming under my feet when I walk without my boots. I plan to raise a tower here and a house, and perhaps begin a small village at the far northern end. I purchased a sailing dinghy for my own use. I have a wagon bring supplies each month so there is a constant flow of people to this area. Perhaps some of them will remain and build a town with me. Before I left, I had been approached by several elders in the Plimouth Colony, some seeking a husband for a daughter. If I do marry, she will have to be very special. I will leave that to fate.

My journal has been my closest companion at times. I am placing it within a cedar box, wrapped in its sailcloth. I have imbued it with a small bit of magik so that anyone finding it will not want it. Unless that person has magikal powers, they will not be able to read it anyway. I must submerge myself in my studies and stay out of the way of the witch hunters. May the magik be with me.

    Aaron Audran of Indian Island, Maine

BACK AT THE ISLAND, SOME VILLAGERS SUSPECT SOMETHING IS AMISS

"Well, I heard that she *is* pregnant, and they've *cancelled* the big expensive wedding, and are going to sail around the world on that gigantic sailboat her father built. You know he won an award in France for that thing?"

"Oh, I know, he won some money, too, and they probably inherited all of it. I'll bet Pauline is some upset now she doesn't have the contract for all those flower arrangements."

Both ladies suddenly lowered their voices, because in through the door walked Addie Bradley, mother of the groom, to order a birthday cake for Keevan. She asked to have all her grandkids to be put on the automatic birthday cake list, but she could only guess Luke's birthday month. Addie's cheeks began to turn pink, because she could sense the ladies behind the counter had been gossiping about her family.

"I'm not sure what kind of cake Luke will want, probably chocolate with jellybeans for decorations," Addie told the woman who took down the notes. "And we will be having a cake for the baby shower, too, but I'll have to get back to you on the date." That will get them talking, Addie thought to herself.

John Bradley was minding the store. A bunch a kids rushed in to get candy and popsicles. He got them their candy bags and motioned for them to put their money in the giant candy jar. They knew when the jar was full it would be a free candy bar day, so they were in nearly every day to buy stuff. John grinned to himself, knowing that some days he put money in it himself. He listened them making their choices of vintage candy and arguing whether or not Bit O'Honey or MaryJanes were the best. A lot of the older generation came into the store to buy the vintage candy that reminded them of their youth. Almost everyone had a story of going to the general store as a kid with just a nickel or a quarter and getting a ton of candy that would last them all week. He looked out the window to the waterfront, absently watching the men load up their boats for the afternoon. As the seagulls flew overhead, crying, he was amazed to see Keevan riding by followed closely by a huge black raven. His grandson parked his bike in the bike rack and locked it up. The raven perched on the seat of the bike for a while. When John checked later, the raven had moved to the handlebars, but stayed with the bike until Keevan was done with class. John stepped out of the store to wave to the boy, who waved back but sped off, the raven in hot pursuit.

"Of all things!" he remarked to Lemuel Dunbar, who was sitting on one of the benches outside. "My grandson has a trained bird!"

"Yah, them birds are some smaht!" Lem agreed. "Had one when I was a kid. It used to find spahkly things for me and trade them for treats."

John Bradley wondered why his grandson didn't stop in for a soda drink.

"Oh, boys that age have other things on their minds. Fifteen, isn't he now?" Lem asked his old friend. "You and me were always ridin' around the island like we had important stuff goin' on."

John nodded his head in agreement. He saw his wife come out of the bakery and could tell something was up. He scooted back into the store before she could see him. He didn't feel like listening to her complain about the villagers gossiping again.

Addie walked across the street with angry purpose. She nodded to Lem as she strode into the Post Office side of the general store. John could hear its door slam and knew soon she'd be coming over to his side. He readied himself. But she did not come. He waited a few minutes and she still didn't show. Now he was worried. What on earth was she doing? He couldn't stand it anymore and went through the doorway to her office. He found his wife staring at her notepad.

"Well, at least the wedding's still on, I got an email," she snapped. "I'm surprised we're invited at all!"

"Oh, come on, now, we wouldn't be uninvited! Marcus wouldn't stand for that!"

"Oh, you know he'd do anything she wants! He's been in love with that gal since they were kids! You know he only married Cynthia because he came home from college to find Marji and Jeremiah engaged. I remember the day he carved their initials in that old apple tree near us. M.B. & M.D. It's funny how life can surprise you after all these years!" Her stinging retort had softened as her words faded. Now she was looking out the window toward the shore with binoculars.

"Did you know they had a widow's walk built? When did they have that done? I looked up their house on the internet. It wasn't there two days ago," she told him.

"How can you see their house from here?" he asked her, incredulously.

"No, silly, I used a pair of these at our house. From there, I can see their house."

He smiled inwardly. She was going into the 21st century kicking and screaming, but she was slowly seeing the benefits of technology.

She handed him the binoculars, pointing toward the wharf. He saw Marji's Island Catering crew loading their gear and supplies into one of the boats to get ready for another trip back to the house. He shrugged. Irritated, she took the binoculars from him for another look.

She asked him, "Why don't any of them have a car? Where are they all sleeping? Probably the barn or in a tent." She answered her own question. "It's good that Marji will have help for the wedding, even if there is only going to be a small, private dinner at the house." She turned around to ask her husband what he would like for the wedding dinner, but he had silently left. So, she replied to the email for him, choosing the chicken cordon bleu for both of them instead of lobster quesadilla. Add a salad and baked asparagus from the drop-down choices and voila! Wedding planning in the new millennium, all done by tapping and swiping, Addie thought to herself. She also wondered if her own daughter, Augusta, would be able to make the new date, two months ahead of the original wedding date, and if Marji's former in-laws would be attending. They had been invited. No wonder people were gossiping, she thought to herself. This family certainly gave them much to gossip about!

WHAT HAPPENED IN THE BARN

Daisy was enthralled with the unicorn, Aborath. She still loved Golden with all her heart, but the sheer joy of the unicorn as he trotted around inside the barn with his newly formed nicorn made her cry happy tears. Everyone had been in the barn—well, not everyone, as Luke, Ellora, and Keevan had been out battling again (which made Daisy really anxious). All the ravens had taken flight toward the meadow where before the blue flames and yellow fire had lit up the sky. She wondered if the meadow would catch on fire. Then later Sarisha exploded into the Barn with the wounded Unicorn. The shielding went up immediately, making all the barnies and the animals upset. Daisy hid her head in Golden's mane, trying to block out the mayhem. Golden knew immediately who Sarisha had brought. She rushed over to him, nuzzling him. Then Golden touched her nicorn to the little nub that was left of his. Sarisha may have added some of her own magik, too, before she exploded out of the barn. Daisy did not know how magik worked, except that it did, and sometimes in wonderful ways. The barn was quiet for one minute, and then she heard a little pop! And his nicorn began to grow! Everyone cheered! The stern looking queen faerie was crying and holding her hands to her heart. There was so much emotion flying around, mixing with the swirls of dust from the hay-strewn floor.

The queen stood up and spoke. "Friends!" Then, more softly, "Friends, we have met on this occasion to celebrate the healing of my dear old friend, Aborath. I do not know this creature who healed him, but I thank her from the bottom of my heart."

Since no one spoke in reply, Daisy stood up. She felt she had to say something. She cleared her throat. "May I speak?" she asked quietly.

"Who art thou?" demanded the queen.

Daisy curtsied. "Daisy Day Donovan. My mother named me, guardian of this house. I have news of what you seek." Daisy tried to speak as Blouette would have done. She faltered, but Golden turned to nuzzle her as if she was giving her courage. Daisy continued, "Much time has passed, O queen, and there's a lot to explain, but Golden is a magikal mixture of the unicorn who was Axoparia and a Maine coon cat. It happened all so quickly. Blouette was there. My sister Ellora and my brothers, Luke and Keevan, all know about what happened if you want to ask them. Oh, and the house brownie, Gitchie, will have it all written down in the journal too." She added as many names as she felt would sway her story just in case the queen did not believe her.

"Child of the guardian, I thank thee for your news. But is there some explanation as to how a dragon, a ninja warrior, the cat in question, and my captain of the guard were sent to rescue me?"

"I don't think they knew anything about you, Your Highness. We read Audran's journal and found out where Aborath was taken after ... after what they did to him! Oh my gosh, that must have hurt him so bad!" Daisy was almost crying again. The barnies were busy bringing Aborath some fresh hay and grain. The raccoon was busy filling the water trough as if they all were trying to be somewhere else, immediately.

"What! Audran's journal?" The queen exploded angrily. "No one was sent to rescue me? How absurd, how utterly..." (her words were lost as she began to sputter in her native language). "How utterly funny! I am the luckiest faerie in the world!" She laughed out loud. But to herself, she thought, what if I had not been in the garden with Aborath this day? I would have been left behind. Her friend would not have come so willingly, she liked to think. He would have not left her behind. Happenstance and good fortune had smiled upon her this day! Her heart was filled with so much gratitude and love for all. She gestured for a feast to begin. "Go forth, my distant kinsmen, gather for the feast!"

The barnies scattered in different directions, some going to the foresters for fish, some gathering mushrooms in the glen, some searching the food bins for enough grain to make bread. And the raccoon went down into the root cellar to fetch some of Charlie's bottled sarsaparilla. He had trouble bringing up more than one bottle at a time, so Brayle went to help, and since Daisy was not doing anything, he politely asked her to lend a hand. Daisy told him she would. This made her feel a part of the celebration and helpful, instead of the kid-in-the-way, as she had been feeling lately. As she handed the queen a drink, Daisy felt her necklace become hot. The queen's crown blossomed into a faint pinkish-red color. Merritt had a look of astonishment as she gestured for the human girl to come forward. Touching her own gemstone as she reached for the ones Daisy was wearing, the queen felt a faint vibration.

"There is magik within the stones you wear. You must be related somehow to a wizard, female or male, to have such a gift around your neck," Merritt told her.

Daisy did not know what to say except, "My mother gave it to me."

"The guardian of whom you spoke?" the queen gently asked, for she saw tears welling up in the girl's eyes.

"No, not really a guardian of this place, but she was my guardian. She died a while ago and I miss her sometimes. But my dad is marrying the real guardian of the house and he'll be the new master and—"

Now thoroughly confused, the queen held up her hand imperiously, so Daisy stopped talking.

"I will ask my captain what has transpired since my abduction."

When Blou heard these words, she dreaded having to explain to the queen where she had been all these moons, but she knew the queen would not like to hear Myster was the wizard Audran or hear about what was left of him.

Marcus suddenly realized that Daisy was, again, nowhere to be found. He quietly slipped away from the celebration in the house. As Marcus opened the barn's side door, everyone stopped to look at him. What he saw astounded him: the fully-grown unicorn with his nicorn restored, the queen ordering everyone about, the nice hustle and bustle to the place. The queen greeted him as if he were some royal servant.

"Greetings! and salutations, come join our feast of celebration!"

Marcus grinned and answered, not knowing whom she was but guessing that, if she wore a crown and was riding the unicorn, she was someone special. "Many thanks, O Queen. My thanks to thee for caring for my daughter Daisy." He then bowed to her.

The queen looked surprised and turned to the girl at her side, asking, "Is this your father, child?"

Daisy nodded, grinning, and ran to her dad. "Dad! She is the queen of Faerieland. See her crown? And Golden healed poor Aborath, and he's better and so happy! Everybody's so happy!"

Her words were true. The Barnies were singing a snappy song while some of them did aerial acrobatics over Aborath's nicorn whenever he lowered it just enough to make it a challenge. Someone was barbecuing mushrooms, someone else was drinking from a beaker with good smelling root beer, and it certainly was a party! Everyone was a bit tipsy, in fact. He should have known that Charlie had brewed some real sarsaparilla.

"I am queen of Balaktria, a province within Faerieland, dear child."

He bowed to the queen again. "May I have my daughter? It is soon to be her bedtime and tomorrow we have much to do. Please, come to the house tomorrow, at your convenience."

The queen nodded and gestured for Daisy to kiss her goodnight. Golden looked confused. She wanted to go with Daisy, but she also wanted to remain with her mate. Finally, after one more forlorn look from Daisy, Golden set off at a trot after her girl. Daisy's heart was never so full of love for her dear Golden. She put her arm possessively around the back of the Lunicorn.

After they left, the queen gestured to her captain to sit by her side. Aborath came over and let it be known that he was grateful for her assistance in the rescue. This was the cue for Blouette to begin her narrative. She chose her words with great care. The queen knew nothing about what she and Raid had done, she hoped. Should she be caught telling an untruth she would be severely punished. Perhaps her wings would be clipped!

"It began for me when the human child, Ellora Donovan, transformed me out of my cast-state, a blue glass bottle, using the magik fire in the house. After awakening I determined that there was much magik here and in the surrounding lands. Next, we set Golden free from her glass prison, which was difficult because she was a merged being. She, in truth, was the unicorn Axoparia. At the time she was cast, the wizard Audran was also reduced to his original state, that of a large cat. His memory is torn and tattered. He recalls only fit and starts of his long, glorious life as a wise wizard. In some ways, this was true retribution for his part in the abandonment of Balaktria by the unicorn and for the Battle of Dingley! The battle was the cause of much strife within the village of this island, and who knows how much damage was done elsewhere. For Dingley used blue magik and thrust it into the very ground of the island. The Others were defeated at the cost of eight human lives and one house brownie. Their bones and blood sealed the cracks and rifts sent to destroy this place."

Blouette hesitated, then continued: "There is more, O Queen. None of us knew that you had been abducted! Ellora found the wizard's journals and read the what and where of Aborath's imprisonment. I assure you that if we had known, I would have come sooner! We have become allies with a dragon named Sarisha Chandi, the anujan of the ancient beings that rule Herstamonix. Of her own accord she came here to aid the humans and to make sure the Others do not prevail. Because should they win the land, Balaktria could be next."

The queen held up her hand to end the narrative. "I wish to know more about this dragon later. Who are the mistress and master of this magik place? Who is this Ellora? Is she the one in the prophecy? If so, she must have a brother who is also a wizard. We must have a meeting soon, for I have not been idle. I have much news to add to the narrative of the Others and their plans. And, I wish to know, where is Captain Raid?"

A TOUR OF THE CAVERN

Marji woke in the morning to the smell of coffee and the cheerful bustle of her crew in the kitchen downstairs. Today she would get married to a man she had known since she was seven. He had carved their initials in an old apple tree long ago. Now that was coming true. How different her life would have been if she had married Marcus first! The old woman she'd met when she was eighteen had been right—she would travel a path of love until it betrayed her. She would find love again and have very special children. Then the old soothsayer, who was also a crystal reader, had looked deep into her eyes and smiled. She had told Marji she would, indeed, have very special children who would help bring balance to the world. At the time, she had thought it was hokum, a trick to get money from her, but the old woman would not take any from her. She said it was an honor to read the destiny of a Blue Guardian. *Now why hadn't I remembered that until now?* she demanded of herself.

Because, Mommy, you had only been touched by magik, not immersed in it like you are now, said someone.

"Luke?" Marji asked out loud. "Was that you?" Silence greeted her. Who was that talking? It was hard to figure out sometimes, because both Luke and Ellora would practice using telepathy. Keevan and Daisy could not initiate this skill, but they could hear someone talking within their minds. Marcus didn't want to try. He said it tickled too much. She sighed. It certainly was a better summer than she'd planned way back in April! Was it only in April that she had catered that odd wedding on Orr's Island? She had to buy the food in Portland, bring it up to Cook's

Lobster and Ale House, and serve the guests. There James had run the barbecue pit spectacularly. Thinking of that April wedding made her think of her upcoming nuptials. Instead of a wedding gown, I am simply going to wear whatever will fit me. She had looked in her mother's things, but they were all much too small to accommodate her pregnancy.

Abequa tapped on her door. Surprised, Marji motioned for her to come in. "What brings you to my lair?" she asked.

"Mistress, my Gitchie tells me that a gown is awaiting you down in the storage compartments. Shall I have one of your young ones bring it up?" asked Abequa.

"Yes, certainly, I would love to see it. But it's not one of those from Victorian times, is it? Because some of those looked like they were more for a funeral than for a bride. I wouldn't mind if it were sea green or cream colored," Marjorie told Abequa.

"I also asked my Gitchie what type of gown it is, and he assured me it is made of Belgium lace, silk, and some other fancy fabrics. Apparently, it was going to be Cassandra Drake's wedding gown. It was worn by previous Drake women and I believe there is a picture of it in a book in the library. Gitchie told me he sent its picture to your email account."

Marjorie was surprised when she saw the gown. It was elegant and not too fancy, but would it fit her?

Sarisha had a surprise for everyone on the day of the wedding. She also said that she would let family members come visit her treasures. She told them proudly that she had just found something special and new. It was hours before the wedding ceremony, so it was actually a good way to spend time for everyone not involved in wedding prep. She advised the mistress not to come, because magik can have ill effects on the unborn. Excitedly, the guests gathered in the library for the tour. The only ones not going were Gitchie, Maemaegwin, James the chef, and Fern, who said she did not like caves. (Gitchie had cast a charm on all of the catering crew to not "spill the grains," as Blou incorrectly told Marcus. Gitchie assured Blouette that no one would spill any beans, grains, or any kind of bead. How he did that with a straight face, he did not know). Queen Merritt had been invited but she had also declined, not wanting to leave Aborath's side. Myster had been quiet after he told everyone where he had been and what had happened to him. He felt that he had been a very lucky cat. At the last minute, Golden changed her mind, nudging Daisy forward into the doorway.

Abequa was quite nervous about being in the cavern with so many people, but she had so much curiosity lately that her husband said to her, "Go! We brownies must be represented as part of the decision making and we need to know what is in there."

Not until the last one trouped inside and the door was shut behind them did all the chatter and talking end. The silence was not golden. The place was eerie, and their breathing echoed. The luminous fungi were quite numerous up in the ceiling. Sarisha motioned some of them to sit on the wooden bench that Grampa Charles had made for her. It was not big enough for all of them, so a few stood in the grayish-green cavern.

Luke broke the silence. "Look, there are some old Christmas ornaments, some really old stuff in this section." They carefully handled the precious things. Ellora had warned them ahead of time that Sari could become nervous when her things were dropped. The dragon said nothing, though, as they began to fan out and explore. It was like a shopping spree except that they weren't going to buy anything, Daisy thought to herself.

Keevan exclaimed, "Look, it's my Red Sox hat! I lost it during the storm with the scarecrow."

Sarisha was very sad as Keevan placed the hat back on his head. He saw her expression and took it off, putting it back carefully where he had found it.

"I'm glad you found it. It's now in the best place where it will never be lost again."

The dragon nuzzled him, happiness lighting up her eyes at how understanding he was. She gave him a small, golden, oval-shaped pin with her gratitude, remarking on how different he was today. Actually, he was different than he was two months ago.

I do feel different, Keevan thought. I don't have that anger and frustration that I used to. He wondered if it was because he felt like his family appreciated him and that he actually had fought an enemy for them. His sister had given away a super-cool magik ring in order to save his life. As if she'd heard his thoughts, Ellora held his hand for a moment, smiling at him.

She whispered, "That will make her so happy. Thank you."

Blou saw this exchange and felt that she should be quiet. She knew that the change for the better in the young man was partially due to her venom, which was a love potion. It made complete sense to inject an enemy with something that would make them friendly and want to please you, instead of wanting to fight. Since Keevan had been bitten not too long after she had been freed, it made sense that her venom was not as strong as it would be normally. So be it. She felt no need to inject him again. He was a good kid and seemed to want to help his family. She wondered why humans called their children after baby goats. Kids were full of energy; perhaps that was the reason. Humans had so many weird mannerisms and ways of speaking that confused her. Blou was starting to get bored, so she flew on ahead.

Luke was talking as if he were the guide. "Yes, and here are Grandpa's glasses and Grandma's slippers, but I think Sarisha has lots more things here that are super old, as she has been hunting and gathering for thousands of years. I think the corridors go way back into the hill. I actually think this area may have been part of an ancient volcano. And these passages were made by lava flows."

Now it was the dragon's turn to talk. "Yes, Master-in-training Luke, this place is proto-ancient, and the world has changed much since it was made. When I arrived, there was no fortress but there was the magikal cave. It was where Axoparia was hidden before the Battle of Dingley. Audran was able to focus this magik to build the tower fortress, which evolved into the house as you see it now. There are magikal items here that simply look like broken parts of things. They have been taken apart on purpose. Here is a lovely thing that belonged to a man named Lord Nelson. I took the large emerald out of it because it had dark power."

Marcus heeded the subtle warning in her explanation. His mouth dropped open when he saw the things stored in the shelf-like grotto. He simply could not believe his eyes! There were more jewels and the flashlight beam caught the tip of a crown, a brilliant large, yellow, oval-shaped gemstone and a long string of pearls. Leaning up against the wall of rough stone was a tall painting that looked as if it had been cut away from a larger one. Marcus looked at it carefully. The horse, ridden by an obvious nobleman, looked a lot like Aborath. If the painter was true to his subject, then it had to be the unicorn, after his nicorn had been cut off! His flashlight beam showed the edge of a partial signature, JvE, which stood for Jan van Eyck. Marcus knew that the painting had been stolen in the 1930's. Quickly he emailed Gitchie to look up the two items. Gitchie's response absolutely floored him. A list of lost world treasures came back in the reply. In Sarisha's cavern were millions of dollars' worth of "lost" items. Then Marcus saw the name "Copernicus" on the edge of a book and carefully picked it up. He made out its name, *On the Resolution of Heavenly Spheres*, second edition, and broke out in a sweat. Beneath that book was the original manuscript of *Treasure Island*. If anyone found out about this, they might arrest everyone in the family! There was no way of explaining this to the authorities. He gently put the books down and covered them with a plain, hand-woven shawl. He saw the tag on it, which read "Ma." He could only imagine whom it had belonged to.

They had a nice time looking over all the treasures. It was kind of like being in a museum. Marcus knew that Marji would love to be here looking at all of it! And there were other tunnels they hadn't even explored yet. Truly it was a touchingly beautiful collection. Sarisha had works of art by famous people, but Marcus also saw on top of one of the piles a carefully preserved drawing done by a child, signed "Victoria" in a childlike script. Sarisha saw him looking at it. She gently picked it up and told him she had saved it from being tossed out by a mournful woman dressed in black. Her husband had recently passed away.

Marcus asked her, "Was she Victoria Drake?"

"No," she replied, "Victoria the queen. It is very powerful, having been made with thoughts of love. Plus, the queen was in truth a guardian, like Mistress Marji. She was granddaughter of a wizard and was also married to one."

Gitchie sent a message that all was ready in the Garden of Roses. Only a half an hour had gone by in the cavern, yet three hours had gone by outside. After they all trouped back into the library, Marcus quietly closed the door. He promised himself to return as soon as possible to look at everything more carefully and make a list.

A ROSE GARDEN WEDDING

The ceremony in the rose garden was short but very sweet. Marji wore the gown that had been Cassandra's, so it was the "something old" along with the pins for her hair came from Queen Merritt, and she held a bouquet of blue wildflowers. To fulfill the marriage custom, she needed something new. Shyly, Maemaegwin handed her a short veil she had made from the cast-off repairs of the dress! Marji was impressed with her sewing talents and promised to find a way for Maemae to continue fashioning garments. Mr. Bradley walked her down the grass path to the rose-covered archway, where Marcus stood with Elias Alexzander Dorr, who officiated their vow taking. Elias was not only a singer-songwriter, but a minister as well! The reception dinner was delicious. They ate outdoors under a medieval style tent with a few friends and family members that could attend. It was a lovely afternoon. The older Bradley's and their few friends left after the cutting of the cake. Marji had insisted they give away pieces of it in old fashioned wedding boxes, like people did in the past. They waved goodbye to them all. But that was only the beginning of the dancing!

As soon they left, the barnies took over, playing some wild lively Celtic-like dance tunes on their own miniature instruments. The music continued far into the night. Queen Merritt danced with the solemn Brass, the very tall brownie from the barn who had helped the Queen during her first day in Terra. Blouette actually danced with some of the younger brownie children who'd had their naming day two years prior. (She felt it was not proper for her to dance with the older male barnies, plus she could not pick them up and twirl them around). Luke and Daisy danced together, and even Keevan and Ellora took a turn or two around the dance floor. Marji danced the slow dances but felt too tired to continue. She motioned for the party to go on as she and her husband made their way to the house to find the girls had decorated their suite with flowers and a bottle of non- alcoholic sparkling apple-pomegranate juice on ice. A miniature version of a harp played by itself softly in the corner, and beeswax candles glowed gently in the night. They looked down from the upper porch at their wonderful extended family, who were laughing and having a nice time just being normal. Well, as normal as it could be with a charmed harp, a unicorn giving rides in the moonlight, and short and tall people dancing an ancient jig. They could see the glowing eyes of Myster, who was up in the apple tree with Kassa. The raven was now commander of the Second Regiment. The music played well into the night. Finally, when all the humans had gone to bed, Myster jumped down from the tree perch. This was the signal for the night watch to begin. All was good in the kingdom.

THE BEGINNING OF THE END

Abequa and her husband were having concerns about the spell they wanted to put upon the catering crew. They were discussing this with Blouette. Myster walked in and jumped up on the couch.

"As you know, the charms we are able to cast lose their power after time. We cannot take the chance that this will happen whilst the young people are talking with others among the Village and beyond." Gitchie began.

Blou was not convinced and sat still with her arms crossed.

Abequa decided to add her thoughts "Honorable faerie sprite, we need your assistance. We fear that for the sake of the newborns, Mistress Marji, and us all, we shall need your help."

Blou sighed, rather dramatically, then told them, "It is rather simple, really. I can sting them all with my venom, they will sleep for a day, and then as they awaken we shall tell them all it is forbidden to discuss in any manner the House and its secrets."

Gitchie asked her why her venom had anything to do with this.

"Why? My venom is not deadly. It merely makes one sleep. It also is a love potion that makes the subject want to please and also seems to make humans less anxious. I have witnessed this with Keevan. Is he not more agreeable of late? Is he not more confident and happier than when we first met him?"

"We should ask the master and mistress first," cautioned Myster. "They are the ones to make this decision. But also does Blouette know how long it will last?"

"It lasts a lifetime."

Marcus was sitting at his desk, but his chair was turned around to face the window. He was actually reading a text on his phone. It was from James, who was concerned about Fern. Apparently, she was very interested in a young man and had been telling him about strange happenings on the island. James had said that he had tried to fend off interest, but since Halloween was around the corner, he felt that kids would try to see whether or not the stories were true. He had an idea that might work.

Marcus replied back, "Good idea! That was quick thinking. I'll give you the money to set up a haunted ride through town. My dad will join in and maybe he'll have a surprise up his sleeve. We have a month to get things ready."

When Marcus swiveled his chair around, he was thinking of how James had become much like an assistant. The young man was proving his loyalty more and more. Marcus then felt eyes looking at him, so he looked up to see the cat, the brownies, and Blou were all staring at him.

He cleared his throat before asking, "Is there something wrong?"

After hearing what they had to say, Marcus was uncertain of how ethical it was to have Blou inject the catering crew with venom. Still, he thought, they would get a good night's sleep and nothing bad would happen. If this would help assure her family's safety, then he decided to go along with it. The queen had assured them that the potion would last a very long time. It would also set up a pattern of thinking and behavior that would become good habits. Myster and Sarisha had also agreed. Now all they had to do was ... do it. When Marji heard of the plan, thought to herself, I should have some of that venom myself to use later. I wonder if Blouette would give her a tiny vial of it.

The weather was not cooperating. The sunny warm days had suddenly turned quite cold. The crew could no longer sleep in the medieval-looking tent at night. James had suggested the barn, but Gitchie made the decision that they should venture downstairs into the cellar to see what the house had for them down there.

While Daisy was making cookies (she was getting better at this), Gayle, Bethany, and Marcus cautiously went down into the cellar. James did not go because he was busy with a project in town and had a meeting with Mrs. and Mr. Bradley. Keevan also declined to go because he was reading! He had taken an interest in Audran's journals. For some reason the cellar-goers were all nervous. Daisy had told them of finding the weird talking books down there. Marcus was remembering all the things stored on shelves. Then he remembered the wine and decided that he should investigate. What they found astounded them all. There was a source of light down in the cellar that could not be clearly defined. Somehow the walls glowed, and giant, chrysalis-shaped lanterns were hung in every corner of the first space they encountered. Gone were the rows of shelving with wrapped clothing and food supplies (they had been recycled by the house). A nice couch sectional wound itself about the room, which gave it the feeling of a college dorm space set up for multiple users. Bethany and Gayle plopped down on the couch, pronouncing it nice and comfy. An archway led to another area divided by one wall. Each small room held a bunk with a bureau beneath it. There were two windows, but upon closer inspection they turned out to be photographs with a luminous quality to them so that the light within changed as the day progressed. Gayle said excitedly that they would go dark at night and light up again with the sunrise. Each girl seemed delighted with this, Bethany choosing a view of the Barn while Gayle chose the open sea toward the east. The room design was an efficient use of space. Should either houseguest need privacy, a heavy curtain could be drawn across the entrance. One other plus consisted of an intercom link system so that Gitchie, or anyone, could message either girl should the need arise. The girls linked the system to their smart phones, entering their passwords. Marcus thought the entire thing was ingenious. Furthest back was a slightly larger room, with an oak door, that held the huge wine rack, but this now had a padlock on it. Another bunk was here, again slightly larger and longer (for James was nearly six feet tall), a larger workspace, and a monitor/wall screen (that Marcus wanted for himself!). James had his own shower unit that looked like it had come from an RV. When the girls exclaimed that they should have a shower too, Marcus explained that the one on the first floor of the house could be shared by the girls. He warned that too much water use would drain the well.

Then Bethany squealed. "Oh my gosh, I just got an email that you've given us a huge gift certificate! Can we borrow the Jeep to go today? I need a warmer jacket, and all of Gayle's stuff was stolen last week while we were waiting for the ferry."

"I'll drive," said Marcus. "Maybe Daisy can come along with you ladies." Privately, he wondered why there was no space for Fern in the newly renovated quarters. That did not bode well. He hoped that Fern would be here tonight because they planned to have them all bitten by the sprite!

Daisy, indeed, did want to go shopping in Freeport, which led to going for lunch and then a movie at the theater. Everyone was exhausted, including Marcus, when they returned. He had ordered pizza, which they picked up at Zach's Store on their way through town. Marcus felt like he had never been in a vehicle with so much non-stop chatter. But he didn't regret this day at all. It gave them a chance to have some normalcy before the big events, which, he felt, were sure to come. They had several holiday catering dates ahead, the Haunted Halloween Tour (which they were catering with cookies and cider), and Thanksgiving *and* Christmas were coming. Marcus put a note in his phone to order two turkeys from Two Coves Farm this year. One was for Sarisha Chandi. Ellora and Keevan had agreed to work on the weekends to help out. Luke and Daisy were too young to work, but they could help decorate. Maemaegwin had been making wonderful garlands and twisted vine creations for all of the events. Her mother told them she was excited to be considered important and wanted to prove herself. Marji assured her that even though she was tiny, they did consider her part of their family.

After dinner, everyone, including the brownies, the sprite, Myster, and Kassa were gathered in the family room. Some sat on the floor, while others were on the couch. A blue fire burned merrily in the fireplace. They were watching *The Hobbit*, again, as it was Luke's choice because it was near his birthday. At the end of the movie, Blouette went up behind the catering crew, and gently stung them one by one, injecting each with the right amount of venom. As they grew drowsy they all trouped downstairs. Marji assured them the couch bed had been turned down for Fern. She felt sorry for her. Blou had injected her with a "forgetting venom" which would make her forget everything about the magik of the house. This dinner had been a goodbye for Fern, because she had announced she was leaving to go live with her boyfriend. That was why the house had not made a room for her down in the cellar, Marcus thought, somehow it knew she would not become a trusted part of the family.

A SAYING GOODBYE

As the days became more and more cold, the leaves left the trees, and the barn readied itself for winter, as did the house. Various family members were busy with their plans for Samhain, Sarisha noted. A lot was going on, which was exciting but also worrying. Although Marji was feeling much better, she knew there had been a lot of magik around her unborn. Marcus had put the sailboat up for the winter, bikes had been put away, and in two days it would be Halloween. The dragon knew what that could mean, but she had not told anyone. She knew the forces of evil that could be unleashed on All Hallows Eve, the half second before one day ended and another began. It was when all time stopped so the portals would converge and open. During that time, the Others would most likely strike. The full moon would make the tide very high, which was good, for the wizards of the sea would not allow anything to access their portal under the island. None of the family knew about this second portal. She was certain even the Others did not know. But should they find out, it would spell disaster for the land dwellers, for the sea beings might bring a tsunami to wipe out the invaders, with no regard for the innocent. She did not wish to lose this human family. She had known many humans in her lifetime, but these were special. In this moment, she received reassurance from an unlikely ally, the beautiful blue sphere that now dwelled with her. Sarisha had made sure that everyone forgot about the eternal entity that Aaron Audran had saved. It made itself known only to the dragon now. Sarisha felt confident that with its aid she could help repel any forces that got past the house. She did not know how the Others had kidnapped Aborath so long ago. Somehow they had been lucky to find their way to Herstamonix through the vortex. John of Gaunt would not prevail this time. Queen Merritt had told them all she knew- about the powers of the infrit, the jinn, and the identity of his master. She also told the dragon of the fatal flaw in their plans: Since the queen had memorized all their names, now Sarisha Chandi also knew their true names. She could wipe them from Terra using blue magik, but only in defense. Merritt, Blouette, Aborath, and Golden would not be there to help, though. They had made plans to travel back to Faerieland.

Golden knew this human girl loved her, but she also had the instinctual knowledge that Daisy must be free to have her own life. The human girl acted as if she were slightly dazed every day. Blou had said it was the venom. Golden snuggled with the girl as she slept by the fire. They'd had a busy day in the village at the Haunted Tour, the Wiggly-Wriggly Lunch, and the evening bonfire. They had seen for the first time, the haunted form of Dingley on the hilltop. It had been a very exciting moment. Now, it was nearly eleven o'clock, and almost everyone was asleep. Quietly Golden touched her nicorn to the girl's forehead. Daisy shook her head as if to say "no" in her sleep. Golden tried again. This time the girl did not struggle. Marji and Marcus had allowed Daisy one more night with her darling Lunicorn. Maemaegwin had made a tiny woven replica of Golden for Daisy to have for her own. The toy was now held tightly in her arms.

"It is time," Queen Merritt softly told her. "We must be there by the appointed time or we shall miss the opening."

Golden nodded in response. Blouette and the queen rode on her back as they went out of the house by the kitchen doors, which slid open for them. Myster was waiting on the porch railing.

"Doth thee wish to join us or wilt thou remain with thy humans?" the queen asked him, but she felt she knew the answer.

"If I am allowed, I shall accompany thee on your walk, but I shall remain here in Terra, where I will live out my final days as I began them," the cat replied, with some sorrow in his tone.

The queen nodded her head, and Blouette made room for him to perch on Golden. As they walked toward the meadow, Aborath greeted them. Myster jumped down, and then up onto the male unicorn to ride the rest of the way with him. It was a solemn walk of honor. Kassa and his regiment were waiting for them, as were the eagle and her two younglings. More friends came quietly out of the bushes, some seeking to say goodbye and some wishing to join. They were all waiting for something, not quite knowing what would be coming. Brass was especially full of sorrow. He had asked the queen to remain with him. He had vowed to become her king. But she had gently told him her faeries needed her.

As they waited together, a white fog began to form on the hilltop near a grave marker. Slowly, the apparition of Dingley came into view. He did not talk. But he looked as if he were trying to communicate some words of warning. He kept pointing to the sky. Back at the house, the barn shielding came on. Out to sea, several sea beings abruptly rose out of the water. They were all armed, some with spears, some with nets, and one held a trident that glowed blue. They were all looking in toward the east at the full moon.

Kassa knew to be vigilant in all directions. He sent his best scouts out. He enlisted a few other birds, like the mighty osprey, to keep watch on the edge by the shore. They heard it before they saw it. A low flying helicopter, armed with weapons, flew from the east, the moonshine glinting off any chrome it came in contact with. Keevan came out from the bushes, talking into the box in his hand and lighting his sword. He held the sword up high, its blue light pulsing, becoming a beacon for the army he had raised: all the forest folk and the barnies, even a tusked friend or two, being ridden by Brayle and Ket. Nearby, as always, Grunge rode Jack.

Keevan's voice boomed out across the hill, for the walkie-talkie had been upgraded into a megaphone. "Wait for my signal! You all know who we face! No evil shall come to this island!"

Many voices answered his as the helicopter neared and then veered off to make a circle around the island. Keevan took something out of his pocket and began to read, loudly, over the speaker. It was an ancient poem, hidden inside the golden pin that Sarisha had given him. Keevan had opened the locket to find the ancient paper. He had asked Gitchie what the words meant, then researched more while reading Audran's journal. It took him nearly three weeks, but he finally realized it was a spell written in ancient Sanskrit. Keevan thought it would be more powerful if read by many voices at once. He had also figured out how to accomplish this. He had Gitchie make some copies, then he taught the words to those who could not read. And they taught it to their folk, not saying the last word until this night. He knew that by now, Ellora was at home up in the widow's walk reciting the exact words. Luke was hidden in the cave (he was the only human small enough to fit inside), also with a copy of the spell. Queen Merritt knew the words by heart. She took her place at a compass point. Aborath was on the southern end, with Golden opposite him. Blouette and Myster together took the western point. Although very small, the queen looked calm and confident. Luke's wizard wind began to blow, gently at first, and then a stronger wind began to flow down from the upper air mass where crystals form into snow.

A blast came from the helicopter, and near the hilltop a tree burst into flames, but no one ran away. Instead, they grew angrier at the death of the old tree. How many more innocent things would die because of the Others? Keevan was mad, but then he felt a voice in his head speak calming words to him: *Strike not! The timing is everything! We will tell you when! Don't lose your cool!*

He thought it was Ellora or Luke, but it sounded like two voices at once.

Keevan centered himself, as Gideon had taught him. They had to speak the spell before 12:01 post-midnight to stop the vortex from opening so they could destroy the helicopter with the Others on board. Keevan only hoped they could take down as many as they could. It was 11:50. Then he heard the voices again: *Now! Say it now!*

Keevan raised his blue flaming sword for a second time. That was the signal for all the voices on the hilltop to begin chanting the same words, repeating them over and over.

"We, the people of Navaratna, know our hearts are pure, our minds are our own. We seek the freedom and health of our souls and those of our descendants in perpetuity, so say we all!"

Suddenly, the helicopter stopped in midflight over the ocean, right at the compass point of east. Not one thing on the machine moved. He didn't know how long it would last. Audran's vision, written in the last journal, had been a bit vague on that crucial detail. Keevan had worried over that for the past two weeks.

Luke's wizard wind grew in strength until it became a controlled tornado that whipped the helicopter higher into the air. It had to be farther away from the island so no one would get hurt from flying parts and pieces. Then Sarisha emerged from the hidden cave and grew in size to match the chopper. She blasted it with a mighty blue flame. Surprisingly, the sea being with the trident added his own blast of blue flame. The helicopter blew into a million pieces, scattering over the waves.

A great cheer came from many voices, but Aborath did not look happy. His gaze went out over the water. All the sea beings also turned toward the south, from whence came another helicopter, but it was much smaller and looked a lot less threatening. Something was dangling from ropes under it. The ones with long sight could see a small mare was buckled into a harness, and she was nearly scared out of her wits. She began to neigh and almost scream as she saw land approaching. Kassa took flight to investigate, but he was turned back by the force of the helicopter blades. The wind did not help, either. No one knew quite what to do. The helicopter hesitated, then, as slowly as it could, it came forward and dropped in the sky until the horse's hooves nearly touched water. They could see there was only one pilot in the cockpit. He was having trouble disengaging the harness! He couldn't fly the thing and unlock the cable at the same time. The dragon came to the rescue. She flew across to the rope attached to the horse and severed it with a huge bite as she held onto the dangling ropes. As soon as the weight was off, the chopper lurched sideways and upward. It began to fly out of control, spiraling out toward the sea. They saw the pilot eject just before it plunged into the water and broke up on impact. The sea being motioned with his arm to two of his lieutenants, who dove into the water to rescue the pilot. Once that was done, all the sea beings dove into the sea. The waters calmed down. They would not be seen again for a very long time.

The pilot was Richard Lambert! He was unresponsive. They laid him on the very end of the wharf jutting out into the water. The house shielding would not allow him to be brought up into the meadow. Lots of creatures were milling around, not knowing quite what to do. Luke had sent a telepathic message to Ellora about what happened. She came running down the path to see what was going on. The little mare was fine, but rattled and scared. Aborath did his best to calm her. After a few minutes it was discovered that she was his daughter, one of the wild ones the Others could not tame. Brayle and Ket knew how to calm her down. They sat astride her back, singing softly to her in their native language.

Sarisha spoke to them all. "Friends, the time for the vortex opening is near. Some of you will enter the Lands of Faerie with the queen. Some of you will travel to Herstamonix. You must join near the cave."

Luke and Keevan stood by, watching, along with a few barnies. Some of them were leaving with the queen. Two tusked suidae were also joining her. As the magik hour grew close, they could hear the hole in the stone widen with a grinding, screeching sound. Then abruptly, the hole shrunk, only to reappear much, much bigger! It was like an eye opening up, wide enough so that Aborath was able to stride through. Golden had one last look for the children she loved, and actually spoke to them for the first time!

"Miss Daisy!" was all she said, but it was enough, they understood what she meant and how she felt. She would miss the little Daisy who had been her loving friend.

At the last possible moment, a raven and a young eagle flew with them into the unknown world of Herstamonix. The portal divided. Each tunnel was showing the distinct color of each world. Sarisha thought she glimpsed some of her kind near the portal, the yellow sky of Herstamonix. She knew that there were posted guards now on every Hallows Time. Some were there to keep ghosts and spirits from entering, some were simply wanting some excitement. She saw one of the golden-haired beings raise a hand in greeting, hands splayed open over her heart.

"Mother!" Sarisha shouted. Her voice held a mixture of happiness and sorrow. Then the vortex closed. Tears formed in her eyes. She let them drop into the soil. They burrowed down into the rocks, following a slim vein of gold, then slowed to a stop by the eye of the portal. When it next opened her tears would flow into Herstamonix and find their way home. She went back to her Terran home, the cavern behind the house.

The Coast Guard showed up because Keevan had called 911. They simply had not known what to do for the pilot, otherwise known as Jinn. He was unhurt, yet unconscious. All they could tell the reporting officer was they had seen the two helicopters break apart in the ocean during their Halloween bonfire on the island. When questioned, the boys had hemmed and hedged their answers until the officer said, "Fine, I'll need all of you to take an alcohol test."

Luke had explained that it was his birthday and the only others there were a large Maine coon cat and their trained raven, Kassa. Everyone at their house was asleep. To prove it they had returned home to a house full of snoring adults of varying ages who would not awaken even if they were shaken. (It took hours for them to feel fully awake.) The coastal paramedics left with the unconscious John Doe. As they did so, one of them thought he saw a white figure up on the hilltop.

Unknown to them all, a letter had arrived at the post office that partially explained why Lambert had flown the small helicopter across a vast stretch of ocean to deliver a small horse to her father. But until they read it, they had no idea why this had happened. The next morning, Grandpa Bradley brought the letter for them to read while they were about to have breakfast. Abequa's tea was warm and soothing for the slight headaches the adults all had. The children were the only ones unaffected by the previous night's antics. The letter was postmarked from Drake's Island, England, and addressed to "Occupants of the House, Wizard friends of the Unicorn, and Queen Merritt, Dingley Island, the House by the Meadow." Acting nonchalant, they ate their pancakes, but as soon a Grandpa left, they ripped the envelope open to read it. But first, the parents wanted some answers.

Keevan said, guiltily, "I guess you want an explanation."

Marji and Marcus certainly did. As the boys and Ellora rushed over one another's words in order to tell their parents what, why, and when—mostly the reason why they had not included them in their plans. Marcus could not but admire how they had put the clues together, formed a plan, enlisted the aid of other friends and had won the day somehow.

A HARSH DECISION

The house and the barn seemed a little empty. Daisy cried herself to sleep during the day after she found out that Golden was really gone. They had told her the queen was leaving along with the unicorns, but Daisy had not truly believed. No more Blou and her sarcastic but insightful comments. No more queen and no more worry about anyone seeing a unicorn by the moonlight. Everyone was a little bit sad. Sari especially felt the weight of missing them, as she had missed so many in the past. Yet she looked forward to the future people she would meet.

It was now November and the season of holiday events were well underway. Luke felt he needed to return to the hilltop. He stood by the burned tree. He knew that one of Kassa's regiment had followed him, just in case. Gitchie had been the one to put that plan into motion. Each human had a raven guard. Luke wondered where Rahven had gone. Many of the animals were also gone, either into hibernation or migration. He found himself wishing for spring, even before the first snowfall. He decided to go back home. The raven called out, so Luke gave him a signal, and his new black friend settled down on his shoulder.

"Hi, I have decided to call you Tripp. Winter's coming," he said cheerfully. He had not had any visions about it. But that could be a good thing.

The letter written by Richard Lambert:

I am not certain whether or not you know who the Others are (all of them are named John or Jean), or perhaps you do know, since you have a dragon fighting for you. Please let me explain who I am. Once I, too, was a warrior fighting a great war for a master so incredible that we could barely compre-hend him. We were not born, we were made, not in a creative sense but in a necessary sense. Many of us were lost in the bat-tles. I was imprisoned within a blue diamond and left upon this world, buried deep within the crust. Apparently, there are laws that even gods must obey.

Unknowingly, a sly and lucky merchant was given a spe-cial tool that he used to break my diamond into many pieces. I was released and had to serve this new master. I have done so for over five hundred years. The Others desire these blue dia-mond pieces, which have magik powers to extend life. That is why they collect magikal things, to drain them of their power. Jean-Baptiste Tavernier, now known as Lord Tavernier, but was formerly Sir Francis Drake, the Pirate Yates, Honorable John Lansing, and Ambrose Joseph Small, to name a few. He was all these men through use of my magik. As I used up my powers doing Tavernier's bidding, I came across you and your dragon. I must say now, I regret my involvement in that. I don't know why this has happened but after that event I found that I was becoming human! The last conjoining reverted to me and I took on the life of Richard Lambert, orphan and assistant to a very rich and power-hungry Tavernier. Please believe me that your magikal island is not immune to his influences.

To prove my good intentions, for I wish to join your forces. I know this may seem incredible and you have every right to be wary of me. Here is the only way I could show you my good intentions by saving the mare that they plan to use in place of Aborath. For you see they had been bleeding him by drinking his blood on every new moon. I will take her to Bermuda by helicopter, in a safety harness. She is wild but highly intelligent. I told her I was bringing her to her father, and I believe she understood me!

I shall be dropping her off along the shore of your island. I am using the last of my powers to keep her safe. Her name is Resilience. I call her Encey. I shall take up residence under an assumed name for I, too, wish to hide away in Maine. Here is my email address. I have never used it and only you will know the name. BewaretheJeans@gmail.com. I wish to begin atoning for the things I have done over the centuries. I feel I can be of some help to humanity.

Sincerely,
Richard Lambert

THE COURT OF THE FAERIE

The astonishment at the Balaktrian Court was unnerving. All serving this day were quick to spread the word: the kidnapped queen had returned with Aborath and another creature they were told was Axoparia! The Lunicorn looked like no other creature that anyone had ever seen. Queen Merritt was made to wait. She began tapping her foot with increasing annoyance, which was gradually turning to anger. Aborath's nicorn was glowing and some greenery that had been burnt brown was already regaining its green colors. Golden, ever curious, was sniffing and looking at and under everything. She was also hungry. Fairly soon after their arrival a small luncheon had been served, which was very meager. The food was not delicious. If this was the best Balaktria could serve, it was an embarrassment, Merritt thought. Queen Marigold was nowhere to be seen, but her king was silently sitting on the smaller throne. Queen Merritt's king was also absent. But she knew he must be dead, for he would have never stopped looking for her. His devotion was well-known. Suddenly, a twinkling of bells announced the arrival of the queen. Her captain arrived first, and, as they all took their places, they bowed to the "old" queen.

"Mother!" a young voice called out. Marigold spoke as she strode forward. Her mother held out her arms to grasp her daughter in a hug. All the other sprites were her daughters, too, but the queen only truly loves one daughter, the one who will replace her. It would be against protocol for any queen to acknowledge any others, for that would send a mixed signal that perhaps the chosen daughter was not fit to rule. The two queens hugged one another, and then stepped back. The rare show of affection could only be brief. Merritt reached up and removed her own crown to place it upon her daughter's head. It fit perfectly.

Marigold quietly said, "We shall talk later. But now I must do the duty that I was voted to do." She turned to address the assembled court. She snapped her fingers and her guards formed behind her. She pointed at her ex-captain. "Take her into custody!" Strong hands grabbed Blouette before she could fly away and calmly but forcefully placed her in the grievance circle in the middle of the room. Once there, Marigold activated a ring that arose from the floor, surrounding Blouette to keep her in place.

In a stern tone Marigold announced, "Captain of the guards, sister to me, Blouette, thou art charged with *treason* for leaving your post on the night of the abduction of my mother, your queen!" The anger in her voice was felt by all in the room. Blou, for her part, stood with her head down, her wings drooped, and her tail looked lifeless.

"Have you nothing to say for yourself?" asked the older queen. She knew some of the reason, having had a long talk with the cat who was once her foe.

"Only that the choice had to be made so that this world would be safe." Blouette's fiery spirit blossomed for one moment, then faded as the younger queen spoke.

"You, then, admit guilt to this charge?" questioned Marigold.

"Yes," Blou replied in a sad, quiet voice.

Queen Marigold continued. "As in olden times, as it is today and will be tomorrow, we pay tribute and give honor to the old laws. Blouette, one-time captain of the guard sisters, is found guilty of treason to the Queendom of Balaktria. Let it be known that we are witness!" She gestured for all of her guard to stand behind her, each one stating her name as she did so. Umbria, Bree, Bray, Grayne, Umbriathe, Maighread, and, lastly, the new captain, Izelay.

"May I have the gift of remembrance?" desperately asked Blou.

They all hovered for a moment, tails uplifted with a closed hand over their hearts. Slowly, as one, all their tails dropped downward. When all the guards of the new queen alighted upon the grassy floor, they spun around to show their backs to Blou. Everyone in the court turned their backs to her. She was lucky to be shunned, not stabbed to death. She did not feel lucky. What would she do now? Where could she go? The land of Balaktria would be closed to her. The vortex portal would open in one year's time, but that was a long time to wait. Golden came over to nuzzle her, but she barely responded. He wings felt glued shut.

Aborath let it be known that Blouette had been very brave while rescuing the queen. He let it be known that he was not happy at her treatment. Golden let out her ear-splitting whinny and stomped her hooves. Aborath joined in the hoof stamping. Queen Merritt reached up to touch their muzzles. Then she spoke.

"As a queen, I beg forgiveness for the traitor! She was led astray by an even worse criminal, Raid. It was he who committed the larger crime. He is still in the land of Terra. Let Blouette return to join with him. For even traitors can be useful. It is not *our way* to punish those that help us. I know—she raised one hand as many voices began to sputter—I know the law! But are we so rigid in our laws that we cannot see the larger truth?"

At the end of a long and heated debate, it was decided that the portal would be opened so that Blouette could return to Terra. It was not fair, but it was the best Merritt could do. She was no longer the reigning queen. Although she had great honor and respect, her words were not law. She had already rescinded her name and announced that she would answer to the name "Merry" from now on.

Not all of her guard sisters were present at the opening of the portal. Aborath was to use the magik in his nicorn to call forth the vortex. Merritt, now Merry, had hugged her goodbye in a rare show of emotion.

She whispered to Blou, "Please tell Brass, I shall never forget him. I hope to return one day. I hope he will wait for me." Golden nuzzled her. Izelay was there, most likely to make certain she did leave the queendom. Little did Blou know that some of the males were requesting that she, Blou, be turned over for training exercise, to be part of a never-ending chase and capture. Izelay hotly refused. How dare they? It was *their* captain that had led her sister astray.

A regiment of males flew in, they sounded like a pack of Herstamonix hyenas! Captain Izelay called her sisters, who appeared instantly to the summons. They began to hotly argue. Blouette was so sad and dismayed at their actions. Never had the warriors of her land been at one another's throats!

"Aborath, quickly! I am ready!" Blou said to him. Her wings were outspread, and as the vortex opened, she quickly reached down to grasp a handful of sand and dirt near the cave opening. She would take a piece of her homeland with her. She shoved the fistful into her grabsack. And then she was gone.

The End

LIST OF CHARACTERS

Ellora (Ell) Charlotte Donovan: Soon to be sixteen, has red hair and blue eyes that are slightly lavender. She has magikal powers that are manifesting themselves; powers of persuasion, empathy, telepathy and telekinesis. She is very kind but in many ways a teenager coming to grips with growing up.

Luken (Luke) Aaron Donovan: Eight years old, has yellow hair with deep purple-blue eyes, is showing magikal powers at his young age of eight; telepathy, fire-wielding, and storm-making. He could be the Wizard of the prophecy. He is able to create a 'Wizard Wind' at a very young age. This is often useful when you wish to get rid of an adversary. He also has 'Vulcan' hearing.

Marjorie (Marji) Ellen Dorr Donovan-Bradley: Reincarnation of an ancient Guardian of the Temple of the Goddess, mother of Ellora & Luke. Owner of *Island Catering* married her college sweetheart, Jeremiah Donovan and then her childhood friend, Marcus Bradley.

Jeremiah Donovan III: Father of Ellora & Luke, Owner/Designer of *Donovan Boat Designs*, died in a speedboat accident.

Marcus Drake Bradley: Co-Owner of *Dingley Island Boats*, married his college sweetheart, Cynthia Day Hamilton, father of Daisy Bradley and Keevan Bradley. Then he married his childhood friend (and secret love) Marji.

Cynthia Day Hamilton-Bradley: Famous country music singer/song-writer, loved the high life. Her fast lifestyle and singing career was cut short by the same speedboat accident that claimed Jere's life. Mother of Daisy Day Bradley, Keevan David Bradley. She had her blue 'sap-phire' earrings made into a necklace for her daughter, not knowing how valuable they were.

Keevan David Bradley: Age 13, friends with Asinwin, a House Brownie. Keevan loves the outdoors and his dog, Boris.

Daisy Day Bradley: Age 9, shows some signs of having magik, falls in love with the Lunicorn named Golden. Daisy's mind is not able to cope with all that has happened; her Mother's death, the magi-kal things that are happening, and she is slowly losing her sense of reality.

Charlotte Ellen Drake-Dorr: Blue Guardian, the Village Librarian, lover of animals, has a way with plants and gardening. She gave her fancy blue gem ring to her eldest granddaughter. Her essence lives on in the Sanctuary within the Library of the House. Mother of Marji Ellen Dorr and Elias Alexzander Dorr. She frequently talks with Ellora through use of their family's magik mirror.

Elias Alexzander Dorr: Minister and musician, he was given a beau-tiful piano by the House. Elias tries to visit his family once a year because the noises inside his head become too much for him to han-dle. He hears the voices of people of the past but doesn't know who they are. He is also afraid to tell anyone, so he writes about them in his songs which are more like ballads.

Charles William Dorr: Brown Wizard, Captain of Axoparia, an award-winning sailboat. He was a reincarnation of an ancient Guardian. Father of Marji and Elias Dorr. He imbued the sailboat with love and protection to keep safe whomever sailed her.

Doctor Isaac Joseph Drake: Father of Dingley and Katherine. His essence lives within the Sanctuary of the House. He was one of the first to connect with Ellora when she turned the magik mirror on. His heart broke when his only son died battling the Others. He felt guilty over the death of the House Brownie, Pilchie. He had many arguments with his son about the upcoming battle. Isaac felt it was too risky.

Victoria Underwood Drake: Shows magikal talent with flowers, roses specifically, but suppresses it. Her essence lives within the Sanctuary within the Library. Victoria was the mother of Dingley and Katherine Drake. She too, through her Mother's lineage is a descendant of the Von Grimms. Dr. Isaac was her second husband.

Dingley Isaac Drake: Thought he was the Wizard of the prophecy, had purple eyes, was Captain of the secret Wizard school- everyone who met him grew to love him. He lost his life battling the Others. He had use of a blue sphere of plasma/power that he brought forth with an incantation he found in an ancient scroll. Best friend of Pilchie, the House Brownie.

Katherine Victoria Drake: Sister to Dingley. She has mesmerizing green eyes. A lover of animals. She became the caretaker of the Library and eventually the House Mistress. Married Doctor Isaac Solomon Day. Mother of Mathias Day.

The Bradleys: They lived down the road, closer to the Village. They are on the Town Council and run the Post Office & General Store. Jonathan Henry Bradley and Adeline Augusta Drake, both born in Maine. Addie knows the house is haunted from her childhood experiences. Parents of Marcus and his sister, Augusta Bouvier Bradley (she is invited to the wedding but could not attend).

Island Catering Crew: The four members of the crew that Marjorie relies on the most and always work for her even though they have other part time jobs; James White, Bethany and Gayle Gobspeak (twins, also granddaughters of the town Witch, Greta Gobspeak) and Fern.

James Day White: does not know he is the illegitimate son of Cynthia Hamilton-Bradley, went to school to be a Chef, works for Island Catering and attends a Karate class in town.

Gideon Garrett: Karate Sensei. His wife, Amye, is pregnant.

Greta Gobspeak: Town Doula. Daughter of Muriel Gobspeak, a Brown Witch.

CHARACTERS THAT ARE NOT HUMAN

Brownie Family: Acrobatic yet wingless Faeries that live within the Library to help care for the House. Some past masters have forbidden them to leave the House. They love to use modern technology and have complete access to the Library computer. They have a funny way of taking Humans literally so one must be careful when using sarcasm or humor around them. They speak in a sing-song manner that can be annoying. They dress in rags, foraging whatever leftover materials have been tossed out by the Mistresses (old curtain, potholders, cloth napkins etc.) Daisy gave them her Barbie and Ken doll clothes.

They chose to flee Balaktria. Each group tends to take on attributes of the place where they thrive. Barnies are strong. House Brownies are smart. Forest brownies patrol the island.

Pilchie: Friend of Dingley but sworn to obey the Master Isaac, who told him to keep his son safe or to never return. The Grandfather of Gitchie. Pilchie's wife was Namewin.

Gitchie: Current Head Brownie, always tries to do what Master Marcus tells him yet sometimes goes too far. He is bound to serve the Master and also the House, which can come into conflict. Should that happen, serving the best interests of the House always prevails. Their love of technology can also bring misfortune as his wife and children learn about Terra and 'the rest of the world'.

Abequa: His wife, brews an excellent tea, Arctium Cynareae, which enhances health and prolongs life. She has knowledge of herbology. Whenever she needs to be in the forest, she wears armor.

Aisinwin: Their son, loves to ride Polly, the smallest dog in the current Household, befriends Keevan, loves animals and is quite emotional about their safety He became an apprentice to the Forest Brownies.

Maemaegwin: Gitchie and Abequa's daughter, hardly ever speaks but has a knack of finding the correct scroll to prove a point or to give the correct password. She is tiny and cannot go outdoors for her own safety.

Barnies: A large group of wingless faeries that live in the barn and help with the animals. They are very strong for their small size. They wear the hides and skins of animals they have found perished in the woods. They eat whatever they can find in the nearby woods, chicken eggs, fungi and mushrooms, cornmeal and worms.

Dawson Barn Clan:
> **Mulch:** An Elder, brother to Brayle.
> **Belle & Brayle:** Elders of the Barn.
> **Playne:** Sister to Belle
> **Mulch:** Mate to Playne
> **Brass:** Huge Barnie that always seems to be able to do most anything. Friend of Queen Merritt.
> **Ket:** Rides the goat Mama
> **Yoke & Haul:** Also very strong but none communicative.
> **Grunge:** Always rides the rabbit, Jack.

Forest Brownies: Live outside and are almost never seen by Humans. Should someone need their help they must ask, politely, at a conclave. They like to make things especially out of spider silk, moss, branches and wool. They can disappear entirely if the need arises. Each Clan takes a moon's turn watching for the Light in the Barn.

Eukan Clan:

Euka: A recently retired Watcher.

Oomy: On his first watch he sees the Light.

Chitin: The best Forester in the Clan

Zoosporia: Leader of the Clan.

Blouette or Blou: A strong willed, winged Sprite, Guard Sister to Princess Marigold. She is in love with Raid, a Court Spy. She is critical of other Faerie creatures and quite sarcastic. She does not want to admit when she does things that are wrong- not taking responsibility for her actions. She is very protective of Golden, the lunicorn.

Myster/Audran: A large Maine Coon cat, once a wise and powerful Wizard who has lived a very long time. He has had contact with the Others in the past. When Dingley drove the magikal blue sphere into the hilltop, some of the magik spilled over, came into contact with Audran. Dingley wished the magik to not harm him. So Audran was changed into his original form, which was a cat, which somehow merged with the unicorn at the same time.

Golden the Lunicorn: In the past she was a Unicorn, Axoparia. She was affected by the same magik that changed Audran. She was turned into a golden bottle. Her whinny sounds like scratching on a chalkboard combined with a pterodactyl.

Mr. O'Dran: The Schoolmaster of the Village school. Once a trusted member of the community. He disappeared the night of the storm and the death of the seven young persons under his tutelage. In secret he was the wizard Audran who built the Fortress and the original Tower, which is hidden from outsiders.

Sarisha Chandi: The Dragon also known as the Anujan, little sister to the other dragons that live in Herstamonix. She is an eternal entity that has taken an interest in Humans and has chosen to live at the Fortress, caring for the magikal artifacts that are hidden within the cavern/cave where she lives. She is obsessed with lost items or things she deems that no one is taking care of. Some of her things are lost items from antiquity that are very valuable. She is a shape shifter that has hands and feet. She can teleport and is telepathic.

Axoparia the Unicorn: Part of the Court of Queen Merritt. Her magik helped Balaktria thrive. She went on the quest with Dingley to rid Terra of the Others and to take revenge upon them for kidnapping her mate, Aborath. The sailboat built by Charlie Dorr is named after her.

Aborath: A prisoner of the House of Ghent (also known as the Others). The Lord John of Ghent stole the fabulous Unicorn from the world of Herstamonix in a daring raid. His nicorn was cut off and ground it into a powder. It then was offered to the Prince, but it gained him nothing. Losing his nicorn nearly made Aborath lose his mind. He was brought to Drake's Island off the southern coast of Britain. The Others hoped to mate the Unicorn and succeeded with one filly, Resilience, born to Aborath and a Lipizzaner mare named Barba.

Resilience: Sire was Aborath, Dam was a mare named Barba. She is very fast but also wild.

Queen Merritt: Reigned Balaktria in Faerieland for a long time. She did not trust Audran. She sent Raid in secret to follow the Wizard and the boy, Dingley. She was kidnapped during the Battle of Dingley because somehow the vortex portal was left open, enabling two of the Others to gain access. They took the Queen after killing her King. She still wears her crown which has in it a huge white diamond, which is not the gem with power. One of the sapphires is really a rare blue diamond. It is the true source of her magik. She must willingly take the crown off though, it cannot transfer its power any other way. She tried to trick the Others by offering up the diamond in exchange for her freedom. It almost worked.

The King: Each time the consort marries the Queen, he loses his personal name and becomes simply known as the King. Queen Merritt's King was murdered by Prince John of Ghent.

Princess/Queen Marigold: Angry leader of the Sprites, voted in by her people after her Mother is abducted by the Others.

Princess Marjoram: Still a baby. Infant Faeries do not have use of their wings. Her guards include six sisters and one brother, which has never happened before in Balaktria history.

Others: All named John or Jean, no one knows how many there are, but they seek to reclaim all the blue diamonds that were once part of a single 1001 carat gem. They have a powerful Jinn/Infrit that does their bidding except he cannot knowingly kill for them, but he can cause accidents that maim and harm.

    Jean Chameau: De facto leader.

    Jean Du Chardin

    John Fayen: In secret the founder of the Johnsonian Institute

    Jean Le Clerc

    Jean Du Temps

    Jean Surhon: In secret an evil infrit Genie

    Monsieur John Morgan

    Jean Philippe Rameau

Jinn: An entity that can ride the air on a flying carpet. He looks like a human/alien. Jinn is losing his power as the decades pass while he is forced to do the bidding of his master, Tavernier. He has the ability to enhance and extend life by allowing one soul to take over the body of another. But as the Jinn is using up his power the 'conjoining's' are not working. The latest attempt failed, and the conjoining merged the jinn with that of Tavernier's secretary, Richard Lambert.

Jean-Baptiste Tavernier: Lived many lives since he left his original body which was buried in Russia. Over the centuries he has taken over the lives of some famous people. (One of them was Sir Frances Drake). Tavernier is slowly losing his mind. He is now in the body of a very rich man in the world but is crazy and dangerous for he doesn't think of the possible consequences of his actions. He is known as Lord Tavernier, Earl of Lancaster.

The Queen's Guard: Umbria, Bree, Bray, Grayne, Umbriathe, Maighread, Captain Izelay.

Raid: A Spy, possible mate of Blou, possibly one of the red bottles on the fireplace mantle.

Boris: A large dog belongs to Keevan.

Molly: A medium sized dog, a past family member that disappeared, shepherd that seems to be able to understand language, belonged to Charlotte.

Polly: Little daschund that belongs to Marji, ridden by Aisinwin.

Rahven: Large white raven, Keeper of knowledge, Storyteller and Judge. No one can tell an untruth in his presence.

Honey: The Bay mare that is ridden by Rahven because he is old.

Eagle: Lived on Eagle Island, she joined the fight with the scarecrow and ultimately helped defeat it. Her mate was lost.

Jeremy the Field Mouse: First Witness to the Battle if Dingley. He forswore a truth telling of the events that happened that night. He is telepathic so was able to read the thoughts of everyone during the battle. Because his feet were burned by the ground fire after Dingley drove the magik back into the Earth, he cried out for help. Sarisha came to rescue him and brought him to the safety of the House. Katherine Drake nursed him back to health. But he was never the same afterwards and developed a twitch he could not control. His essence lives on within the Sanctuary of the Library. Friend to Audran.

Other types of Faeries:

Kelpies: Have shape shifting abilities in water and on land.

Pookas: Cause a lot of mischief. Often rides upon people's shoulders.

Merrow: Sea people or Saeries. One of them is named Moruadh.

Ballybogs: Love puddles.

Oakmen: Spring from trunks of cut down trees.

Sanders: A mysterious creature that lives in the sand.

Spriggans: They are like tall, willowy Shadow people. They are dangerous because just a few seconds in their shadow can kidnap your mind and bend your will. The effects can be long lasting.

Akamu: The Fire Faeries.

Brownies: Often live with humans and have abilities of seeming to be invisible. They can also send charms of forgetfulness but those fade in time.

PLACES

Palandine: Also known as the Temple, where Tavernier cheated the temple priest by giving him very little money for the 1001 carat blue diamond, claiming it was merely a sapphire. The Temple hosts a secret doorway/portal. Access to Palandine is now closed like the world of Chamavi.

Herstamonix: Also connected to Terra. Here live wild, hippy-like Pixies, Dinosaurs, Gnomes, Trolls, and other fantastic creatures. The platypus lived here but a pair escaped to Terra. Here the Dragons rule the land and the Saeries rule the Sea. It doorway is guarded 365 days, 5 hours, 48 minutes and 46 seconds each year. In fact, it is never unguarded so the Sentries must double up their shifts at the beginning and ending of each year so that no Others may enter.

Chamavi: Closed to everyone without permission. King Kornelius Khronus Alexzander rules there. Not much else is known about this world. Khronus is the twin of Veah, who chose to become a mortal of Terra, also known as Earth.

Ghent: Flanders, Belgium. Birthplace of John of Gaunt, a cunning Other with a dark destiny. He captured the Unicorn, Aborath and kept Queen Merritt prisoner. The name of John is cursed is Balaktria. He is one of the Others currently hibernating in Egypt.

The House Fortress: It is a giant computer, replicator and 3-D printer combined. It seems to be able to morph into whatever the family needs, adding rooms and staircases as required. It enables access to each compass point, the cellar is a strange place that can also turn into whatever needed. The House also has the final say in who becomes the Master and Mistress. Sometimes it does not like certain people. It did not like Cynthia nor was it very friendly to Addie.

The Barn: Has its own magik barrier that is automatic.

The Library: The heart and soul of the Fortress. Its purpose is to protect the magik inherent within the island. The barrier for the Barn is separate from the House and comes on automatically, which is a good indicator that trouble is near. The Library needs upgrades constantly. Its shelves are full of trinkets, books and scrolls from the past that have been collected by previous Masters. There is a magikal portrait hanging on the wall of Dingley Drake

The Ocean Saeries: help keep the islands safe also, due to their hatred of the Jinn and the Infrit. The only drawback is sometimes the tide is out. The Saerie or Merrows are Witches and Wizards of the Ocean. They have a lot of power that can rise up out of the water to attack the winds of the Infrit. Their leader is Oodoon.

The Sanctuary: A wondrous place, much like Heaven, some see it as a continuation of the Library, some view it as a vast garden. Past Wizards, Masters and Mistresses are within- you can only enter if you have died. Sometimes Rahven accompanies Spirits who have lost their way to the Sanctuary.

The Village: The northern part of Dingley Island, where many descendants of the original settlers of Harpswell live and work. It hosts a flower and Chapel and meeting House, Medical clinic, small Library, Post Office/general store, an Inn, a Cafe, working waterfront, gift shop, middle school and the historical museum in the old School for the Gifted.

MAGIK THINGS

Sailboat Axoparia: Built entirely by Charles Dorr. He won an award for its design. As he built it, he imbued his love for his family within the wood thus the boat will try to keep safe anyone who sails it. The image on the sail is a Kraken.

The Journal: Written in by the Mistress and Master, detailing the events surrounding the House, Village and occasionally the world.

Scroll of passcodes: Created by each Master, some change the passcodes for security reasons. Charles changed them to well-known phrases from movies so he would remember them easily.

The bridge and the Kraken: A magik causeway joining the island on the southern end to the mainland. A command, "release the kraken" causes the bridge bolts to explode.

Scarecrow: Purchased by Marji while on a trip to a Catering Conference. It was an impulse purchase that turned into a spy for the Others and came alive during the storm.

The Oriental carpet/rug: Also a purchase while on the same trip. It had curses written on it that were discovered by Blou. It became animated and went to rescue the Jinn (hooded fighter that killed some ravens and tried to kill Sarisha).

Meadow of barley, clover and wild oats: Katherine Drake imbued it with a wish for Peace. Some days you can find a giant Spriggan napping there, wrapped up in his or her shadow.

Portrait of Dingley: Hangs in the Library—who painted it? The eyes seem to follow you, and the expression on the face changes with the mood of the day.

Vortex portals or doorways: There is one between the Hill on Dingley Island and a subterranean cave beneath the island There may be other Vortexes perhaps one on the moon? They allow passage to other worlds that are connected to Terra (Earth). To open these 'doorways' you need a large travel stone (diamond or a ruby), or the power of the nicorn of a living Unicorn. To travel thusly is not for the faint hearted, the swirling tornado tears at your skin, and if you touch it in the wrong place, you will find yourself where you did not expect (perhaps back in time?)

The shining blue sphere: Aaron Audran Capuchin found it as a young orphan at the Capuchin Monastery...It broke free when the gem, of the Goddess of Palandine, was broken into pieces. When it escaped, it naturally found its way to the young Wizard. It inherently flees from evil. The sphere was part the diamond used to capture the jinn.

Truth candle: Has the ability to relight itself when it blown out. It is currently down in the cellar, far in the back by a small bedroom. It is used as a truth candle when a witness tells the truth of an event.

THE FIRST REGIMENT OF RAVENS

First Regiment, motto: "We fight for this world"

Commander Taldassa: The eldest.

First lieutenant Kassa: Chooses to stay and aid the Eagle.

Soldiers/Searchers/Finders:
    Second lieutenant Kissa: Took part in the scarecrow fight but was not injured.
    Skur: Killed in the scarecrow fight
    Skrass: Killed in the scarecrow fight
    Krane: Killed in the scarecrow fight
    Kaldassa: Audran's personal raven. First of the Regiment that guards the Island. He fathered Taldassa.

LANGUAGES USED

Latin, Lithuanian, Frisian, English, archaic French, Sanskrit, courtesy language of gestures (similar to sign language), Abenaki, Algonquin, Cherokee, Aramaic, and Ojibwe. All Native American languages were researched for names in hopes of honoring these languages in the best possible manner.

ACKNOWLEDGMENTS

I would like to thank all the people who donated money so that this book could be published, and especially the following who read it and/or encouraged me: Fran Norton, Pat Erwin, Debbie Yates, Debbie Brisbois, Denise Perry, Mary Maloney, and Myrna Koonce.